SHE DID

IT CO

SHE DIDN'T SEE IT COMING

Shari Lapena

PAMELA DORMAN BOOKS / VIKING

VIKING
An imprint of Penguin Random House LLC
1745 Broadway, New York, NY 10019
penguinrandomhouse.com

A Pamela Dorman Book/Viking

The PGD colophon is a registered trademark of Penguin Random House LLC.

VIKING is a registered trademark of Penguin Random House LLC.

DESIGNED BY MEIGHAN CAVANAUGH

LIBRARY OF CONGRESS CATALOGING-IN-PUBLICATION DATA
Names: Lapena, Shari, 1960– author.
Title: She didn't see it coming / Shari Lapena.
Other titles: She did not see it coming
Description: New York, NY: Pamela Dorman Books/Viking, 2025. | Summary:
Identifiers: LCCN 2025007107 (print) | LCCN 2025007108 (ebook) |
ISBN 9780593832448 (hardcover) | ISBN 9780593832455 (ebook) |
ISBN 9798217060535 (international edition)
Subjects: LCGFT: Detective and mystery fiction. | Novels.
Classification: LCC PR9199.4.L366 S54 2025 (print) |
LCC PR9199.4.L366 (ebook) | DDC 813/.6—dc23/eng/20250310
LC record available at https://lccn.loc.gov/2025007107
LC ebook record available at https://lccn.loc.gov/2025007108

First published in hardcover in Great Britain by Transworld,
an imprint of Penguin Random House Ltd., London, in 2025.
First United States edition published by Pamela Dorman Books/Viking, 2025.

Printed in the United States of America
1st Printing

The authorized representative in the EU for product safety and compliance
is Penguin Random House Ireland, Morrison Chambers, 32 Nassau Street,
Dublin D02 YH68, Ireland, https://eu-contact.penguin.ie.

To public libraries everywhere, and

to those who support them

Acknowledgments

The more books I write, the more grateful I am to all the people who help make the magic happen. In today's crowded marketplace I have the great good fortune to work with some of the best people in publishing. I try to write the best book I can, but I have help all along the way—from editing the book to make it the best it can be, to getting it onto the shelves and into readers' hands.

In the U.S., I'd like to thank Brian Tart, Pamela Dorman, Jeramie Orton, Kate Stark, Mary Stone, Jason Ramirez, Natalie Grant, Kristina Fazzalaro, Magdalena Deniz, Rachel Wainz, Raven Ross, and the rest of the team at Viking Penguin. In the U.K., I'd like to thank Bill Scott-Kerr, Sarah Adams, Alison Barrow, Becky Short, Nina Lewis, Jen Porter, Tom Chicken, and the rest of the team at Transworld. Thanks to Richard Ogle in the U.K. and Ervin Serrano in the U.S. for their brilliant cover designs. In Canada, as always, my thanks to Kristin Cochrane, Amy Black, Bhavna Chauhan, Megan Kwan, Emma Ingram,

Kaitlin Smith, Keara Campos, Val Gow, Kate Panek, and the rest of the team at Doubleday Canada. Thank you all.

As always, special thanks to my editors, Sarah Adams, Jeramie Orton, and Bhavna Chauhan, for helping me shape the book into its final form. Thanks once again to Jane Cavolina, the best copyeditor out there. Thank you also to my agent, Helen Heller, and to the Marsh Agency. And special thanks to Luke Speed, my wonderful TV and film agent.

As always, any mistakes in the book are all mine.

Lastly, I'd like to express once again my appreciation to my family, especially to Manuel, for all you do. It's too bad that our new cat, Ginger, doesn't seem to be particularly interested in crime fiction, but fortunately, my pony, Nutmeg, is a good listener.

SHE DIDN'T SEE
IT COMING

Prologue

Six weeks ago

Bryden Frost is running late. She has to pick up her daughter, Clara, from day care within the next few minutes or she will get a reprimand and a lateness fee. She doesn't care about the fee, it's the reprimand she wants to avoid. She knows to expect traffic at five o'clock on a Tuesday in late January, in Albany, New York, a city of about one hundred thousand, but today it's worse than usual. It's stop and start. She glances down at her cell phone in the coffee cup holder to her right, anxious that it will light up with a call from the day care. Or a text. Why do they text her when they must know she's in the car, on her way?

She fumes behind a large truck that blocks her view so that she can't see what's going on ahead. What the hell is the problem? She thinks of adorable little Clara, the light of her life, waiting for her at the day care. Is she the only one left? No, she can't be. Some kids and staff stay later, kids whose parents work longer hours. At three, is she old enough to realize her mother is late to pick her up? To feel sad, forgotten? Have they put her in her little pink corduroy jacket already? And is her little heart falling as all the other children are swooped into eager arms? Or is she distracted by some kind childcare worker—Hilda perhaps, who is so caring and adept at addressing any potential hurts before they happen? That woman is worth her weight in gold. But if it's Sandy, she will be looking at her phone, thinking about her own plans, not caring about Clara's feelings. And Clara is such a sensitive thing. Her little orchid child.

"For fuck's sake!" Bryden mutters in exasperation at the delay. It's now 5:04 p.m. and she was meant to pick up Clara by 5:00. She should ask if she can work from home more. It would make things easier. Traffic begins to move again, and she spots an opening to her right. She nips in quickly, hoping to get out from behind the tall truck and to make up time. An intersection is just ahead of her, and she prays the light won't turn red before she gets through. There's a sleek black Tesla in front of her. She hears the ping of a text and automatically glances down at her phone. She sees the name *Dandylion Day Care*, and then she is thrown forward against her seat belt, assaulted by a horrific screeching noise.

She feels the crash, the shock of it, the extraordinary sound of it, even at only twenty miles per hour. She looks up in disbelief and realizes that she has plowed into the Tesla in front of her, which has come to a halt in front of a yellow light that turns red as she looks ahead of her. *Fuck!*

She sits there for a moment, dazed, both hands on the steering wheel, staring straight ahead, telling herself surely it can't be that bad. The airbags haven't deployed, and it probably sounded and felt worse than it was. Her heart is racing and she realizes her breathing has become quite shallow and quick. The person she hit is driving a fancy car, just her luck, and as she hesitates, she sees a tall man in a dark suit under an open wool coat get slowly out of the Tesla and close his door. He looks toward her, and his eyes meet hers behind her windshield. Then he walks slowly toward the back of his car, toward her.

Fuck, fuck, fuck. She can't tell yet if he's angry or not. What strikes her most as he approaches is how good-looking he is, like a character in a film. She scrambles awkwardly out of her own car, an older Volvo, built like a tank—it's probably crumpled the entire back end of that Tesla. She narrowly avoids getting hit by a passing car while she does it as the traffic has now started to move forward again. They're holding up the cars behind them in the busy intersection. She takes a deep breath and faces him.

He doesn't look angry. He looks—civil. Like he's prepared to be reasonable. Thank God. She doesn't think she could take another driver's rage right now. She will be apologetic. She will pay whatever it costs. It will be fine.

"Oops," he says to her. And for a moment she can't read him at all. She's too struck by his looks. He's tall and well built and wears his good suit and coat with ease. He's got thick black hair, blue eyes, a slight stubble on his face. His appearance makes her wonder what he does for a living. There's something edgy about him, like maybe he's pissed off after all, but he's trying not to let it show. Of course he's pissed off, she thinks—his car looks brand-new. It's so clean; hers is filthy with January grime. And he's probably late getting to where he's going just like she is.

Then he smiles, and it transforms his face. As if he's decided to let bygones be bygones, he's forgiven her, he's going to be charming, and he's not going to make her life more difficult. She's grateful. Her husband might be more annoyed when he sees the bill.

"I'm *so* sorry," she says, flustered. She's never been in an accident before. "I'm late picking up my daughter from day care," she babbles, attempting to explain, "and they texted, and that distracted me—I'm so sorry, it's entirely my fault." Any hope of getting to Clara quickly has completely died away, of course. She must call them and tell them she's been in a minor traffic accident. They can't hold that against her, can they?

He continues to look intently at her, and she feels herself blushing. She brushes her hair away from her face, suddenly self-conscious. She wonders what he's thinking. She's a mom now, and usually forgets that men find her attractive. For no reason at all, she finds herself glancing at his left hand and sees a gold wedding band on his ring finger. That reassures her that he's not flirting, he's just listening.

"Let's check the damage, shall we?" he says easily, then turns away from her and looks at the back end of his car. He bends down and studies it.

The bumper is crushed in. It looks so unsightly on his beautiful car; it looks as if he just picked it up off the lot. She fervently hopes that's not the case. Her car hasn't been washed for as long as she can remember, and she doesn't even think to look at it for damage—she's watching him touching his damaged car. It's almost tender, the way he runs his hand along the surface of the bumper. He glances up at her, the smile is gone now. He looks at her car and she does too. "Yours looks fine," he says. "Mine, however—"

She's grateful that he's not yelling and swearing at her for destroying the back end of his car. "I'm sorry," she repeats. "Will it be expensive to fix?" And then she feels stupid for asking. Of course it will be expensive to fix. He winces at her and she says, "Excuse me, I have to call the day care." And then she turns away and calls Gwen, Dandylion's director, and explains why she will be late, and to just charge her for the extra time and please reassure Clara that everything is fine, and she will be there as soon as she can. "Can you have Hilda tell her, please?"

"Of course," Gwen says.

Gwen knows that Bryden likes the way Hilda interacts with her daughter—all the parents love Hilda. "Thank you," Bryden says warmly, and turns back to the matter at hand. He's waiting for her to finish her call.

"Do you want to do this through insurance, or would you prefer not?" he asks.

She doesn't know. "I'm not sure. I've never had a car accident before. I don't know how it works. I'll have to speak to my husband about it," she says.

He nods. "Okay. We'd better exchange information." He gives her his name, address, phone number, and car insurance information via his cell phone. She does the same.

"I'll take the car in tomorrow and get an estimate for the repair," he says. "Then I'll get back to you and we will figure things out."

"Yes, okay," she answers. "I'm really sorry," she repeats. He smiles, again, and she finds herself charmed.

"These things happen," he says. Then he gets gracefully back into his damaged Tesla and drives away.

She climbs into her own car and drives more carefully the rest of the way to the day care, thinking now about how much the repair will cost. It's not the end of the world, they can afford it, but it will make a dent.

Then she tries to put it out of her mind in the happy anticipation of seeing her daughter.

1

Now

Bryden encourages Clara to eat her breakfast of Cheerios and a banana. She needs to get Clara ready for day care. She's working from home today, Tuesday, at their condo in Buckingham Lake, because she has a lot to do, and she gets more done at home, away from distractions, than she does at the office. She's an accountant with a busy midsize firm on North Pearl, downtown, and they don't have a problem with it.

Her husband, Sam, enters the kitchen dressed for work, tightening his patterned silk tie. He kisses her on the cheek and heads for the coffee maker. He has his back to her, pouring out his coffee, when he asks, "What's on for today? You working from home?"

"Yes, I told you last night, remember?"

"Right." He turns around to face her and smiles. "And you're in your work-from-home outfit."

She laughs and looks down at her sweatshirt and yoga pants. "It's nice not to have to dress up for work once in a while."

He makes himself some toast and eats it sitting beside their daughter at the kitchen table, entertaining her with silly faces, making her laugh, while Bryden gathers everything together to get Clara ready.

Sam leaves the condo first. He's a portfolio manager with Kleinberg Wealth, and he's got an early meeting. Bryden picks up Clara and they have a group hug in the front foyer, and Sam and Bryden kiss each other goodbye before he puts on his coat. Bryden and Clara wave from the doorway as they watch him walk down the corridor and enter the elevator to go down to the underground parking garage, where he'll get in his car and make the fourteen-minute drive to his office downtown.

A few minutes later, Bryden gets in the elevator with Clara, descends to the parking garage, and buckles her daughter into her car seat in the Volvo to drive her to day care.

THAT AFTERNOON, Sam Frost is in a meeting with a high-networth client. They're sitting at a long table in front of glass windows with a panoramic view of the city, when Sam gets a signal through the glass wall from Connie that he's wanted on the phone. He shakes his head at her. He turns his cell phone off during meetings for a reason. But she's insistent, making faces and gesticulating at him. He excuses himself and leaves the room.

"What is so important that you have to interrupt my meeting?" he asks her.

"It's your daughter's day care."

"Is she all right?" he asks quickly.

"Yes, she's fine, but your wife hasn't picked her up."

He glances at his watch. It's 5:30. Bryden always picks Clara up at 5:00. "Seriously?"

"You'd better talk to them."

He follows her to reception and picks up the phone. "Sam Frost," he says.

"Mr. Frost, sorry to bother you, but Bryden hasn't been in to pick up Clara, and she's not answering her phone or texts."

"She's probably in her car on the way," he says. "Can you wait a little longer?"

"We're here for late pickup till six thirty. But someone must come get her by then."

He makes a mental calculation. "Look, if Bryden doesn't arrive there by six, I'll come get Clara. It's only a few minutes from here. But I'm sure she will get there any minute. I'll try to contact her."

"Thank you, Mr. Frost."

He hangs up the phone. Connie is looking at him.

"Everything all right?" she asks.

"I'm sure everything's fine," he says. "Something must have held Bryden up." He texts her. *You okay?* He watches his phone for a moment, but there's no reply. He calls her, but it goes directly to voicemail. "She must be in the car, running late," he says to Connie. He returns to his meeting, which soon comes to an end. When he hasn't been able to reach Bryden by six o'clock, he phones the day care. The director, Gwen, answers.

"We were just about to call you, Mr. Frost. Bryden still isn't here. I hope she's okay."

"I don't know what's happened to her," he says, allowing worry to creep into his voice. "But I'm leaving now. I'll be there soon."

He turns to Connie, who is hovering. "This is really odd. I've called and texted her, and the day care has too, and she's not answering. She should have got there by now." For good measure, he calls Bryden again while Connie stands by, but again, there's no answer. He leaves another message. "I'm really worried now, Bryden. Can you please get in touch? I'm going to pick up Clara."

Sam quickly leaves the office and drives as fast as he dares to the day care, which is located about midway between downtown and their condo in the northwest part of the small city. The first thing he does when he arrives is gather Clara up in his arms and smother her tearstained face with kisses until she giggles. Then he turns to Gwen, who has been waiting, and says, "I'm sorry, I don't know what's happened to Bryden. I'm sure there will be some simple explanation." Nothing like this has ever happened before. He puts his daughter down and takes her by the hand. "Let's go find Mommy, shall we?" They walk out of the day care as if nothing is wrong at all. It's important to act as normally as possible in front of his daughter, he thinks, even if things aren't normal at all.

They arrive home via the underground parking garage, and the first thing Sam sees is his wife's car sitting in its usual spot. He parks beside it. "Look. Mommy's car is here," he says to Clara. His voice sounds fake, with a forced optimism. He gets out of the car and glances quickly through the windows of his wife's Volvo, but the car is empty. Then he helps Clara out of her car seat.

They take the elevator from parking level 1B directly up to the eighth floor. The doors slide open, and Sam walks down the quiet corridor holding his daughter's hand. Their feet make no sound on the carpet; he can feel the thudding of his own heart.

When Sam opens the door, he spots Bryden's handbag on the small side table in the foyer beneath the mirror. It looks so familiar, so normal. He calls out her name as he closes the door behind them.

"Bryden?" There's no answer.

The foyer and short hall give way to the living room, a large, open space, with the dining room to the left. He sees his wife's computer sitting open on the dining-room table, where she likes to work. Her cell phone is resting beside it. He makes a hurried check of all the rooms, while three-year-old Clara follows him like an eager puppy.

He pops his head in the kitchen, then checks the master bedroom and en suite bath, then Clara's room, the den, the other bathroom. Everything is undisturbed, just as it should be. The apartment is tidy, as it usually is. But there is no sign of Bryden. He rushes back to the dining room. His wife's computer is on but has gone into sleep mode. It looks like she's just stepped out for a moment.

Then he goes through the apartment again, more carefully. There's no note left on the fridge, or anywhere else. Clara is beginning to realize that something is really wrong.

"Where's Mommy?" she asks, her lower lip trembling, on the verge of tears.

"I don't know, sweetie, but I'm sure she'll be back soon. She probably had an appointment and I forgot I was supposed to pick you up. Silly Daddy. We will find her, I promise."

He scoops the little girl up in his arms and leaves the apartment and knocks on the door of unit 808, two doors down. He realizes he's practically hammering on the door and tells himself to calm down.

Angela Romano opens the door with a look of surprise. She takes in the sight of him with Clara in his arms, the troubled look on his face. "Sam, what is it?"

"Do you know where Bryden is?" he asks quickly.

"No. I got home about an hour ago. I haven't seen her."

"She didn't show up at the day care to get Clara. She's not home. I don't know where she is."

Clara begins to cry.

Now Angela looks concerned. She reaches out automatically for Clara and takes her in her arms.

"Clara, do you want to say hi to Savanah? She's in the living room." She puts her down and gives her a little pat on the bum to send her off. The two little girls are best friends; Clara and Bryden spend a lot of time with Angela and her daughter.

Once Clara is out of earshot, he doesn't have to try to pretend that everything is okay.

"Her purse and phone are in the apartment, and her car is here," Sam says. Angela glances at her watch. Sam knows it's almost 6:30. "She was supposed to pick Clara up at five. Where the fuck can she be?"

"I don't know," Angela says, her voice low but tense. "Leave Clara with me for a bit. Text me when you find her, okay? Let me know what's happening." He can tell she's trying to be calm for him, but she's clearly worried.

"Okay. Thanks." He hurries back to his own apartment and calls Bryden's sister, Lizzie, who lives not far away, in the center of town.

"What?" Lizzie says, when he tells her that he doesn't know where Bryden is.

"Have you heard from her today?" Sam asks.

"No, I haven't. When was the last time you spoke to her?"

"This morning when I left for work. Her phone is here, and her purse, but she's not here." Anxiety has taken hold of him; he lets it infect his voice. He paces the apartment. In the dining room, while he's talking to Lizzie, he picks up Bryden's cell phone and scrolls quickly through it. He knows the password for her phone, and she knows his. He sees the messages and texts from the day care and from him—she hasn't responded to any of them—but nothing to indicate where she might have gone. "What should I do?"

"Have you called Paige?" Lizzie asks. "Try her and call me right back." She disconnects.

Sam calls Paige Mason, Bryden's best friend; it goes to voicemail. He sends her a text: *Is Bryden with you?* But he doesn't get an immediate answer. He calls Lizzie back.

"There's no way she wouldn't pick up Clara, unless something was really wrong," Lizzie says uneasily.

Sam swallows. "I know."

"I think you should call the police."

"I'll call them now."

"Okay. I'm coming over."

"Yes, please come," Sam says.

2

Detective Jayne Salter, of the Albany Police Department, is at dinner at home in her apartment near Washington Park when the call comes in. She picks her cell phone up off the table, glances apologetically over the flickering candle at the man across from her, swallows her mouthful down, and says, "Jayne Salter."

"Sorry to bother you at home, Detective, but we've just had a report of a woman going missing. Failed to pick her child up from day care. The husband called it in. Uniforms are on the way to the home now."

She glances at her watch. It's 6:51 p.m. "I'll be right there. What's the address?"

"It's a condominium building—Constitution Drive, unit 804. In Buckingham Lake."

She writes it down and disconnects the call. She looks at her boyfriend, Michael Fraser, who has stopped eating and put down his knife and fork. He's observing her with dismay. It's March 7, the one-year anniversary of their first date, and he wanted it to be special. He'd made her favorite meal, linguine with seafood, and bought champagne. She's only had half a glass, she'll be fine to drive, she thinks to herself. And then she realizes that she is doing it again—she's putting her job first. Her first thought should have been for Michael, who'd made all this effort.

And then she thinks, *but should it?* Should she be more worried about his disappointment than about finding this missing woman? She realizes that she feels defensive already, because she can tell that he's not happy about it. Well, he knew when he met her what she did for a living.

She rises from the table. He stands too. "I'm really sorry about this, Michael, you know I am. But a woman is missing, a woman with a child."

He nods, resigned. He kisses her goodbye.

She gathers her coat and bag. "You eat, I'll warm mine up when I get back." She adds, "I'll try not to be late."

"Sure," he says, with a rueful smile. "I'll eat in front of the TV. I'm sure there's something good on Netflix."

JAYNE ARRIVES IN less than ten minutes. A police cruiser is parked on the street outside the luxury condo building, and she pulls up behind it. The condo is a large, sandstone-colored building of about ten to twelve stories. It looks like most units have balconies. There's a curved drive leading into it from the street. The front entrance is rather grand, with an arch with *100 Constitution Drive* emblazoned on it. It's an attractive building, in a good neighborhood. Jayne enters through the glass doors, quickly taking in the concierge desk to the left; the bored-looking young man sitting behind it doesn't even lift his head. The floors are glossy and the interior appears to be well maintained. The bank of elevators is on the right. She makes her way to the desk and holds up her badge. "Is the building manager here?"

He looks at her badge with alarm and says, "No."

"Get him here urgently, will you?"

"Yes, ma'am." He's reaching for the telephone as she turns from the desk, walks across the lobby, and takes the elevator to the eighth floor. She glances up for cameras but doesn't see any. The elevator pings as she arrives. The doors slide open and she walks down the corridor, the soft carpet deadening her footsteps. She greets a female uniformed officer standing outside unit 804, then opens the door and enters the foyer. At first glance, she can see that the apartment is spacious and decorated in light, neutral tones. She can see beyond the foyer and short hall into the living room, which is carpeted in a tasteful beige. A man and a woman are sitting side by side on a large, plush sofa and look up quickly as she enters. She's met by Officer Hernandez, who steps away from the couple and speaks to her quietly.

"We just got here. The husband's pretty upset," he tells her. "The missing woman's sister is here too."

Jayne makes her way into the living room and sits down. Officer Hernandez stands beside her. "I'm Detective Jayne Salter," she says. She studies the man sitting across from her, his knees apart, hands clasped tightly. The husband. She knows that when a woman is missing, it's often because of the husband, one way or another, but she tries to keep an open mind. He looks distraught. He's attractive and well dressed, although a little disheveled; he's thrown off his suit jacket, loosened his collar, and removed his tie—the jacket and tie are on the arm of the sofa, the tie a splash of red—and he's obviously been running his hands through his hair. She notes that his hands are trembling slightly; he clasps them in an attempt to hide it. The woman beside him is average looking, petite, with medium-brown, chin-length hair. Her blue eyes are alert.

"I'm Sam Frost," the man says, "Bryden's husband."

"I'm her sister, Lizzie Houser," the woman says.

"We'll do everything we can to find her," Jayne says, leaning in. She focuses on Sam. "When did you first realize your wife was missing?"

He swallows nervously and says, "I got a call from the day care. Bryden hadn't picked up Clara. That was about five thirty. She usually picks her up at five. They'd been calling and texting her without any answer. I tried to reach her then too, but she didn't answer. I picked up our daughter and got home at about six thirty. I left Clara with a neighbor and called the police. Bryden's phone is here, on the dining room table. And her purse is here. I just can't imagine her leaving home without her purse and phone—"

"What about her car?"

"It's here, parked in the underground parking lot."

"Okay. Excuse me a moment," she says to Sam. She walks into the kitchen beyond the living room and makes a call to Detective Tom Kilgour, who she knows has already been apprised of the situation and is on his way to the police station. "I need you to get a team here at 100 Constitution Drive to do a full search of the entire building."

"Got it," Kilgour responds.

"It's a condominium. The missing woman's car is here, and she's left her phone and purse behind, so she might still be in the building somewhere. Have them check all the common areas—the exercise room, the storage facilities, the parking garages, the roof, everything."

"Maybe she's fainted somewhere or fallen in one of the stairwells," Kilgour suggests.

"Maybe. If she doesn't turn up in any of the common areas, we'll need to go to every unit, see if anyone saw her. I'll get you a full description and a photo."

"I'll let you know when I arrive with the search team."

"When you do, I'll come down and we'll speak to the property manager. He's on his way. We'll want access to all CCTV in and around the building."

She finishes the call and returns to the living room. She sits back down across from the anxious man on the sofa. "Tell me about your wife, Sam."

Sam says, "She's a very good mother, very reliable. She would never just leave; she would never abandon Clara."

"Does she work outside the home?"

"Yes, she's an accountant with Rolf and Weiner. She was working from home today."

"Does your wife have any physical health problems—epilepsy, diabetes, anything like that?" Jayne asks.

"No."

"Any mental health issues of any kind?"

"No, nothing like that."

"Where might she go, inside the building?" Jayne asks. "Laundry room? The gym?"

"We have laundry facilities inside our apartment. She doesn't use the gym. The basement garage, of course. She goes to our neighbor Angela's a lot, but I already went over there before I called you, and she hadn't seen her." He adds, "Clara is with her now. She's our daughter. She's three." His voice catches.

"What unit is Angela in?" Jayne asks.

"It's 808." Then he remembers. "Bryden's been going to the storage locker lately—she's been moving stuff down there."

Jayne nods. "We'll check it out." She asks, "Any problems recently that you know of?"

"No," he says, as his sister-in-law shakes her head in agreement.

"Have you noticed any changes in her mood or behavior recently?"

"No."

"No financial problems?" she asks.

"No."

"And you two haven't had any difficulties lately, in your marriage?"

"No." He shakes his head. "Absolutely not. We're very happy." He lurches forward in his seat. "Please, you have to find her. I'm afraid something has happened to her."

"This is completely unlike her," Lizzie agrees, a little breathless.

She's very tense, Jayne observes. They both are. But that's to be expected. "When was the last time you spoke to your wife, Sam?"

"This morning, when I was leaving for work. At about eight o'-clock. I left a bit early because I had a meeting first thing. As I said, she was working from home today, but she would have dropped Clara at day care at about nine."

"I see. And you didn't hear from her at all during the day? Not a quick text about anything?"

"No."

"Do you usually talk or text each other throughout the day?" Jayne asks.

"Sometimes. Most days. But I know she had a lot on her plate today, that's why she was working from home, and she didn't want to be disturbed, so I wasn't surprised I didn't hear from her."

She looks at Lizzie. "And you didn't have any contact with her today?"

"No."

"Okay. We'll need a recent photograph of Bryden, and a full description, including what she was wearing when you last saw her this morning. Can you do that for me?"

He nods. "She's five foot three, about one hundred twenty pounds. Thirty-five years old. Shoulder-length blond hair, green eyes. She was wearing black yoga pants and a gray sweatshirt when I left this morning, and she had her hair in a ponytail." He's thumbing through his phone for photos.

Jayne watches as Hernandez takes the details down. "If we don't find her quickly in the building, we'll need to take her phone and her computer. Is there anything out of place in the apartment, anything missing?"

"No, nothing."

"Are you absolutely sure?"

"Yes. I looked."

"Was the door locked when you arrived home?"

He looks confused for a moment. "Um, I used my key to get in, like I always do, but I don't really know if it was locked. I didn't try it first."

"Do you mind if I take a look around?" Jayne asks.

"No, not at all."

As Jayne stands up, she says to Hernandez, "Get the description and photo out to the full team immediately." She turns back to Sam. "If we don't find her quickly, we'll need all her banking information to see if she's accessed her accounts recently."

"She hasn't run away, if that's what you're suggesting," Sam says sharply.

She doesn't answer. She knows that sometimes people do run away. In fact, they do it all the time. They have enough, and they suddenly snap. Or they plan it carefully. And she knows nothing about this woman and her family. It all looks perfectly fine, but that doesn't mean it is. You might leave your phone and purse behind if you wanted to walk away and start over.

Or perhaps she has simply fallen somewhere in the building and hit her head. Or it might be something worse. Perhaps she's been taken from this apartment against her will. Or perhaps her husband killed her. It's possible that this condominium is a crime scene. She takes Officer Hernandez aside and speaks to him quietly. "Treat the apartment as a possible crime scene. No unnecessary persons in—clear anyone with me first—and make sure everyone is documented."

3

Lizzie, in her sister's condo, with the uniformed police officer standing nearby and the female detective looking around, watches with close attention. Sam is distraught. It's good that Clara is at Angela's, not seeing all this. Lizzie thinks she should go check on her niece, but she doesn't want to leave the apartment in case something happens, in case there's an update.

She doesn't want to miss anything. She knows that something has happened to Bryden; she would never abandon her family. Lizzie feels as if a current is surging through her, like electricity, as if she is a human tuning fork, humming, humming. But she doesn't think anyone has noticed. She's a nurse; she's good in emergencies. It's her job to keep everyone else together, to manage her own feelings as required. She's used to it.

She's already made the difficult call to her parents, who live in Tampa, Florida. Her mother had become hysterical on the phone. Her father was so shocked he barely spoke. They all know that Bryden would pick up her daughter—unless she couldn't. They said they would fly to Albany immediately. They will stay with Lizzie at her apartment in Center Square, which isn't too far from Bryden and Sam's, only a ten-minute drive. Lizzie tried to reassure them, but her reassurances rang hollow. This isn't like Bryden at all.

JAYNE MEETS DETECTIVE KILGOUR and the search team in the lobby. Tom Kilgour is in his early thirties, just a bit younger than Jayne. He's tall and broad shouldered and exudes quiet strength. One would be mistaken to think that his brawn is his best asset; he's a smart, talented detective and she's glad he's here. They work well together.

The building manager, Ravi Sabharwal, has arrived now too and is standing behind the desk with the young man who was here before, but who is looking less bored now. Ravi, a worried-looking man of about forty, will accompany the search team. He knows every part of the building and has the necessary keys to gain access. Jayne has already made a preliminary inquiry about the Albany Police K-9 Unit, but they are currently engaged elsewhere. Perhaps that won't be necessary.

"How many apartments in the building?" Jayne asks Ravi Sabharwal.

"There are one hundred thirty-five units," he answers. "Twelve stories. They range in size from six hundred to four thousand square feet."

"What about common areas?" Kilgour asks.

"There is a party room on the twelfth floor, as well as a gym. They require keys, and all residents have access. The floors and elevators and stairs, of course—they are open to anyone who lives in the building. There are two levels of underground parking below. Also a storage area, with lockers for the residents, which also requires keys. There are some maintenance rooms and a garbage and recycling area. Residents don't have access to those." He adds, "Most units have balconies."

Jayne already knows that Bryden Frost's unit doesn't have a balcony—they hadn't wanted one because of safety concerns for their little girl.

Kilgour will accompany the search team. Meanwhile, Jayne will start the door-to-door, interviewing residents on the eighth floor first. She advises Ravi that if Bryden isn't quickly found, she will want to review any CCTV with him, so he's not to leave. "What kind of CCTV coverage do you have here?"

He looks slightly uncomfortable and says, "Coverage on the front and back doors of the building. Nothing on the floors or elevators."

"What about the underground garages?"

"There's CCTV there, but it's not working right now."

She looks back at him in disbelief. "Why not?" She'd expect better security in a building like this.

"We put in a new system a couple of weeks ago, but there's something wrong with it."

She watches the team set off to start the search on the lower levels and then rides back up to the eighth floor.

It's a fairly new building, about five years old, in good condition, and expensively appointed. The lighting fixtures are tasteful, the carpet good quality. Jayne was impressed by the spaciousness of the Frosts' apartment—the large rooms with lots of windows; the modern, high-end kitchen; the expensive finishes. She wonders how much a unit in this place costs.

She begins with the neighbor who was friendly with Bryden, in unit 808. A woman in her thirties, her dark hair swept up in a ponytail, quickly answers the door, looking anxious. Jayne holds up her badge. "I'm Detective Jayne Salter of Albany Police," she says. "Are you Angela Romano?" The woman nods. "Can I talk to you for a minute?"

"This is about Bryden, isn't it?" she says nervously. "Have you found her?"

"Not yet."

Angela's face falls. She lets Jayne in, lowering her voice to a whisper. "Clara is here. I've got her and my daughter settled in front of the TV. We can talk in the kitchen."

At a glance, Jayne can see that this unit is very similar to the Frosts' down the hall. But where the Frosts' unit is decorated in Scandinavian style, with pale woods and washed-out beiges, this one is much more colorful. It's also messier, with kids' toys everywhere. Angela leads her through to the kitchen, where they sit down at a marble island, after Angela clears away some dishes.

Jayne had learned from Sam and Lizzie that Bryden spends a lot of time with Angela Romano. She's the only other person on the floor with a young child, so they have naturally gravitated to each other. The two little girls are both three years old and good playmates. Angela is clearly upset that her friend is missing.

"Angela," Jayne begins, as they sit in the messy kitchen. "We want to find Bryden, and I'm hoping you can help us." The other woman nods. "How well do you know her?"

"We've been close since the girls were born—our daughters are almost the same age. We spend quite a bit of time together, mostly on the weekends. We both work full time and have the girls in day care—different day cares—during the week."

"When was the last time you saw her?"

"On Sunday. The girls had a playdate here in the afternoon, while Bryden went out."

"Do you know where she went?"

"Yes, she went to get a haircut. We often spell each other like that."

"Do you have any idea where she might be?"

She shakes her head. "No."

"Has she mentioned anything out of the ordinary to you recently?"

She shakes her head again. "No, nothing."

"Anyone she's had problems with at all? Here in the building?"

"No."

"Any problems with anyone else? At work maybe?"

"No. She really likes her job and the people there."

"Does she confide in you?"

"Yes. I think so. I mean, we confide in each other."

"About what?"

"Everything. Our kids. Balancing work and motherhood. Our husbands. Our plans for the future. Everything."

"How would you describe her relationship with her husband?" Jayne asks.

"I know she's very happy with Sam. They seem perfect for each other. I mean, we both complain about our husbands from time to time, but who doesn't?"

"What does she complain about?"

"You know—just that she feels she does more of the childcare and household chores than he does, even though their salaries are about the same. I feel the same, to be honest. A lot of what we do seems to be invisible." She shrugs. "My husband travels for work a lot. It seems like he's never home." She emphasizes, "Bryden and Sam are solid." She pauses. "I know they're trying for another baby."

Jayne files that in the back of her mind. "Did she ever mention that she was worried about anything?"

"No."

"She never mentioned anything unusual in her life in the last little while, any changes? Did she meet anyone new?"

Angela shifts uncomfortably in her seat. "What are you suggesting? Bryden would never cheat on Sam."

"I didn't necessarily mean it like that. Just—was there anything new in her life, any changes? Anything odd, or troubling her?"

Angela shakes her head again. "I honestly don't think so." She adds, "She would never just leave, not of her own free will." Her expression changes, as if she's considering something.

"What is it, Angela?" Jayne urges. But the other woman looks uncertain, apprehensive. "Tell me."

"One of the tenants here had a problem, a couple of years ago." She hesitates.

"What kind of problem?"

"I think you should talk to him about it. I don't want to be a gossip. He lives down the hall, unit 811, with his wife. She and I used to be friends."

"Okay, thank you, Angela," Jayne says. She hands her a card. "If you think of anything else, please give me a call."

4

Jayne knocks on the door of unit 811. The door is opened by a woman whose friendly expression changes immediately when Jayne introduces herself and shows her badge. As if she's on guard. Almost as if she is expecting trouble. "May I come in?" Jayne asks.

The woman lets Jayne into the foyer and closes the door behind her. She turns to face Jayne, crossing her arms in front of her chest, and says, "What now?"

A strange thing to say, Jayne thinks. She says, "One of your neighbors, Bryden Frost, has gone missing. She lives in unit 804. I'm going door-to-door asking if anyone has seen her."

The woman goes very still. "I haven't seen her." She adds, becoming more animated, "I know what she looks like, we say hi, but that's about it. I don't remember exactly the last time I saw her."

Jayne glances toward the living room. "Can we sit down?"

"Why?" The edge is back in the woman's voice.

"I just have a few questions."

She reluctantly leads Jayne into the living room, where they sit.

"Your name?" Jayne asks.

"Tracy Kemp."

She jots it down. The other woman looks at her nervously.

"How long have you lived here?" Jayne asks.

"Almost three years."

"Do you live alone?"

"No. With my husband."

"And what is his name?"

"Henry Kemp."

The name is familiar. "Does your husband know Bryden at all?"

"No." The answer is firm, almost angry.

Jayne presses the sore spot. "I understand your husband, Henry, had some difficulties a couple of years ago."

Now the other woman looks at her with open hostility. "That's why you're really here, isn't it? I know what you people are like."

Jayne waits, lets the silence do the work.

"He was completely innocent. He wasn't even charged. But even so, it's pretty much ruined our lives. So pardon me if I seem bitter."

"Can you tell me about it?" Jayne asks.

Tracy Kemp sits rigidly, caught in a situation she can't get out of. Finally, she says, "A woman made a false claim against him. He was arrested, but as I said, he was never charged, and they released him. There was no evidence whatsoever. She made it all up. And we've been paying for it ever since."

"What did she accuse him of?" Jayne asks, although she remembers perfectly well.

At that moment, the door opens, and they turn to look at the man entering the foyer, dressed in a business suit. He drops his keys with a clatter onto the side table, then turns and seems startled to see a stranger sitting with his wife in his living room.

"Why don't you ask him?" Tracy says coldly.

Henry Kemp walks into the living room, slowly loosening his tie. "What's going on?" he asks, looking at Jayne, and then at his wife.

Jayne stands up and introduces herself, holding up her badge.

"What the fuck is this?" Henry says.

Tracy stands up too. Jayne sees her swallow as she addresses her husband, her eyes fixed on his. "A woman down the hall, Bryden Frost, has gone missing."

There's a strange, electric vibe between them, Jayne notices. Tracy is protective of her husband, but is she afraid he has something to do with Bryden's disappearance?

"Oh, I see," Henry says, with heavy sarcasm, turning to Jayne. "And you think I've got something to do with it."

TRACY WATCHES HER husband's face darken as he stares at the detective. She feels a knot in her throat; she can't seem to swallow. There's a churning in her stomach. She thought all this was behind them. How quickly the panic returns, how familiar it is.

Now Henry says to the detective, "I don't know her, other than to see her in the hall. When did she go missing?"

"Sometime today," the detective answers.

Her husband looks nervous, but speaks offhandedly. "I was at work all day. People can vouch for me. Ask them."

"Where do you work?" the detective asks.

"I own a car dealership." He pulls out his wallet and offers her a card. "As you people know perfectly well."

"We'll check that out," the detective says, taking the card.

"You do that," he says acidly.

"I'll need a list of all your employees and their contact information," the detective says.

Tracy feels something pressing on her windpipe. It's fear. Fear that it's happening all over again. The accusations. She remembers the questions, the denials, the doubt. She got through it once; she doesn't think she can do it again. The detective glances at her and Tracy turns away, afraid the other woman can see right through her, smell her fear.

The detective waits while Henry fires up his laptop and emails her his employee list and their contact details. Tracy can't look at the detective, and she can't look at her husband either. The silence in the room only emphasizes the tension. She can hear the loud ticking of the clock on the sideboard, a ticking bomb counting down to something.

When she has received the emailed list, the detective thanks them for their time and stands up. Then she asks, "Mind if I have a look around?"

"Not at all," Henry says smoothly. Tracy can't even speak.

The detective walks down the hall toward the bedrooms, and Tracy's husband follows. Tracy remains standing in the living room. She knows there's no one here. Does the detective honestly think her husband would abduct a woman and keep her in the apartment? That she would let him?

Finally, the detective leaves. Tracy watches the door close behind her and begins to shake involuntarily. Her husband observes her in dismay, and she sees his anger blossoming. "Why are you shaking like that?" His voice is quiet; they are both aware of the detective outside in the corridor. He steps closer to her. "You know I had nothing to do with that woman going missing!"

"I know," she answers.

"For fuck's sake, Tracy, I was at work all day."

"I know. It's—I think it's just reaction. After what happened last time, everything we went through, because of that woman's lies." It's been two years. They have almost no friends left; funny how people don't stand by you, how they fall away, make excuses. Family too. All they have left is each other.

It's put such a strain on their relationship.

"Look, I don't like it either," he says quietly, "but we have nothing to worry about. They'll soon realize that and leave us alone. It won't be like last time." He strokes her hair. "They're just going door-to-door, like they have to. It's just our shitty luck that a woman on our floor has gone missing."

"We have all the luck, don't we?" Tracy says bitterly.

5

Jayne walks down the corridor away from the Kemps' door and quickly calls Kilgour.

"Nothing yet," Kilgour says automatically.

"Henry Kemp," Jayne says. "Remember that case?"

"Sure. I wasn't directly involved though. Why?"

"He lives in unit 811." She hears Kilgour suck in his breath.

He says, "A woman accused him of abducting her in a van, holding her there overnight, raping her, and then letting her go. He wore a mask, but she was sure she recognized him. She worked in a Dunkin' Donuts near his car dealership."

"That's the guy," Jayne says.

"There was no evidence," Kilgour continues. "She was credible, but she didn't come forward immediately, didn't have a rape kit done. When she did report it a few days later, they tried to find the van, but couldn't. He runs a used-car dealership, and they checked every van on-site. He has access to all kinds of vehicles, and they thought he might have something that hadn't been put on the books, something he kept hidden somewhere."

"He was arrested but never charged," Jayne says. "I just spoke to him. Seemed defensive, a bit nervous. His wife too."

Kilgour says, "He always claimed she'd either made the whole thing up, or she'd mistaken him for someone else." As if reading her mind, he says, "What if Bryden's hidden in a van somewhere right now?"

"Then he's not likely to let her go, is he? After the last one ID'd him?" Jayne answers. "He says he was at work—I'll call it in and have them check out his alibi. Maybe he *was* at work all day. But in the meantime, I'm going to talk to the officer stationed at the Frosts' front door. If she sees Kemp leave his apartment, we need to know."

After Jayne makes the call and speaks to the officer at the door, she continues canvassing. At the unit next to Angela's, a man answers and she introduces herself. She takes his name and writes it down. She asks, "Do you know your neighbor, Bryden Frost?"

"I know her by sight. Why?"

"She's been reported missing." The man's expression changes to concern. "Did you see her today at all?"

He shakes his head. "No. I was at work all day, got home a short while ago."

"Does anyone else live here with you?"

"Yes, my wife." He calls, and a woman appears.

He quickly explains, but she hasn't seen Bryden that day either.

At the next apartment, another resident reacts with dismay. "The woman with the little blond girl?" But she has nothing helpful to offer.

Jayne carries on down the hall, but none of the neighbors she speaks to have seen Bryden that day or noticed anything of a suspicious nature. Some doors aren't answered; she will have officers follow up on those.

Jayne hears a ping and checks her phone. A text from Kilgour tells her they've been through the basement floors—the storage locker area, the parking garages, the maintenance rooms—and found nothing. They've swept upward, checking the stairwells and corridors on the way up to the exercise room and the party room. They have only the roof left. Jayne has a bad feeling.

Finished with the eighth floor, she returns to the lobby, where Kilgour and the search team soon arrive and report they've found no signs of Bryden or of foul play. Jayne sends the team out to search the surrounding area, but keeps Kilgour back. There's a park across the street, with a children's playground, surrounded by bushes and trees. There's also a ravine behind the building. Maybe Bryden went for a walk in the park or somehow fell in the ravine. It's already dark and it's March—it's cold outside.

Jayne turns to face the manager, Ravi, who is looking increasingly worried. "I'd like to see whatever CCTV footage you have."

"Right." He leads them behind the concierge desk in the lobby, which doubles as a security desk, and they step in behind him. The younger man watching the desk steps aside.

Jayne can see two monitors showing grainy black-and-white views of the front and back of the building. Two others are blank. "We have camera coverage so we can see everyone who comes in and out," Ravi explains.

She remembers what he said earlier about the cameras in the underground garages not working. "But not anyone who comes in and out through the two levels of underground parking garages," Jayne points out.

"No. Like I said, I've been trying to get them fixed."

Jayne tells Kilgour to get someone to check and see if the cameras have been tampered with. As he gets on his phone to do that, she turns back to Ravi. "Why aren't there cameras on the floors and in the elevators?"

"I don't know. I'm just the manager. I don't own the building."

She leans down and says, "Show us what you've got."

Kilgour has finished his call, and they all look at the footage of the front door first. They skip quickly through periods when there is no one entering or exiting, and slow down when they see someone. But it soon becomes clear that Bryden Frost had not left the building that day through the front doors. They check the footage on the back door, but they don't see her exiting through there either.

"So she didn't leave through the main floor, we know that much," Jayne says. "She could have exited through the parking garage, if she was with someone with a car."

"Or a van," Kilgour says, glancing at her.

"Do you need a key card or anything to get out of the parking garage?" Jayne asks Ravi.

"No, just to get in. The barrier goes up automatically at the exit."

Kilgour points out, "She could have walked out of the underground garage, on her own, if she wanted to leave without being seen."

Jayne nods and continues. "Or she could still be here, somewhere, inside one of the apartments." She turns back to Ravi. "Are there any empty units?"

He nods quickly. "There's one on the second floor and one on the eighth."

"I'd like to see them."

Ravi leads them first to the empty unit on the second floor. He unlocks it and steps inside, and Jayne and Kilgour follow. It is unfurnished, and their footsteps echo on the polished floor. They do a quick search of every room, closet, and balcony. Nothing.

They leave and go back up to the eighth floor. They're walking along the corridor to the unit at the end of the hall, but before they reach it, the door to Sam and Bryden's unit opens and Bryden's sister, Lizzie, steps out. "I was just going to check on Clara," she says. "What's happening?"

Jayne turns. "We haven't found her. We would have notified you if we had." Lizzie remains standing there, watching. They carry on to the unit at the end. Ravi unlocks the door. Jayne and Kilgour enter behind him, and Jayne realizes that Lizzie has followed them and is hovering in the doorway. Again, they do a quick search of every empty, unfurnished room and closet and balcony.

But there is no sign of Bryden Frost.

6

Sam has been texting Angela, checking on Clara. The two detectives, Salter and Kilgour, had returned to the condo and reported to him and Lizzie on their fruitless search—and had shared the troubling information about Henry Kemp. Then they'd left, leaving one officer still stationed outside their door. Sam tells Lizzie he's going to get Clara and put her to bed.

He knocks on Angela's door, realizing it's after ten o'clock. He can see immediately that Angela is more distressed than she was earlier. She looks up at him with questioning eyes.

He says, "They haven't found any sign of her."

She invites him into the foyer and closes the door.

He blurts out, "They told us about the guy in 811—did you know about him?" She nods, looking frightened. "And you didn't say anything?"

"I hadn't thought of it when I spoke to you earlier. But I told the detective."

He takes a deep breath, lets it out. He doesn't want to get angry at Angela. "I just can't—you just don't know who's living around you, do you?" His voice turns into a hiss. "What if he took her? What if he's holding her somewhere? She's not in his apartment, they looked. They've got the cop on our door watching in case he goes anywhere. *Christ*—I want to go over there and hammer on his door, grab him by the throat!" He feels himself sweating.

"Let the police handle it," Angela urges. "We don't know if he ever did anything wrong at all. His wife believes he's innocent."

"You know her?"

"We used to be friends, but . . . we drifted apart."

All at once Sam feels himself sagging. "I don't know what to tell Clara," he says. Angela looks back at him with watery, sympathetic eyes. "How do you tell a three-year-old that you don't know where her mother is?"

"I don't know." She reaches out and hugs him. After she releases him, she says, "I gave her supper. She's asleep now. And Sam, if there's any way I can help, if you need anything at all, just let me know."

"Thank you, but I've got Lizzie here to help. And her parents are coming in."

She nods. "Sure. But if you don't want Clara around when the police are there, just ask. I can take some time off."

He nods gratefully and makes his way into the living room. He looks down at his sleeping daughter. She looks so peaceful; he takes in her round, soft cheeks, her long eyelashes. He wishes he could protect her from whatever is going to happen next.

JAYNE HAS NOT BEEN ABLE to return home early, as she promised Michael. She calls him and apologizes, tells him not to wait up. She has her hands full here. He has recovered from his disappointment and tells her he loves her, not to worry about him. That's the thing about Michael, he is inherently unselfish, doesn't hold a grudge, and she loves him for it.

It is now after ten. She is back at the police station, heading up the missing persons team. She has Detective Kilgour, and a group of uniformed police officers to conduct inquiries and aid in the investigation.

"Right, listen up, everyone," Jayne calls out, and the team settles and falls quiet. Behind her is a whiteboard with an enlarged photo of Bryden Frost stuck to it. Jayne turns and looks at it. Bryden Frost is an attractive woman, and clearly photogenic, with her large green eyes and shoulder-length blond hair. She smiles back at them from the photo. No one ever thinks their photo will one day be on a police station whiteboard, Jayne thinks. She turns to face her team. "We know Bryden Frost dropped her daughter off at Dandylion Day Care this morning at approximately eight forty-five. We know she returned home because her car is in her underground parking space, and her phone and purse were found in the condo. Her husband confirmed that she was working from home today. Her office didn't call her all day, at her request, and she didn't contact them. She appears to have had no contact with her husband, her sister, or anyone else we can find all day, at least nothing we can find on her cell phone or on her computer. Just a couple of brief work emails she sent just before ten a.m. It's interesting that she told her office and husband not to try to reach her. Why? Did she just want to work free of interruptions? Or did she have another reason?

"For now, given those work emails she sent in the morning, we're assuming she might have gone missing anywhere between approximately ten a.m. and five p.m., when she should have turned up at the day care to pick up her daughter. We're looking at her phone and computer for whatever we can glean that might be of interest. There was no sign of forced entry, and we don't know whether the door was locked or not when her husband and daughter returned home. The husband, Sam Frost, says nothing is missing from the apartment. I took a look around myself and there were no obvious signs of a struggle, no obvious signs of foul play. She may have just walked away.

"We've done a thorough search and found no sign of her inside the condo building. She's not on the property in any of the common areas, as far as we can ascertain. There is a possibility that she may be inside one of the other units, and that is a real concern, because we can't search those without warrants, and we can't yet show sufficient probable cause. But officers are continuing to go door-to-door in the building, asking if anyone has seen her and looking for anything suspicious. Unfortunately, the security in the building is rather lacking. There is coverage of the lobby, but not the elevators or the floors. We've checked the CCTV, and Bryden does not appear to have left the building via the front or back doors. But the CCTV in the underground garage hasn't been working for a couple of weeks, so anyone who might have accessed or left the building through the underground parking garage is not on CCTV." She adds, "The cameras don't appear to have been tampered with; they're just brand-new and apparently defective.

"We have one person of interest, Henry Kemp, in unit 811. He says he was at work all day, at his car dealership. But the employees that have been spoken to so far can't confirm that he was on the work premises *all* day. It's possible that he might have stepped out for a time. The dealership is only ten minutes from the condo. If he'd used his pass to get into the garage we would know. He didn't. But it's possible he buzzed Bryden to let him in, saying he lived in a neighboring unit and lost his card. Maybe he's been watching her. Maybe he knew somehow that she was working from home that day. Maybe he saw her this morning in yoga pants instead of work clothes and deduced it. So we're keeping a close eye on him. If he—or his wife—leaves his apartment, we will have someone tail him."

"Would he try something like this so close to where he lives?" an officer asks.

"It seems unlikely," Jayne answers, "but you never know. Kilgour will follow up on his alibi. Meanwhile, we're conducting background checks on everyone living and working in the building. We're looking at Bryden's banking info for any suspicious activity, checking all the hospitals and hotels in Albany and the surrounding area, following up with cabs. It seems unlikely she could have taken an Uber without her phone.

"You've all got your jobs to do. Bryden's description and photo have gone out over all the usual channels, and I'll be making a statement to the press at nine o'clock tomorrow morning with a full description and a plea for public assistance if we haven't found her by then. The search team continues to cover a widening area outside the condo, and I've got a request in to the K-9 unit." Jayne takes a breath. "She seems like a stable woman, a mother who dotes on her three-year-old child, who works a steady job as an accountant. No physical or mental health problems." She pauses, lets her voice drop. "Foul play seems likely. I don't need to tell you that time is of the essence. Let's find her."

7

Tracy Kemp rises from the bed, careful not to wake her slumbering husband. The anxiety she's felt ever since the detective knocked on their door earlier that evening has not abated. Instead, she feels an escalating hysteria. She goes into the kitchen and makes herself a cup of chamomile tea, careful to stop the kettle before it screams. She takes her tea into the living room and stands staring out the windows at the darkness outside, unseeing.

Her husband is a cipher. She wishes she could get inside his mind. She wishes she knew if he was telling the truth. She'd loved him once. She'd trusted him. And then that woman happened, and everything went to shit. She told everyone she believed him.

And she did. She believed him 90 percent. But not 100 percent. There is that small part of her that has doubts. Because she's a woman, and she's always felt that women should be believed when they make a claim of assault. She's a feminist, or at least she was. Is she anymore? Her former friends don't think so. They believed the woman. As she would have done, automatically, if she hadn't been married to the man accused of abducting and raping her.

The thing is, even though Henry is a good husband, and loves her, she thinks it's unlikely that the woman was deliberately lying. Tracy tells herself that she was more likely mistaken. That she'd pointed out the wrong man, that's all. But what niggles is that she can't deny that she was relieved when it became clear that his accuser had waited too long to collect the evidence a rape kit would have provided. Tracy herself had pointed out to the investigating officers that it was highly suspicious that the woman hadn't gone to the police immediately. She'd had to listen while a female officer gently explained that there are many reasons why a woman might not come forward right away—which Tracy knew perfectly well. She'd felt like such a fraud.

If only she knew the truth. Without knowing, she's trapped. Trapped in a life of constant anxiety. She remembers her instinctive terror when the detective arrived at their door. If she knew the truth, then she could make a choice. And what would that choice be? If he did abduct and rape that woman, if she *knew*, then she would leave him. But as long as she doesn't know, as long as he might be innocent, she feels honor bound to stand by him.

The detective's visit has made this clear to her. For the last two years she has lived in a state of outrage, denial—and doubt. Now it's all coming into focus. She must learn the truth, one way or another. But how?

Maybe it will all be made clear for her. Maybe her husband has abducted Bryden Frost. And maybe this time he won't get away with it.

THE NIGHT SEEMS ENDLESS to Sam. He barely sleeps at all, getting up every time Clara starts to cry. He and Lizzie have told her that they don't know where her mother is, but they're sure she'll be back soon. Clara isn't soothed; she doesn't believe them. She's terrified, and

Sam doesn't blame her—he's terrified too. Lizzie has stayed at the condo overnight, sleeping in the den on the pullout sofa, and she also gets up every time the child cries. They take turns lying in bed beside her until she goes back to sleep.

The last time Sam rises quietly from Clara's bed, the sun is already coming through the windows. He gives up on trying to sleep and makes his way to the kitchen to find Lizzie already there, in Bryden's borrowed pajamas, sitting at the kitchen table with her head in her hands. She looks awful. She hasn't had any sleep either. She must be as scared as he is, he thinks.

"I'll make some coffee," Sam says, and moves to the granite counter. The fact that the night has passed and Bryden hasn't been found hangs heavily over them. They don't speak as the coffee is brewing. Then he brings their mugs and the milk to the table and sits down heavily. He takes a gulp of the caffeine, hoping it will clear his head. He looks at Lizzie, summons his courage, and asks, "What do you think has happened to her?"

Lizzie looks back at him with frightened eyes. "Do you think it might be that guy in 811?"

"Maybe."

She whispers, her voice intense. "I can't stand it that he's there, just across the hall."

"I know." After a long pause, he asks impulsively, "Do you know anything I don't? About Bryden? About her life?"

"What? What are you talking about?" Lizzie asks, startled.

He stares at her as she observes him with dismay and then says, "I'm sorry. I—just don't know what to think."

Lizzie takes a deep breath, lets it out, and says, "I don't know anything about her that you don't, I swear. Do you think she was keeping something from you?"

"No, of course not." But he can tell that his question has unsettled her. Has made her wonder if things weren't so perfect between them. He wishes he hadn't asked.

Lizzie says, "There was nothing, and Bryden tells me everything. We're very close, you know that."

Her statement annoys him slightly because he knows that isn't strictly true. She and Bryden are up and down, they have their issues, and now she's pretending they don't. They're not so close that Bryden would necessarily tell her everything.

"I know she was happy with you and Clara," Lizzie says, reaching over and covering his hand on the table with hers. "I'm afraid for her. I'm afraid that she answered the door to someone, someone like Kemp, and they took her. She wouldn't just walk away, leave her phone and purse behind. Leave you and Clara behind. She wouldn't. It's like she was . . . interrupted. And just vanished." Tears begin to spill down her face, and he squeezes her hand helplessly.

After a while she says, "Mom and Dad are arriving today. I have to go pick them up at the airport. Will you be okay on your own? What are you going to do about Clara?"

He hadn't even thought about it. Should he keep her at home, or would she be better off at day care, where she'd have a normal routine? But everyone at day care will know her mother is missing by now. Or soon will. He has to call the office. There's going to be a press conference at nine, and then everyone will know. Maybe he should ask Angela to take her?

"Let me take care of her," Lizzie suggests. "You've got too much to deal with. I'll call the day care and tell them. Then I'll take her to the Albany airport to pick up Mom and Dad. She'll be happy to see them. It will distract her. Make her feel secure to have us all around her." She adds, "But Sam, you're going to have to figure out what to tell her soon."

He nods. "I know." He closes his eyes briefly, then opens them and whispers, "Thank you."

"We're all here for you," Lizzie says.

He nods. "I'm here for you too," he answers. "This is hard for all of us."

8

Jayne is back at the police station early the next morning. Bryden Frost has not been found. Her computer has revealed that the last time she saved the document she was working on was at 12:42 p.m. Other than that, her computer and her phone have revealed little of interest. Just work and friend emails and texts, completely normal internet shopping and so on. Bryden was not particularly active on social media, except for the odd Facebook post. Bank records show no unusual activity except for one cash withdrawal, of $2,700, several weeks ago. The timing corresponds to a couple of phone calls she had from a number in her contacts—from a Derek Gardner. That number had never appeared before or since. She will ask Sam Frost about that. In fact, Bryden's life appears almost dull. She married Sam five years ago when she was thirty years old. They both have stable jobs. Clara is their only child. They are comfortably well off.

Jayne does the planned press statement and public appeal for information at nine. There is a lot of interest from the press, as is typical in these missing persons cases.

After the press conference, Kilgour leaves to follow up on Kemp's alibi, and Jayne returns to the condo to speak to Sam Frost again. She arrives there shortly after 9:30. There is a different officer stationed outside the door today. Jayne knows that Henry Kemp had not left his apartment until 8:15 that morning, at which time a plainclothes officer followed him to his workplace. The officer will remain there to keep an eye on his movements, just in case, while Kilgour looks into Kemp's alibi more closely.

Sam is expecting her—she'd called ahead to tell him she was on her way. As he lets her into the apartment, she notes how drawn he looks—he clearly hasn't slept. He hasn't showered either. He's in old jeans and a plain white T-shirt, and his hands shake when he brings her coffee. None of this is extraordinary. It's just what you'd expect in a man whose wife is missing. It's also what you might expect in a man who'd gotten rid of her.

She sits in the armchair while he sits across the coffee table from her on the sofa. The apartment is noticeably quiet. No sounds of a child, and the sister isn't here either. They appear to be alone. "Are Lizzie and Clara not here?"

He shakes his head. "She has to pick up her parents at the airport later and she offered to take Clara—to distract her. To give me a break. She wanted to get her place ready for them first." He sighs heavily. "Clara was crying for her mother off and on all night. Christ," he mutters and slumps on the sofa, the picture of exhaustion and misery.

"How are you holding up, Sam?" Jayne asks sympathetically.

He doesn't answer, just shakes his head.

"I'd like to ask you a few more questions, if that's all right?" she says quietly. He nods. "I assume you were at work yesterday?"

"Yes. I'm a portfolio manager at Kleinberg Wealth."

"And where is that?"

"On Broadway, downtown."

"I see. And you were there all day?"

He looks at her, and she can tell that something is wrong. There's something he doesn't want to tell her. She waits.

"Not all day. I stepped out for lunch."

She nods. "And when was that?"

"I don't know exactly—around noon?"

She writes it down. "Where did you go for lunch?"

Now his face is flushed, and she watches him with interest.

"I picked up something and went to the park."

"Were you with anyone?"

"No."

"And where did you pick up lunch, and which park?"

"At Gino's. It's a food truck, near Washington Park. That's where I went."

She nods. "And what time did you return to work?"

"At about two."

She writes it down. Then she looks up at him. "We've been looking into your wife's financial records and her phone records, and one thing stood out."

She has his attention now. "What?"

"Her banking is all very regular, except for one day, several weeks ago, when she appears to have withdrawn twenty-seven hundred dollars in cash from her bank account. Do you know what that's about?"

He looks blank for a moment and then he nods. "Oh right. She had a minor car accident a few weeks ago. Hit a guy's Tesla at a red light. We decided not to put it through on insurance. She paid the guy cash. It was twenty-seven hundred dollars to repair his car."

"I see." Nothing of interest there. "That would explain it." She thinks about it. They exchanged information. She's quiet for a moment, considering. It's worth checking out. They haven't found any sign of anyone else coming into Bryden's life or crossing paths with her recently. Just her usual friends, the people she works with, the other moms she knows casually. There was nothing else out of the ordinary. They have this person's contact information in Bryden's phone. Derek Gardner. She will pay him a visit.

Jayne lets her eyes move around the living room again, wondering if she's missing something. Then she studies Sam, leans forward with her elbows on her knees. "Sam, I know this is difficult, but if there's anything we should know about Bryden, anything you've been holding back, you should tell me now." She notes the flicker of anger in his eyes. Or perhaps it's fear?

"I'm not holding anything back," he says. "I don't know what's happened to her. We had no secrets between us. We were very happy. I just want you to find her." He looks anguished.

She smiles kindly at him and nods. "Of course. We all want to find her. We're doing our best." She wonders if he realizes that he just slipped into using the past tense in reference to his wife.

9

---

erek Gardner is working from home this morning. He and his wife live in Loudonville, an Albany neighborhood of people with high incomes. The Gardners' house itself is large, modern, and striking. He works for himself—he is not someone who likes to work for someone else. He is a cybersecurity expert and owns a small, profitable company with offices downtown on Bryant Street, with half a dozen employees. But he often works from his office at home because he finds it pleasant.

His wife, Alice, after earning her PhD in chemistry from Princeton, got a part-time job at the University at Albany as a researcher in the Chemistry Department. Her specialty is computational chemistry. Alice needs the mental stimulation, but she doesn't want the responsibilities of a full-time job, doesn't have the patience for the people and the politics. She mostly keeps her own hours but puts in two or three days per week. She went to work early this morning, so he's home alone when he hears the doorbell chime. He's not expecting anyone.

He answers the door to a woman he has never seen before. She's quite lovely—of medium height, with a trim build; short, deep brown hair; and rather striking dark eyes.

"Are you Derek Gardner?" she asks.

"Yes. And you are?" he asks curiously.

She holds up a badge for him. "Detective Jayne Salter, Albany Police."

He looks at the badge and then back at her. "I've never met a detective before," he says. "Would you like to come in?"

"Thank you." She steps past him and looks around.

His home is impressive—lots of glass and open space. It cost a small fortune. He watches her forming an opinion of him.

"What do you do for a living, Mr. Gardner?"

"I'm in cybersecurity," he says.

"I see."

"I'm sorry, I have no idea why you're here."

"Can we sit down?" she asks.

"Of course." He leads her into the living room, with its deep designer sofas. They sit.

She says, "I'm investigating the disappearance of a woman, Bryden Frost."

He feels his eyebrows rise. "She's—disappeared?"

"Yes. Sometime yesterday, from her home. Have you not seen the news?"

He shakes his head, frowning. "No, I've been busy with work."

"We're concerned about her well-being. We're talking to people who know her," the detective says.

"Well, I hardly *know* her," Derek says. "I met her, briefly, a few weeks ago, when she ran into the back of my Tesla with her Volvo."

"But you exchanged information, you know where she lives."

"Well, yes, that's standard procedure, isn't it, when there's a minor car accident? I wanted her to pay for the damage. Which she did, in cash."

"Can you tell me about it?"

"It was all very amicable—it was clearly her fault. I called her when I got the estimate, we agreed not to go through insurance, she said cash would be fine. I called her again when the work was done and I had the bill, and we met after that, at a coffee shop near where the accident occurred. I showed her the bill, she gave me the cash— twenty-seven hundred dollars, I think—the actual amount was a bit over that, but I rounded down—and that was it. I never contacted her or saw her or heard from her again."

"You were never at her home?"

"No, as I just said."

"And what's the name of the coffee shop you met in?"

"It's called the Daily Grind, at the corner of Chandler and Dover."

"Do you remember the day and time you met?"

He's annoyed at her now. "No, I don't. What does it matter?"

"I'm just making inquiries, Mr. Gardner. Do you prefer not to answer the question?"

His annoyance deepens. She's probably a good detective, but he doesn't like it. He doesn't like her. He no longer finds her attractive.

"Let me look at my diary," he says smoothly, not letting his feelings show. He walks farther into the house to his office and grabs his leather diary off his desk. He pages back to several weeks ago. He finds the appointment for the work on the car, and there it is, the note in his diary the next day to meet Bryden Frost at the Daily Grind at 4:30 p.m., January 26. He takes the diary back to the living room and shows it to the detective.

"And you never saw her or spoke to her again after that time?" the detective asks again.

"That's right, as I just told you."

"All right, that's it then." She rises from the sofa, and he shows her to the door.

"Have a nice day, Mr. Gardner."

He says, "I hope you find her." He watches her as she gets into her car and reverses out of his driveway.

JAYNE DRIVES AWAY from Derek Gardner's house. She found him rather full of himself. But she has no reason to believe he wasn't telling her the truth.

She returns to the police station. No one has come forward with any solid information, even after the statement and appeal she'd made earlier that morning. There have been some reports of a woman matching Bryden's description that have turned out to be otherwise explained. They are still looking into the backgrounds of all the people living or working in the condo building—particularly to see if there's anyone who has a criminal record. She should have a full report soon.

She gets a call from the plainclothes officer watching Henry Kemp. "Yes?" Jayne says.

"The prick hasn't gone anywhere except to Dunkin' Donuts."

"Stay with him for now," Jayne says.

Detective Kilgour taps on her door. He's back from Henry Kemp's car dealership, where he interviewed Kemp and his employees. He shakes his head. "Kemp left the dealership twice yesterday. Once was for about an hour to grab lunch at a nearby restaurant, and at least two servers vouch for his being there for almost an hour. Another time, in the afternoon, he went on a test drive with a customer. I've spoken to her and that checks out too. The rest of the day he was at the dealership. CCTV confirms it. He's not our guy."

"Okay," Jayne says, deflated. "I'd better call off the surveillance then."

Another officer taps on the door. "I went to Bryden's firm, Rolf and Weiner," he says.

"Anything interesting?" Jayne asks.

"They do accounting for a lot of midsize to large businesses in Albany and the environs. Nothing sketchy at all, as far as I can tell. She's respected and well liked at the firm. When I asked if it was possible she was involved in anything shady, they looked at me as if I was nuts. They all seem very worried about her, and everyone agreed that she would never just walk away from her life."

Jayne nods. "No. It doesn't seem likely, does it—we see no signs of any kind of preparation for that. She hasn't been hiving off money anywhere to make a leap. Not that we can find anyway."

"Every penny of her paychecks is accounted for," Kilgour agrees.

"Thanks, Martin," Jayne says, and the officer departs. "If it was some kind of accident or misadventure," she says to Kilgour, "we should have found her by now—we've searched that building inside and out, and the surrounding area too." Jayne looks her colleague in the eye. "More likely it's foul play: either some stranger—someone who knocked on her door—or someone she knew." She adds, "And they either took her out through the underground parking garage, or she's still inside the building—possibly in one of the units." Detective Kilgour nods. "Let's talk to the people who were closest to her," Jayne says. "I'm not so sure about the husband. He told me he went out for a couple of hours yesterday, from noon till two, alone—says he picked up lunch and went to Washington Park. That's a long lunch." She pauses, then continues. "But before we bring him in, I want to talk to the sister on her own, and the parents too—they're on their way in from Florida. And I want to speak to her best friend, Paige Mason. Sam mentioned her. We need all the background on the missing woman we can get, before we question the husband."

10

izzie has picked up her parents at the airport and brought them back to her apartment in Center Square, not far from downtown. She has a pleasant two-bedroom in an old brick walk-up with lots of historical features and character. It's sufficient for her, and she likes the charm of the building and the neighborhood. It's only a short drive northwest to her sister's condo in Buckingham Lake.

Although she saw them just three months ago, at Christmas, her parents appear older and more frail than she remembers. Perhaps it's the shock of Bryden going missing. They seem to be almost helpless. They're only in their sixties, but they have aged a decade since she last saw them. Her father has always been quiet; her mother is the chatty one. But she isn't chatty now. She's mostly silent. Lizzie also has Clara to manage, and she's a three-year-old, frightened and upset and missing her mother. Lizzie has been trying to comfort her, to keep her occupied, to stop her crying. The little girl has picked up on the emotional distress of the adults. Her routine is upset. She wants her mother.

This morning, Lizzie took indefinite leave from her work at the hospital for as long as necessary. They are understanding.

She puts Clara on her grandmother's knee in the living room and goes into her bedroom to call Sam. He picks up immediately. "Any news?" she asks, though she knows that if there was, he would have texted her right away.

"Nothing."

"We're back at my place. I've got Mom and Dad here." She doesn't know whether she should suggest a visit right now or not—he might not be up to it. Her parents have always been close to their son-in-law, and it would be odd if they didn't go to him. When he doesn't say anything, she says, "They want to see you."

"Of course. Bring them over. We should be together."

"Okay." She pauses. "Have you eaten anything?"

"No."

"I'll stay over again tonight, if you want, to help with Clara. I can drop my parents back here later—they can manage here okay on their own."

"That would be great. Thanks, Lizzie. How's Clara doing?"

"She's okay."

She steels herself to take Clara and her parents over to Constitution Drive. Somehow they have to get through this together. They have to be strong.

AFTER HER TERRIBLE NIGHT, Tracy couldn't face going into work today and had called in sick. So she's in her apartment when she hears her cell phone ring and glances at it. She registers the caller's name with disbelief. Why is Angela calling her now, when she hasn't spoken to her in so long and seems to make a point of avoiding her? Another fair-weather friend. Should she answer? On the fourth ring, she accepts the call. "Yes?"

"Tracy, it's Angela, across the hall."

She sounds nervous, Tracy thinks. "I know."

"You must have heard about Bryden?"

"Yes. Why?" She's not going to make this easy for her.

And then Angela speaks all in a rush, and Tracy can't believe what she's hearing.

"Tracy, if there's any chance that Henry took Bryden, you have to—"

Tracy abruptly disconnects. Her heart is beating too fast. She's lightheaded, and she's absolutely furious. At Angela, at her husband, at everyone.

SAM IS FINDING IT HARD to concentrate. There's a lot of activity around him now that Lizzie's arrived with her parents and Clara, and he almost wishes he was alone again. His brain is full, and he wants to shut everything out. It's midafternoon, and what he wants right now is a nap. He didn't sleep at all last night. Clara is being especially demanding, and he has no patience for her. She's on his knee now, gently slapping his face, trying to get his attention. He grabs her hand and holds it to make her stop.

He was rather shocked when he saw his in-laws. They were together at Christmas, and they look so much older now, so suddenly. But he knows he looks like a wreck too. They are all in the midst of a crisis. He likes his mother-in-law, Donna, and his father-in-law, Jim, but they require a lot of effort. Lizzie runs around getting everyone settled and bringing coffee, and cookies that are ignored, keeping the stilted conversation flowing. No one wants to say much in front of Clara.

He doesn't know how Lizzie does it. She must be as exhausted and as afraid as he is. But they're her parents, and he lets her take care of them, the same way he always let Bryden take care of them. He needs Bryden now, to take care of Clara. *Oh God, how will he manage?*

He stifles a sob, but not quickly enough. Everyone has heard it and turns to look at him with concern. Even Clara has gone still and is staring at him. He runs a hand over his face and says, "Sorry."

Donna says tearfully, "You don't have to apologize, Sam."

Jim's face is rigid; he's trying hard to keep it together. Bryden has been missing for close to twenty-four hours and they don't know what's happened to her. With every hour that passes their thoughts turn darker.

Sam looks up from his phone and says, "Angela's home. She wants to know if Clara would like to come play with Savanah."

Lizzie nods in relief. "That'll be good for her. I'll take her over." She picks up Clara and says, "Let's go see Savanah."

When Lizzie returns and sits down beside him, the life goes out of her, and she seems almost catatonic, staring straight in front of her at nothing.

Sam asks her, "Are you all right?"

She just shakes her head, biting her lower lip.

"What are the police doing?" Jim asks brusquely.

"Everything they can," Sam answers. He tells them what he knows about the search, which the detective had described to him in detail, and the older man nods. They are all unnerved about the man in unit 811.

"I can't believe this is happening," Donna says, her voice trembling.

Sam shakes his head helplessly. "All we can do is wait."

As if on cue, there is a knock at the door. Sam starts at the sound. His entire body tenses as Lizzie rises and walks down the hall. He hears the detective's voice. He feels on the edge of hyperventilating. They all hold their breath. *Have they found her?*

Detective Salter comes into the living room accompanied by the tall, athletic-looking Detective Kilgour. Sam and Lizzie had met Detective Kilgour the night before, when they'd reported on their search efforts, but Salter now introduces him and herself to Bryden's parents.

Sam watches as Detective Salter sits down on one of the armchairs. Detective Kilgour remains standing.

"I thought I'd come see how you're holding up," Salter says, glancing at all of them, then looking directly at Sam.

He meets her eyes and shrugs helplessly.

Detective Salter says gently, "Henry Kemp's alibi checks out. His every moment yesterday is accounted for. He didn't take Bryden." She looks at each of them in turn. "No one has seen her. The last time she saved the file she was working on was at 12:42 p.m., and she seems to have a habit of saving her work roughly every fifteen minutes. So we think that whatever happened probably happened around one o'clock—that's our best guess."

The detective looks again at Sam; she knows he was out of his office at that time. Sam feels a chill run over his body.

"We know Bryden didn't leave the building through the lobby via either the front or back doors. There are cameras on them, and we've been through the footage. If she left the building, it could only have been through the underground parking lot, where there are no functioning cameras. Apparently, they've been down for almost two weeks. She looks at Sam again. "Did you know the cameras weren't working?"

"Yes, everyone knew," Sam says. "Management sent a notice that they were getting them fixed."

"She can't just vanish into thin air!" Lizzie exclaims. "She must be somewhere."

The detective continues. "Her description has gone out to all police channels and to the media. We're doing everything we can. Now, if you don't mind, we'd like to speak to each of you. We'll start with you, Lizzie." She glances at Sam. "Is there another room we could use?"

He says, "You can use the den."

He watches from the living room with his wife's parents as the two detectives follow Lizzie down the hall to the den.

11

---

izzie is uneasy as she sits down on the pullout couch. She's glad she hastily folded it back up after using it the night before. Bryden's borrowed pajamas are draped across the back of it. Detective Salter pulls a corner chair up closer and sits down, and Kilgour does the same.

Lizzie thinks they should have found her sister by now. What have they been doing? But that might be unfair. She sees Salter nod at Kilgour. But first Lizzie says, "Are you absolutely sure about Kemp?"

"Yes," Salter replies.

"I know this is difficult, Lizzie," Detective Kilgour begins, "but we're hoping you can help us." Lizzie nods, eager to help. "Can you describe your relationship with your sister?"

"We're very close. She's pretty much my best friend. We tell each other everything."

The detective nods. "Is there anything about your sister that might be relevant to her disappearance that you'd like to share with us privately?"

Lizzie looks at the two detectives. "No. I don't know anything." But before the detective can ask another question, Lizzie says, "But something is bothering me."

"What's that?" Detective Salter asks, leaning forward slightly.

"What if she's still in the building?" Lizzie says. She'd lain awake all last night in this condo thinking, and she wants to share her theories. "I mean, what if she never left the building at all, and she's in one of the other units?"

Detective Salter nods gravely. "We're aware of that possibility. We can't get inside them without either consent or a warrant, and we need sufficient grounds to get a warrant. We're checking the backgrounds of everybody who lives or works in this building, and we're working as fast as we can."

Kilgour says, "That's why it's so important to tell us if you can remember *anything* Bryden might have mentioned. Anyone in the building look at her the wrong way? Anyone give her the creeps? Or anyone she'd become friendly with recently?"

Lizzie shakes her head. "No. I would remember if she'd said anything like that. And I'm sure she would have told me."

"Was she involved with anyone else," Salter asks, "someone maybe she didn't tell Sam about?"

Lizzie stares at her. "Are you asking me if she was having an affair? Absolutely not. She would never cheat on Sam."

The detective nods. "Okay. Any problems with friends, colleagues?"

"No," Lizzie says. "Do you remember that case at the Cecil Hotel in Los Angeles? About the missing girl they found on top of the roof in one of the water tanks?"

"Yes," Salter says. "The Elisa Lam case."

Lizzie swallows. "I just wonder if this is something like that." Suddenly she begins to cry, and the words come out through her sobs. "Like maybe she's still here, hidden away somewhere in the building, in the water tanks or in the boiler room or something, and you've missed her."

The detectives share a glance.

Lizzie pleads with them, sniffling. "Could you check again?" She adds, "Maybe you could use dogs?"

Detective Salter pauses and says, "We've had a request in for the K-9 unit from the beginning, but unfortunately, they're unavailable right now. As soon as we can get them here, we will."

Lizzie retrieves a tissue from her pocket and wipes her face.

The detectives wait for her to pull herself together, then Kilgour asks, "Where were you yesterday, between noon and five p.m.?"

Lizzie is taken aback. "Wait. Am I a suspect now?"

He says, "Please just answer the question."

"I was at home, in my apartment."

"What do you do?"

"I'm a nurse. I work shifts. I was off yesterday."

"Okay. Was anyone with you in your apartment?"

She can see how this is going to go. "No. I was alone. I'm single." She feels herself flushing, as if it's a great failure on her part. The thing is, she feels that it *is* a great failure. She's thirty-two years old and doesn't have a partner. She's a modern, independent woman, so it rankles her that she feels this way. But she just wants someone to love. To be loved. Is that so wrong? Her bookshelves are lined with romance novels.

"Okay," Detective Kilgour says. "And as far as you know, everything was good between your sister and Sam?"

"Yes, of course," she answers firmly.

"You seem very clear on that," Salter says.

"I am."

"He doesn't have a temper?" she asks.

"No! Not that I've ever seen. If he did, Bryden would have told me." She adds, "Sam would never hurt Bryden."

"Okay," Salter says. "Thanks, Lizzie. Stay strong. We'll find her."

Once Lizzie leaves the den, Jayne stands up and moves closer to Detective Kilgour.

"She's not wrong," he says in a low voice.

"I know she's not wrong," Jayne agrees. "Bryden might still be inside this building somewhere, inside one of the units, and so far, there seems to be fuck all we can do about it." She adds, "Do you think they could have missed something, in the other areas? I mean, she has a point about the Lam case. They thought they'd searched everywhere, and they only found her in the water tank because the drinking water tasted off."

Kilgour seems uncertain. "I'd feel better if we had the K-9 unit."

"Me too." She keeps her voice low. "If we don't take another look, the family will complain. And there's a lot of heat on this one—mother going missing from her own home. People don't like it."

12

Sam studies Lizzie when she returns to the living room. He wants to know what the detectives were asking her—he imagines they were asking about him. Donna and Jim rise together to go for their turn in the den, beckoned in by Detective Salter. He waits for them to disappear inside and for the door to close. But before he can whisper anything to Lizzie, he gets a call on his cell. It's Paige, Bryden's best friend. He's been expecting her to be in touch. He'd already asked Detective Salter if it was okay if Paige came over to the apartment, and she'd cleared it.

"Have you heard anything?" Paige asks anxiously.

"Nothing new," he says.

"Should I come over?"

"Yes. Bryden's parents are here. The detectives are talking to them. Lizzie is here too." He adds, "The detectives will probably want to talk to you."

"Okay, I'll be over shortly."

"Who was that?" Lizzie asks when he gets off the call.

"Paige." He knows Paige isn't Lizzie's favorite person. The two of them are competitive about Clara's affections. Paige spends a lot of time at the condo and is Clara's favorite babysitter. But Paige should be here. She's practically family, and she's Clara's godmother. Lizzie doesn't seem to want to talk to him; instead she's scrolling intently on her phone.

Before long, Paige arrives. She doesn't look anything like herself, Sam thinks. She hugs him tightly at the door and then steps back, searching his face with concern. "Oh God, Sam. What could have happened to her? Are you okay?"

At the sight of Paige's familiar face, Sam feels something inside him collapse. He lets it happen and starts to sob. She puts her arms around him again and holds him tight. Finally, he pulls away and wipes his eyes with his hands.

"Sorry," he says automatically.

When they join Lizzie in the living room, Sam brings her up-to-date on everything. His voice is bleak.

Paige looks him in the eye and says, "It hasn't been that long. You can't lose hope, Sam. Bryden is out there somewhere, and they're going to find her."

PAIGE CHEWS THE SIDE of her lip. Bryden is missing, and there are detectives talking to her parents in the next room. Poor Donna and Jim, how hard this must be for them too. It all feels rather surreal. She can feel her anxiety mounting. She doesn't know what's going to happen next. But she knows that she must talk to the detectives, and it worries her.

Donna and Jim emerge from the den looking shell-shocked, followed by a man and a woman, both wearing dark suits. Paige greets

Bryden's parents, whom she's known for years, hugging them both in turn. Then Sam introduces her to the detectives. "This is Paige Mason. She's Bryden's best friend—and Clara's godmother."

"Can we speak to you for a few minutes?" Detective Salter asks.

"Of course."

She feels Sam's eyes following her down the hall.

JAYNE STUDIES THE WOMAN sitting in the den across from her. Paige Mason is a beautiful woman, and it strikes Jayne that she is well aware of it, even in circumstances like these. Something about the way she holds herself and tosses her hair out of her eyes. She's not wearing a wedding ring. Jayne wonders if Paige will know anything more about Bryden's life than her neighbor Angela and her sister, Lizzie. Bryden's parents hadn't been that helpful; they've been living in Florida for the last couple of years. Jayne feels the clock ticking.

"How long have you known Bryden?" Jayne asks.

"We met at college—we both went to NYU. Funnily enough we are both from Albany but didn't meet until we were at college."

"And are you close?" Detective Salter asks.

"We were roommates, and we've been close ever since. We both returned here after graduating. So I guess I've known her for about sixteen years."

"What do you do?"

"I'm communications director at a firm in Albany. Bennett Communications Group."

"From what I hear, apart from Sam and Lizzie, you probably know Bryden better than anyone. Is there anything you can think of that might have a bearing on her disappearance?"

Paige looks back at her and shakes her head.

Kilgour interjects. "When was the last time you saw her?"

Paige appears to think. "Sunday night. I came over for dinner."

"And how did she seem then?" Kilgour asks.

"Completely normal. The same as always."

"No tension between her and her husband?"

"No."

Jayne leans in a little closer and asks, "Did she have any secrets?"

Paige's eyes narrow. "Bryden wasn't the type to keep secrets," she says.

"Maybe she was just very good at keeping them," Jayne suggests gently.

Paige replies, "Bryden didn't keep any secrets from me, and I didn't keep anything from her."

"What can you tell me about her marriage?" Jayne asks.

"I know that Bryden and Sam are good together. They're happy." She adds, "Neither one of them would ever cheat."

But she's glancing away and to the left as she says it. Jayne finds that interesting. It's an indication of a lie.

Now Paige is meeting her eyes again. "Sam had nothing to do with her going missing, if that's what you're thinking."

"What about admirers?" Jayne presses. "Maybe Bryden isn't interested in other men, but maybe someone is interested in her? Did she ever mention anything like that?"

Paige shakes her head, "No, I'm sorry. She didn't."

Kilgour asks, "Did she ever mention anyone here in the condo building—anyone she had a problem with, or who made her feel uncomfortable?"

Paige answers, "She's never mentioned anyone making her feel uncomfortable. She likes it here. And other than Angela, she didn't really know anyone in the condo, except to say hello to, you know? There aren't many young-families living here."

Paige's cell phone rings and she quickly reaches for it and shuts it off.

"What about people at work," Kilgour asks. "Did she mention anyone there particularly?"

Paige shakes her head. "She likes everybody at her office, as far as I know. I can't think of any problems there either." She adds, "Honestly, I'm as much at a loss as you are."

They talk a while longer, but Paige has nothing useful to impart. Jayne gives Paige her card and lets her go, asking her to please call if she remembers anything that might be helpful.

Not long after that, Jayne and Kilgour leave the apartment. As soon as they're in the elevator, Jayne says, "I think she was lying, about the cheating."

"That's what I thought," Kilgour agrees.

"She said, 'Neither one of them would ever cheat.' So who do you think Paige thinks is cheating—Bryden or Sam?"

"Could be either, or both."

She nods. "Everyone is painting a perfect picture here. But I'm not buying it. A woman is missing, and there's got to be a reason."

"Shall we talk to her again? Push her a bit more?" Kilgour suggests.

"Yes. But before we start hammering the inner circle hard, I want to search the building again, with the K-9 unit."

13

onna is waiting in her daughter's condo, telling herself that Bryden walked out that door yesterday of her own free will and that she'll come back at any moment, with some completely reasonable explanation, something simple that none of them have thought of. Like she went for a walk and fainted—maybe she's pregnant, she fainted a bit with Clara—and hit her head and someone helped her but didn't take her to the hospital because she didn't have any ID, and just took her home to take care of her and as soon as she's over her concussion she'll remember her phone number and call them and they'll all just laugh in relief.

But then the facts intrude—she would have taken her keys and her phone with her if she'd gone out for a walk, and her keys and phone are here. There's always some fact that gets in the way of these fantasies. But they are the only thing sustaining her right now.

She spoke to Bryden a little over a week ago. Now that she thinks of it, she didn't speak to her this past Sunday, like she usually does.

Should she have mentioned that to the detectives? But Bryden doesn't call every Sunday. She could ask Sam what they were doing Sunday, around dinnertime. Maybe they were busy.

But the last time she spoke to her daughter, the week before, everything was fine. She seemed her usual self. A little worried about Clara—she's such a sensitive child—but nothing unusual about that. Donna is worried about Clara now. What will happen to her if she doesn't get her mother back? But she can't let herself think that way. She can't bear the thought of losing her daughter, and the idea of her granddaughter losing her mother at the tender age of three is even worse.

Sam wouldn't be able to cope on his own, she thinks. He's a good father, Bryden always said so, and it looks that way to her, but Bryden is the more hands-on parent by far. But it's so often like that, she thinks. The mother doing most of the childcare. That's the way it was for her, although she knows dads are expected to do more these days. She thinks Sam should be more careful about what Clara is exposed to right now. She's grateful that Angela is able to take her when the police are here, so that Clara doesn't hear things she shouldn't. But maybe she's being unfair. Sam's a mess, it's obvious. What could be worse for a man than to lose his wife and the mother of his child? And he loves her, they all know that.

She glances at her watch. She still wears a watch although most people these days just seem to look at their phone all the time. It's almost five o'clock, time to start thinking about supper for everyone. Paige has already left. Lizzie and she will figure it out together. Thank goodness for Lizzie.

She leaves Jim in the living room staring at the floor and enters the kitchen to find Sam and Lizzie, heads together in quiet conversation. She seems to have interrupted something because they look up guiltily.

"What is it?" she asks uneasily.

"Nothing," Lizzie says. "I was just telling Sam about what the police said to me."

But Donna knows she's already told them all about her interview. What is she telling Sam that she didn't tell them? "Is there something you didn't tell us before?" Donna asks.

"No, Mom."

But she stares at her daughter the way she always did when the kids were growing up and keeping something from her. Her stare says *Out with it.*

Lizzie sighs and says, "She asked me for an alibi."

"An alibi?" Donna repeats. Then, her voice shrill, "For what? Do they think she's dead?"

"Mom, calm down," Lizzie says firmly. "It's normal procedure. She probably didn't ask you and Dad because she knows you were in Florida." She adds, "As a matter of fact, I don't have an alibi. It was my day off. I was at home by myself, cleaning the house, taking it easy. I don't get a lot of time to just relax." She turns to Sam. "They must have asked you too. But you were at work, right?"

Sam nods, but Donna can see that he suddenly looks uncomfortable.

Lizzie must notice it too because she repeats, "You were at work all day, right?"

There's a long moment where the tension crackles.

Sam finally says, "She asked me, this morning. And I wasn't at work *all* day. I was out of the office for a couple of hours around lunchtime—I got something to eat and went to the park." He glances at each of them nervously. "I have nothing to do with Bryden going missing, of course I don't. But what if they don't believe me?"

Donna looks back at him, suddenly not sure what to think.

．　．　．

Jayne Salter has managed to get the Albany Police K-9 Unit to come search the condo building at 100 Constitution Drive. The delay has been frustrating but unavoidable. They'll be arriving any minute. She stands in front of the building again now, waiting with Detective Kilgour beside her, her nerves humming. She checks the time. It's 5:35 p.m. Bryden Frost has been missing since sometime after roughly 12:45 the day before; approximately twenty-nine hours now.

The officers have finished questioning every inhabitant and every person who works in the building. No one had seen Bryden the day before or noticed anything or anyone suspicious. Background checks have turned up nothing on the inhabitants or employees, other than Kemp's arrest and subsequent release, and a couple of DUIs on other residents. Certainly nothing suspicious, and nothing to justify a search warrant. But there could be someone in this building who is operating under their radar. Someone unknown to police who might have Bryden in his apartment right now.

Jayne turns her mind to the search. They will start at Bryden's unit, where they will get something with Bryden's scent, an item of her clothing. There will be only one dog, able both to follow Bryden's scent and to sniff out a dead body. Jayne wants to cover all the bases.

She sees the Albany Police K-9 Unit van arrive, emblazoned with signage declaring exactly what it is. The van parks on the street in front of the condo and a uniformed officer jumps out of the van and closes the driver's-side door. People outside the building—residents, media, curiosity seekers—watch with interest. They know a woman is missing from this building, and they're curious. There are several news outfits outside the condo covering the disappearance, preparing updates for the six o'clock newscasts. They are busily taking photographs and footage of the K-9 van. Jayne and Kilgour approach the officer.

Jayne says, "Detectives Jayne Salter and Tom Kilgour."

"Officer Hank Bremmer," he says.

"We're glad you're here." She describes the situation to him.

He nods. "This is my best dog, and he's ready to go."

He moves to the back of the van, opens the door, and she sees a black-and-tan German shepherd on a lead. The large dog bounds out of the van, looking eager. He pulls a little on the lead, but a quiet word from Officer Bremmer makes him sit while he locks up the back of the van. "Let's go, Brutus," Bremmer says.

Jayne has already alerted the building manager, Ravi, about what they're doing; they will need him and his keys once more to gain access to various parts of the building. Now, she signals him from the glass door, and he buzzes them into the building. Ravi stands behind the desk in the lobby looking concerned while they pass by with the dog and make their way into the elevator.

As they arrive on the eighth floor, Jayne takes a deep breath, lets it out slowly. She hasn't let them know they're coming; she wants to gauge their reactions. She glances at Kilgour. He looks wired too. The elevator doors slide open. Jayne says, "Unit 804," and they walk down the carpeted corridor, the dog leading the way, straining at the lead. Jayne raps on the door.

14

---

ayne steels herself for what's coming. It's Donna who opens the door. When she sees the dog, she takes an involuntary step back as if she's frightened of him. Then she recovers herself and calls over her shoulder, "Sam!"

Sam appears in the foyer. He takes in the handler and the large, panting dog, the detectives, and is momentarily speechless. Jayne tries to read him, but she can't.

Now Lizzie comes up behind Sam and says, "Oh good, you've got a dog."

"Come in," Sam says finally.

They make their way into the living room. Jayne notes that Paige seems to have left and there's no sign of the little girl, but she asks, just to be sure. "Where is your daughter?"

"She's at Angela's," Sam says.

Jayne nods, relieved. "We're going to do another search of the building. This is Officer Bremmer. He's going to need something of Bryden's, so that the dog can get her scent."

"A piece of clothing would be good," Bremmer says, "maybe something of hers from the laundry basket that hasn't been washed."

Sam retreats to the bedroom to find a piece of clothing. They are all silent while they wait for him to return, with only the unsettling sound of the dog panting. Jayne finds herself watching Lizzie, wondering what she's thinking. She wanted the K-9 unit, but now she's quiet, as if she's frightened by what they might find. Fair enough, Jayne thinks.

Sam returns with a T-shirt and hands it to Bremmer. They all watch as the handler holds the clothing to the dog's nose. The dog sniffs it thoroughly, rooting into it.

Jayne says gently, "If there's anything to find, this dog will find it. He's trained as both a tracking dog and a cadaver dog." There's a charged silence as *cadaver dog* registers with everyone. Sam's face blanches and Bryden's parents look stricken. Although they always hold on to hope when there's a missing persons case, Jayne knows that Bryden may not still be alive. For the family, it's an idea that needs getting used to.

Sam suddenly looks pale and unsteady on his feet, as if he might fall over. Jayne observes him with concern. She's seen grown men faint before. "Sam, you'd better sit down." He slumps onto the sofa. She observes him for a moment and then turns to go.

"Can I come?" Lizzie asks.

Jayne turns back. There's an avidity about Lizzie that Jayne finds almost distasteful. "No. You should all remain here, in the apartment."

"Let's go," Bremmer says, turning the dog around. Brutus seems to pause, his nose testing the area between the living room and the front foyer. He whines slightly and Bremmer watches him closely. Then the dog seems to settle, and they head out the door into the corridor.

Nose to the ground, the dog goes to the bank of three elevators. Naturally he will be able to detect Bryden's scent here, Jayne thinks. It's whether the dog can track her to somewhere in the building she wouldn't be expected to go that they need to determine. The dog picks up the scent on the path between the front door of unit 804 and the elevators, to Angela Romano's unit, and the trash disposal. But nowhere else on the eighth floor.

Bremmer says, "She hasn't been to any of the other units on this floor." The dog shows no interest in the stairwells at either end of the corridor.

"Let's see if he can pick up the scent on any of the other floors," Bremmer says.

They all get into the elevator and go up to the top floor, the twelfth. They emerge from the elevator, but the dog clearly finds no scent of Bryden on the twelfth floor or in the stairwells. They repeat this all the way back down, stopping at each floor. They arrive on the ground floor, and when the elevator doors open, the dog eagerly puts his head down and clearly follows Bryden's scent to the front doors, and also to the concierge desk and the bank of mailboxes, but not to the exit doors at the back of the building.

"Which level is her car on?" Bremmer asks, back at the main floor elevators.

"It's on 1B," Jayne answers.

"Let's do 2B first."

Brutus does not pick up Bryden's scent on 2B at all. They go back down one floor. At 1B the elevator opens and the dog leads them eagerly through a pair of windowed double doors into the parking garage and directly to Bryden's parked car, which has already been thoroughly searched. Bremmer gives him a treat. The dog then puts his nose down and leads his handler to the car next to it, to the passenger-door side.

"That's Sam's car," Kilgour says.

Bremmer says, "She's obviously in the habit of taking the elevators directly to the lobby or directly to the parking garage and going to her car or her husband's car. Brutus hasn't picked up anything else."

"So, no possibility she *walked* out of this parking garage?" Jayne says.

He shakes his head. "No. And she wasn't taken to a car parked somewhere else down here either, or Brutus would have caught it." He suggests, "He did seem a bit agitated up in the apartment."

Jayne asks, "What are you thinking? That she might have been killed in the apartment?" Jayne knows that a body doesn't have to be dead for long—perhaps only minutes—before a trained cadaver dog can detect something. Perhaps the body was moved too quickly? How would someone move the body without being seen?

Bremmer shakes his head. "I don't know. Brutus didn't seem sure."

They return once again to the elevators while Jayne texts Ravi to come down and join them with the keys. From there, Brutus lowers his nose and leads them down the corridor through another set of double doors toward the storage and maintenance areas. Brutus starts to tug more eagerly on his lead and Bremmer gives Jayne a glance as if to say, *Prepare yourself.* Now the dog is pawing at the cement floor at the base of the locked door marked Storage Lockers. Ravi arrives, fumbling with the keys as he opens the door. Jayne knows that this area was searched yesterday.

The door finally opens, and inside, Jayne sees rows of lockers, all enclosed with wire mesh. She follows the handler and the excited dog down the first row, aware of a jumble of items—bicycles, old furniture, and camping gear—inside the lockers on either side. She reaches locker 804, Bryden and Sam's locker, and glances in, peering through the wire mesh at the contents. It's full of baby equipment—a playpen, a swing chair, a crib, and boxes marked Baby Clothes—all carefully covered in clear plastic, waiting to be needed. Jayne remembers Angela

Romano saying that they were trying for another baby. The dog is barking wildly now, at the end of the corridor, and a terrible feeling comes over her.

Jayne follows the sound. Bremmer and Kilgour are standing at the door to another storage locker, which is slightly ajar. Inside the locker are a number of cardboard boxes, stacked about three feet high, and another open box full of old computer equipment. Jayne turns and tells Ravi to stay back. The handler reaches into his pocket, pulls out gloves, and puts them on. Kilgour does the same, and Jayne copies them. Then Bremmer pulls open the locker door.

Brutus charges inside and leaps on top of the cardboard boxes, barking furiously at something behind them. Jayne can't smell anything, but the trained dog clearly can.

Bremmer follows the dog inside, gesturing for Jayne and Kilgour to come closer. They all lean in over the musty cardboard boxes to see what the dog is barking at, on the floor behind the row of boxes.

It's a large suitcase. And the dog won't stop barking.

Bremmer says solemnly, "I think we've found her."

15

Brutus, having done his job, is now quiet, and Jayne sees Bremmer pass him a treat from his pocket, which the dog gulps down. It makes her feel slightly sick.

She turns and sees Ravi standing stiff with alarm farther back. She asks him, "Who does the locker belong to?"

"The empty unit on the eighth floor. They moved out a couple of months ago," Ravi says, his voice shaky.

Jayne turns to Kilgour and says, "Call in the forensics team—have them come in through the underground parking, level 1B."

She turns to Ravi and tells him, "You let the forensics team in when they arrive. And not a word about this to anyone, do you understand? Those news teams out front will know something's up soon enough. But you're to say nothing about this. Okay?"

He nods quickly. He looks overwhelmed, Jayne thinks. She watches him leave, then takes a deep breath, preparing herself. She nods to Bremmer. "Good work."

The forensics team soon arrives, the white van parking in the underground garage near the elevators. Jayne briefs them and then leads them through to the storage lockers. The forensics team quickly gets to work, its members moving about in white bodysuits and booties, methodically doing their jobs. The area around the storage lockers has been cordoned off with yellow police tape. Jayne dons the little paper booties now available to her. She approaches Detective Kilgour, standing outside the open locker. Together they watch what is going on inside it, both lost in their own thoughts. Someone is taking photographs. The fingerprint people are hard at work. Jayne knows that they and the dog have already contaminated the scene to some degree, but that can't be helped.

"How much longer until they can open it?" she asks Kilgour.

"Not long. About another half hour or so."

As she waits, Jayne starts to think about everything that's ahead of them if Bryden Frost's body is in that suitcase.

Finally, one of the team approaches her and says, "We found a lot of fingerprints on the door to the locker and on the suitcase. They aren't necessarily those of the perpetrator. But lots to process. No discernible footprints on this cement floor. Do you want to open it now or have it taken back to the lab?"

"Let's do it now." She follows him into the locker, and Kilgour comes with her. They watch carefully as the technician now moves the cardboard boxes out of the way and squats down beside the suitcase. She can see it's got a combination lock on it. Jayne finds herself hoping it isn't locked.

He presses the mechanism, and she hears a click. He carefully tries to lift the lid, meeting some resistance. Then he gives it a yank, the lid gives, and he folds it back and steps to the side.

Jayne finds herself staring at the pale, contorted body of a woman, wearing only bra and panties. She's in the fetal position, on her side, her legs pulled up to her chest, her neck and head curved inward. Jayne can see thick blond hair, and she can see enough of the dead woman's face to identify her.

Jayne knows they have found Bryden Frost's body. And this has just turned into a homicide case.

SAM THINKS HE hears someone saying his name. He turns toward the sound. It's Lizzie. He sees her in front of him, staring at him, repeating his name. Now she has her hand on his shoulder and she's shaking him a little. He looks at her vacantly, unable to process the enormity of everything he's facing. Lizzie's eyes look a little wild.

"Sam, I'm going to Angela's to let her know what's going on. I'll make sure she keeps Clara for the time being. Okay? I won't be long."

Sam thinks of the dog searching the building while they sit here, terrified. What's taking them so long? It's been hours. He glances at his watch; it's after eight o'clock. He desperately needs something to take the edge off. Suddenly he can't face any of it. He feels genuine, physical panic. It grips him like a vise. He feels like he is being squeezed so tight he can't breathe. The vise is getting tighter and tighter. He can't catch his breath. His anxiety is overwhelming. He hears himself making a strangled sound and is aware somehow of Jim noticing and turning toward him.

"Sam?" Jim says, looking at him now with alarm. "Sam?"

Lizzie hears from the foyer and comes running back. They're all staring at him.

"Breathe, Sam," Lizzie says, kneeling down beside him. "You're having a panic attack. That's all it is. Breathe." She takes deep breaths beside him, and he breathes with her, and slowly the feeling of being clamped in a vise subsides.

"You're okay," Lizzie says.

She goes out to check on Clara. Sam is grateful. How can he protect Clara from all this? What is he going to tell her?

What if they don't find her mother?

What if they do?

AS JAYNE AND KILGOUR walk silently down the corridor toward unit 804, Jayne prepares herself for the difficult task ahead. It is never easy to tell a family bad news.

Jayne knocks on the door to the unit, opens it, and steps inside. She immediately sees a tableau of the family, the moment before they hear the news. Sam is still sitting where they left him, as if he hasn't moved at all since they began to conduct the search. Donna and Jim are with him, huddled together on the sofa. Lizzie is standing nearby. All eyes immediately turn to her and Kilgour in fear.

"Lizzie, sit down," Jayne says, and she obeys. Jayne and Kilgour sit as well. She leans in to speak to the family in a steady, solemn voice. "I'm so sorry. But I'm afraid we've found Bryden's body."

She watches their reactions. Disbelief, horror, shock, pain. She focuses her attention on Sam. Nothing in his reaction suggests that he either is or is not the one who killed her. No one says anything for a long moment. She waits for it to sink in, for them to absorb it. Donna gasps and begins to sob, covering her face with her hands. Jim puts his arms around her and hides his face from the rest of them. Lizzie has gone strangely mute. She doesn't cry. Neither does Sam. But that means nothing, Jayne knows. People process grief in very different ways. They are all in shock.

Jayne sits silently, waiting for someone to speak.

It's Lizzie who finally breaks the silence. "Where did you find her?"

Jayne says carefully, "The dog found her in a storage locker in the basement. She was inside a large suitcase, hidden behind some cardboard boxes. I'm so sorry."

As the meaning of this becomes clear, Donna lets out an awful, blood-curdling shriek.

16

Jayne watches the dead woman's parents weeping in each other's arms. Sam appears to be in shock, and Lizzie is silent, staring wide-eyed.

After a respectful interval, Jayne continues. "This has now become a homicide investigation. I promise you we will do everything we can to find out who harmed Bryden. You can help by cooperating with us." She pauses. They all look back at her through their numbness and grief.

"Of course we'll cooperate," Sam says at last, his voice shaking. "We want to find out who did this."

"Good," Jayne replies. "First of all, we will need you to leave the apartment while the forensics team does a thorough investigation. And we will need all of you to be digitally fingerprinted, for elimination purposes. We can have that done now. Is there anyone else who visits the apartment, other than Paige and Angela? A cleaning lady? Anybody else?"

Sam shakes his head. "There's no cleaning lady. Angela often brings her daughter." He adds, "And her husband comes over sometimes too."

Jayne nods. "We will have to get them fingerprinted as well, although I understand he's away on business. They should be finished here by the morning, and you can return then." She adds, "I suggest you find a hotel close by. It's only for one night."

Lizzie speaks up tonelessly. "I can arrange the hotel. We could get a suite," she says to Sam, "with two rooms, and I can stay the night and help with Clara. We can't expect Angela to keep her all night." She adds, "I'll take Mom and Dad back to my place."

Jayne watches as Sam nods, as if in a trance. She says to him, "I know it's getting late, and you must be exhausted, but we'd like to have you identify the body and bring you down to the station, now, Sam, and talk to you there. We're hoping you can help us." He looks even more shaken at the prospect of having to identify Bryden.

"I've been thinking and thinking," Sam says brokenly, "but I don't know anyone who would hurt Bryden. Unless it was some sicko who got into the building, or who already lives here."

Jayne and Kilgour wait for Sam to pack an overnight bag while Lizzie packs one for Clara and goes to retrieve her from Angela's. She will take Clara with her to drop her parents off at her own place. She says she will text Sam the hotel information.

Sam comes with them willingly enough. They're badgered by reporters and photographers shouting questions and taking photos as they leave the condo building through the front doors on the way to their car on the street. The media knows they must have found something—they saw the K-9 unit van, and they will have seen the forensics van pass by and go into the underground garage. And now the husband is being taken away by the detectives for questioning. It will be all over the news soon enough. Jayne calls the head of the forensics team from the car and gives him the go-ahead to examine the apartment too.

First, they go to the nearby morgue, where Sam Frost identifies his wife's body, breaking down in sobs when the sheet is lowered from her face. Then they take him to the station, entering through the back entrance. He appears shell-shocked. They escort him to an empty interview room and sit down across from him at the table.

"I hope you don't mind, Sam, but we'd like to record this interview, if that's all right with you," Jayne says.

Sam looks startled. "Why?"

"It's just standard procedure," Jayne assures him. "You're here voluntarily, and you can stop this interview at any time and leave if you wish, okay? Do you understand?"

He nods. "Yes."

Jayne tries to put him at his ease, leading him through questions about how he met Bryden, how long they dated, when they got engaged and married. She asks him about Clara, how their lives changed when they became parents. He gradually seems to get over his shock and, though obviously shaken, answers all her questions willingly and straightforwardly. She doesn't pick up on any problems between them. Certainly nothing Sam is admitting to. Now she must move into more difficult territory. "So, you and Bryden were faithful to each other? No affairs ever?"

"No, of course not. Neither of us was interested in that," Sam says firmly.

"What about arguments about money?"

"No, I've told you. We're comfortable. We have two good salaries, our student debt is paid off. We're saving to buy a house, but money isn't a source of stress."

"Does either of you have life insurance?" Jayne asks.

"Of course we do. We have a child. We both have life insurance policies."

Jayne nods. "I know this is very difficult," she says, "but I'd like to show you a photograph of the closed suitcase, if that's all right with you?" He looks terrified at the idea, but then he nods reluctantly, rigid in his chair. She opens a file on the table in front of her and picks up a photograph of the suitcase. It's a large, hard-sided, burgundy Samsonite, a common brand. She places the color photograph in front of him on the table. He looks down at it and blanches.

"Do you recognize this suitcase?" she asks.

He swallows and says, "That looks like mine."

Jayne observes him calmly. "Where do you normally keep your suitcase, Sam?"

"In the closet. In the walk-in closet that Bryden and I share."

"I see. And it's not there now, is it?"

"I, um, I don't know. This one looks just like it."

"I asked you earlier if anything was missing from the apartment and you said no."

"I didn't think anything was missing. If the suitcase wasn't there, I probably wouldn't have noticed. I don't know."

She says, "The forensics team has already confirmed that there is no suitcase matching this description in the apartment now." Sam looks increasingly nervous. "Sam, how do you suppose your suitcase got into the storage locker?"

"I don't know."

"You need a key, don't you, to access the storage area?"

"Yes, I guess so."

"You guess so," she repeats.

"Yes, you need a key."

"And where do you keep that key?" she asks. He swallows again. She watches his Adam's apple move up and down.

"It's on my key chain."

"Do you have your key chain with you now?" she asks.

He nods and reaches into the pocket of his jeans for his keys. "This one is for the storage room, and this one is for our own locker," he says, separating them out. His hands are trembling.

"Who else has keys to the storage area?"

"Everyone who lives in the building has keys."

"Did your wife have keys to the storage area as well?"

"Yes. She kept them in one of the kitchen cupboards."

"Do you know if those keys are there now? Have you seen them since Bryden went missing?"

He shakes his head. "No. I haven't looked."

Jayne says, "Let's take a break and find out." She pauses the tape for a moment and suggests Kilgour get Sam a coffee as she exits. A short phone call confirms that the keys are in the kitchen cupboard where they belong. She returns and resumes the interview. Sam slumps in his chair, sipping coffee.

"Bryden's keys to the storage room are still in the kitchen cupboard. So how do you think the killer got inside the storage area?"

"Like I said, anyone in the building would have keys," Sam says, visibly sweating. "Anyone from the building could have knocked on our door, attacked her. And then found my suitcase in our closet and taken it down to the storage area and used their keys."

Jayne nods thoughtfully. "It might have been someone who lives in the building. Or the person who murdered her might have come in through the underground garage."

He clears his throat and says, "You need a key card to get into the parking garage."

The detective says, "Unless she buzzed them in."

"She wouldn't just buzz someone in that she didn't know," Sam says.

"Exactly," the detective agrees. "We think it's possible she knew this person. That it was someone she trusted." There's a moment of silence. "We've already got the record of everyone who used their key card to get into the underground garage that day," the detective continues. "You didn't use yours till you came home with Clara. But you could have asked Bryden to buzz you in. You could have told her you lost your card."

"I didn't!"

Then she says, "Sam, you said earlier that you were at work all day, except when you stepped out for a while around lunchtime. Let's talk about that."

"Am I a suspect?" he asks, his voice sharp with fear.

She tilts her head at him. "I'm afraid at this point everyone who knew Bryden is a suspect. We just have to eliminate you from our inquiries. We can do that if we can establish with certainty where you were at the time Bryden was murdered."

He looks at her fearfully. She watches him, waiting.

"As I told you, I went out for lunch, alone, around noon. I got some takeout from a food truck called Gino's and sat in Washington Park. I didn't get back to the office till about two."

"Why is that, Sam?"

"It was a nice day for a change. I wanted to get out of the office."

She observes, "Nice for March, you mean. Still a bit chilly to sit on a bench that long." She pauses. "That's a bit of a hike from your office. How did you get there?"

"I drove."

"I see. Where did you park your car when you were at the park?"

"On the street."

"Which street?"

"What difference does it make?" Sam bursts out, clearly frustrated.

She explains. "We want to be able to confirm, if we can, that you were at that park at the time you say you were. So where, exactly, did you park your car?"

He stammers. "I—I don't know the name of the street. It's on the, the north side of the park."

Jayne knows that park; she lives nearby. Not much likelihood of any CCTV coverage there, but they'd check.

"Did anyone see you?" she asks.

"The people at the takeout place saw me. I was there at about twelve ten, twelve fifteen. I got a BLT and a Coke. I paid with a credit card."

"Okay. Did you talk to anyone at the park?" He shakes his head. "Speak up for the tape, please."

"No." Then he blurts out, "I didn't kill her, I swear." He looks at her, naked fear in his eyes. "Do I need a lawyer?"

"That's really up to you," she says.

17

izzie puts the sleeping Clara down on her living room sofa and covers her with a blanket. It's after nine o'clock. She was asleep when Lizzie picked her up from Angela's. She doesn't yet know her mother has been found. Lizzie's two cats, Pip and Squeak, swirl around her legs as she feeds them. She gets her parents set up in the spare room. They'd barely touched the sandwiches she'd made them at the condo while they waited for the results of the search. They are like her patients at the hospital—weak and uncomplaining, doing as they are told. They are in shock. She kisses them good night, and hopes they can sleep, because tomorrow will be a terrible day. And so will every day after that. She makes a phone call and reserves a hotel suite for the night at the Marriott. Then she checks on Clara, tucking the blanket up around her chin, and retreats into her own bedroom and closes the door.

Lizzie takes several deep breaths, sitting on the edge of the bed. She finds it helps, in times of crisis, to be alone and practice deep breathing. It's how she gets through her most difficult times at the hospital, when a patient dies, or a child is diagnosed with a terminal illness. This feels worse than that. Closer.

She needs to pack her overnight bag but instead gets up and turns on her computer. She has a desk in her bedroom with a desktop computer and a large monitor. She also has a laptop that she uses for most other things. Nobody knows about her hobby. The people she knows online only know her by her other persona. She doesn't want her online life to spill into her work life or her family life or her meager social life. People might think it's weird.

She's not a gamer. She's never found computer games interesting. She finds people interesting; she finds real life interesting. She finds real crimes most interesting of all. She belongs to numerous True Crime Facebook groups, is fascinated by real-life cases. Madeleine McCann. Elisa Lam. Recently, she has even joined some groups that try to solve actual crimes the police have failed to solve—it's an odd community of online amateur sleuths.

One Facebook group she is a member of is called True Crimes in Albany NY. It's a public group, with sixty-six members. It's a community of sorts, and she feels like part of something, like she belongs. Perhaps she is online too much because she is lonely. She knows it's an obsession, and that obsessions are dangerous. But she can't help herself. She can't resist the allure of the group and what they do. She's aware that some people might find it strange, or unpalatable. That they wouldn't understand. Perhaps even more so now, now that her own sister has been murdered. She doesn't want anyone in her real life to learn about what she does. Especially her parents. And the detectives. The police are dismissive of online sleuths, of what they do. They don't like it when they succeed where the police have failed.

It all started when she watched that show on Netflix—*Don't F**k with Cats: Hunting an Internet Killer*. It was a documentary about a group of people online who connected through a public Facebook group because they were outraged by the anonymous posts of some deranged person on YouTube showing cats being tortured. The group was called *Find the Kitten Vacuumer . . . for Great Justice.* They wanted to find out who was hurting these cats, because if there's anything that people on the internet love, it's cats. Lizzie loves cats herself—especially Pip and Squeak. And everyone knows that lots of serial killers start out by torturing and killing animals before they move on to people—it's a huge red flag. But the police weren't much help with the online cat torturer. So the online sleuths, building on what one another learned, eventually discovered who the creep was—someone called Luka Magnotta, a Canadian. And they also figured out that he was responsible for the grisly murder of a man in Montreal. They did the police's job for them, solving the murder and tracking Magnotta down so that he could be arrested, ultimately, in Berlin.

Once she saw that documentary, Lizzie, already an avid reader of true crime, was hooked. She ventured into that world, gently at first. She became obsessed with other cases, just as gripping.

Now, she logs on to the Facebook group True Crimes in Albany NY. She uses her fake profile on here. She suspects some others do too. She calls herself Emma Porter. She logs on to see what people are saying about her sister's disappearance. She goes back to her own first post, that she'd made yesterday evening on her phone from the condo, the one that started it all. She'd posted a picture of the front of Bryden's condominium building, a photo that was already on her phone, that she'd taken when Bryden and Sam had moved in, with the address prominently displayed. And then she'd written:

> A woman has just gone missing from a condominium at 100 Constitution Drive. Police are on the scene. Stay tuned for updates!

She skims the recent posts of people speculating about what might have happened to Bryden; there is considerable interest. Well, it is an interesting case. Perfectly happy woman goes missing from her condo in the middle of the day. Lizzie reviews her own posts, the ones she'd made furtively the day before on her cell phone from the condo, with Sam sitting nearby, oblivious.

> Still no sign of her, and it's been hours. Apparently, she didn't pick up her kid at day care.

> **Michelle Gautier**
> Oh no, she has a kid?

> They've searched the building. I'm on the ground here, outside, and there's police and reporters everywhere.

> **Tessa Workman**
> Post more pics!

She'd ignored that. She couldn't post more pics because she'd been inside the apartment, and she certainly couldn't post any pics from there, unfortunately.

> It's a pretty safe neighborhood, and a nice building— hard to believe it happened here.

> **Michelle Gautier**
> Nowhere is safe for women.

> **Tessa Workman**
> It can happen anywhere. Probably domestic violence. It usually is.

From the sound of it, it looks as if she just stepped out for a minute. Maybe she'll turn up, safe and sound. Fingers crossed!

But Bryden hadn't turned up, safe and sound. Lizzie hasn't posted anything today yet. And now things are about to get a lot more interesting.

Lizzie takes a deep breath and begins to type.

18

After interviewing Sam Frost, Jayne and Kilgour return to the condo. They know for certain now that it is a crime scene. Bryden didn't walk away—she must have been murdered and placed in the suitcase in the apartment, and then taken down to the storeroom.

But it doesn't look like any crime scene Jayne has been to before. It looks as if nothing has happened here at all. There are no bloodstains, no yellow cards laid out by the forensics team marking evidence. Jayne watches as the technicians walk around in their white suits, dusting methodically for fingerprints, looking for hair, fibers, anything.

Jayne is very suspicious of the husband. It's his suitcase. He has keys to the storage room. And most damning of all, he has no alibi.

ALICE GARDNER CURLS UP in bed in a pale-pink satin slip of a nightgown. She has brushed out her long auburn hair till it gleams.

She's studied her porcelain skin in the mirror and smiled at herself. She's plumped up the pillows and now she pats the ones next to her for her husband, who is changing out of his clothes, to join her. She's feeling amorous, and she hasn't seen him all day. She got in late, because she had dinner plans. "How was your day?" she asks.

He gives her a look and slides into bed beside her in nothing but his boxers. "I had a visit from a detective today. A female detective."

"Really? Why?"

"Do you remember a few weeks ago when that woman smashed into the back of my Tesla?"

"How could I forget? You were furious."

"Yes, well. Apparently, she's gone missing."

"Missing?"

"Yes. And the detective was questioning everyone who had come into contact with her for the last few weeks."

"I think I saw something about a missing woman on the news. What a small world. Well, it's not like you knew her." She pauses. "You didn't know her, did you?" She can feel her own eyes narrow, her smile falter.

"No, of course not." He looks back at her guilelessly. "I only met her twice, you know that—the time she hit me, and then later when we met up for her to give me the money for the repairs."

"Are you absolutely sure?" she asks.

"Of course I'm sure."

"Was she attractive?"

"Not really."

She pouts and grabs her phone from her nightstand. "I'm going to google it right now and see what she looks like, so I'll know if you're lying."

"She was attractive, but not as attractive as you." He kisses her.

She smiles at him, puts her phone back down. "Is she married?"

"I think so. Yes, she mentioned a husband and a child."

"Then if she's missing, my money's on the husband."

He kisses her on the mouth, and she feels his warm hand slip beneath the pink satin to caress her breast. She forgets about the missing woman.

SAM LETS HIMSELF quietly into the hotel suite that Lizzie has arranged. He knows she's already there. She'd texted him the information, and the detectives had provided an officer to drive him there. It's almost ten thirty. He uses the key card and slips in the door as if he is in disgrace.

Lizzie hears him, creeps toward the door to meet him, and whispers, "How did it go?"

"Fine." He realizes that he sounds abrupt. He doesn't want her to think he isn't grateful for all she's done. "Thanks for arranging this," he adds after a beat. "I don't seem to be able to manage anything right now." He rubs his hands over his face in exhaustion.

"I understand," she says.

"I've got to get some sleep," he tells her. His nerves are shot. He's not thinking clearly, and he needs to keep his wits about him. That detective thinks he murdered his wife, and she's not going to let up. He must be careful, not give her anything she can use against him. But he can't tell Lizzie that. Lizzie seems to be the one who's coping best—perhaps it's her training as a nurse, Sam thinks; she functions well in a crisis.

He looks in on Clara, in the hotel room cot in the room that Lizzie has taken; there's an adjoining door between them. Clara is asleep, at least for now. She doesn't know her mother is dead. He doesn't know how he's going to tell her. But he has to, soon. He whispers to Lizzie,

"We have to tell her. Tomorrow morning. The two of us, before we go back to the condo."

Lizzie looks back at him and nods gravely.

He makes his way to his own bed and sags down onto it, overwhelmed, trying to think.

He is afraid of what the police might discover.

JAYNE RUBS HER TEMPLES WEARILY. She and Kilgour have stopped at a coffee shop after leaving the condo. It's late, and she ought to be going home. The story of the dead woman in the suitcase will probably lead the eleven thirty news. She's tried to keep the information given to the press to a minimum, but the fact that the body was found in a suitcase in the basement of the condominium building has been released.

The body is now with the coroner, awaiting autopsy. She hopes forensics will come up with something useful. Perhaps they'll find something in the apartment that wasn't visible to the naked eye. She's hoping they can find something on the body, the suitcase, or in the storage locker.

The finding of the body has made things less urgent. It's no longer a missing persons case; Bryden can't be saved. Jayne nurses her cup of coffee and talks it over with Kilgour, who looks as if he's ready to go home too. The adrenaline of a missing persons case has evaporated, and now they're in for the long haul of a homicide investigation.

"It's Sam Frost's suitcase that we found her in," Jayne says. "He has no alibi." She thinks it through. "He might have driven back to the condo once he picked up his lunch. It would take less than ten minutes. We know he didn't use his key card to gain access to the garage, but she might have buzzed him in."

"What's the motive though?" Kilgour asks.

She says tiredly, "Maybe one of them was having an affair—we both got the sense that Paige was lying. We need to talk to her again, tomorrow, first thing." She continues. "If it *was* Sam, and he didn't use his card to enter the garage, that speaks to planning. He knows there are no cameras in the garage, or on the floors or elevators. And he knew she was working at home that day. He kills her in the apartment—probably smothered her, no mess—puts her in his suitcase, and takes her down and puts her in the open storage locker behind the boxes and leaves the way he came. No cameras. Except he could have been seen. And why use his own suitcase and leave her in a storage locker in the building? She was certain to be discovered eventually, from the smell." She looks at Kilgour. "Is he just stupid?"

Kilgour says, "On the other hand, does finding her in the storage locker really make him look any more guilty than if we'd found her in his suitcase in a ditch somewhere? He might have been afraid of being seen or caught on camera dumping it, and he knew there were no cameras in the garage."

"Maybe he's innocent," Jayne says wearily. "Anyone who lived or worked in that building could have gone to her apartment, killed her, found the suitcase, dumped her in the storage locker, and returned to their own unit or even left the building." She pushes her coffee away. "The storage area is kept locked," Jayne says, "so whoever it was would have needed a key. All the residents have keys. Unless—"

"Unless what?"

"Unless the storage area wasn't locked at all. Maybe sometimes it's left unlocked or propped open, in which case the killer wouldn't have needed keys. I'll talk to the manager again."

Kilgour nods. "If that door wasn't locked, it could have been anyone at all, somebody she might have buzzed in through the parking garage."

Jayne says, "Ravi is adamant that no one entered the building through the main floor that didn't belong there. Every person on the CCTV is accounted for. We need to have officers speak to everyone in the building again and ask them whether they saw anyone with a large suitcase yesterday. And we need to look into Bryden's life and find out who she might have let into the building." Jayne thinks quietly for a moment, then asks, "Why move the body at all?"

"Maybe to implicate the husband? By using his suitcase?"

"Perhaps a lover," Jayne says. She looks at the other detective. "Go home. Tomorrow is another day. And it's going to be a long one."

JAYNE DRIVES HOME to her apartment. Michael isn't there. They don't live together, not yet. But perhaps soon. She calls him when she gets there, as soon as she sets down her bag.

"Hey," she says.

"Looks like you've had a busy day," Michael says.

"You can say that again." She finds the remote and turns on the TV for the news, but keeps it muted. It's almost eleven thirty. "We found her," she says, her voice catching. She can let her guard down with Michael. It's something that she needs him for, that she loves him for.

"I heard. I saw it online. Pretty awful."

"Pretty awful," she repeats.

"Do you want me to come over and give you a back rub?" he offers.

There's nothing she would love more. But she really needs to sleep, and she has to be up early. "You're the best," she says, meaning it, "but I should go straight to bed. I've got an early start."

"Okay. I love you, Jayne."

"I love you too, Michael, more than you know."

"Sleep well."

She kisses into the phone and disconnects. She's lucky to have Michael in her corner. Hers is the kind of job that sucks your belief in the goodness of people right out of you. She changes into her pajamas and goes into the living room. The news is about to come on and she turns up the volume.

And there it is, the photograph of Bryden Frost filling her television screen. The details are sketchy, just that her body had been found in a suitcase in the basement of the building where she lived. There is mention of the husband, Sam Frost, being taken in for questioning and released.

As she climbs into bed, she wonders what they will uncover in the coming days. Maybe the news coverage will shake some skeletons out of the closet. Maybe someone saw somebody with that suitcase.

19

Lizzie sits with Sam at the little table in his hotel room, the lights dim. Neither of them can sleep, although they are both drained and exhausted and it's long after midnight. Sam has plundered the mini bar, and Lizzie has joined him. He's drinking scotch, and she's drinking little bottles of vodka, mixed with Coke. She needs its warmth and comfort, needs its numbing properties. Clearly Sam does too, because this is his third.

She studies him anxiously. Fortunately, Clara has not woken up, not yet anyway. Lizzie is worried because Sam is all Clara has now. But then she reminds herself that that is not true. Clara has her, and her grandparents. She is loved, and she will be okay. They'll make sure she's okay. She tells herself that children are resilient. But she recognizes that Sam himself may never recover from this.

She wants to know what happened when he was with the police, but she's afraid to ask again. Instead, she says, "Sam, you should probably get some sleep."

"I know, but I tried that. I can't. I just keep imagining . . . what happened to her." His voice has sunk to a strangled whisper.

She nods. "I know. I keep thinking about it too, even though I try not to." She adds, her voice catching, "We don't even know how she was killed yet. I hope she didn't suffer too much . . ." She watches Sam finish his drink. She hesitates, then finally asks, "How did it go with the detectives?"

He doesn't look so defensive now, like he did when she asked him earlier. Maybe it's the scotch.

"They think I did it," he says abruptly.

She feels a surge of fear. "No, they can't actually believe that," she says, her mouth dry.

"It was my suitcase."

"*Your* suitcase," she says.

He nods. "And I don't have an alibi. They really grilled me about that. Detective Salter hates me, I can tell."

"She doesn't hate you," Lizzie protests. "She has to investigate you, that's all." She says it, but she's afraid Sam might be right about them thinking he did it. Her voice rises. "It could have been anyone. Anyone could have come to the door and knocked. And she would have answered it—why wouldn't she? And whoever it was killed her and looked around the apartment and found your suitcase. It could have been anyone!" She puts her hand out and lays it on his forearm. "And we have to find out who. Because the police are useless."

He looks back at her, visibly surprised. "We don't know that they're useless. They found her. And they've only just begun." He adds wearily, "I have keys to the storage room."

"Anyone in the building has keys to the storage room!" Lizzie exclaims.

"That's what I told them." He downs the rest of his drink. "Maybe they'll find out things." He seems a little drunk.

"What things?"

"I don't know." He looks down at the table.

"You don't know something you're not telling me, do you?" Lizzie asks.

"No, of course not." But then he abruptly staggers to his feet. "I'm going to bed."

Lizzie watches him, uneasy, then returns to her own room. She spends more time on her phone before she finally goes to sleep.

DONNA LIES RIGIDLY on her back in bed, unable to close her eyes, while her husband tosses and turns beside her in a restless, tortured sleep.

Her eldest daughter is dead, her beloved Bryden. Someone murdered her and left her in a basement to rot. She doesn't think she can survive it. Donna hasn't been able to keep even the smallest amounts of food down since she heard her daughter was missing. It's as if her body is trying to heave up the ugliness and horror in the world and expel it. But nothing she does can change anything.

She thinks she understands now why some people go mad. Maybe it's a choice. To go somewhere else in your mind because reality is just too hard to bear. She had a great-aunt who went mad, although the family never talked about how or why, and now everyone who knew her is gone. Maybe Donna will go mad too and end up in an institution like her great-aunt, living in her own, inaccessible world. Right now, that doesn't seem too farfetched.

Her thoughts run on, won't let her sleep. Who would kill her beautiful daughter, who would discard her body that way? Whoever did it is a monster. It might be someone Bryden knew. Possibly even someone close to her. It usually is, isn't it? So—a monster with a friendly, familiar face. She knows that the detective suspects Sam; she could tell, they could all tell. The husband is always the main suspect. Donna wants to think that the idea is absurd. He's always been so good to Bryden. She loved him. She remembers how they were together at Christmastime. They were so happy. Weren't they?

But honestly, how well do parents know what's going on in their children's lives, in their marriages? They might have been pretending. It could have been awful, and Bryden might not have told her. She might have been too embarrassed, or ashamed, or in denial. She and her daughter weren't as close as they used to be, since they'd moved away to Florida. Maybe that was a mistake. Maybe she should have stayed put, been here for her daughter. Maybe Bryden would have confided in her then. Maybe Donna could have helped her. The guilt kicks in hard. She should have been paying more attention.

She thinks about Sam, about his demeanor since they arrived. He's been distressed, agitated, distraught—it's impossible to tell if it's from grief or guilt.

Donna had been deeply shaken when she learned Sam didn't have an alibi. He should have been at work, and he wasn't.

She's always thought she loved Sam, but she could easily hate him.

ON THURSDAY MORNING, Paige wanders tiredly around her apartment. She doesn't think she fell asleep before four. How could she sleep?

She knows they found Bryden's body last night, after she'd left the condo. Sam had called her to let her know, but she had stayed away. It was time for the family to be alone. She told him how sorry she was and tried to comfort him. She'd watched the coverage on the news, followed it all online. She couldn't bring herself to do anything but sit at home by herself, her arms around her knees, thinking about Bryden. Her best friend, murdered and stuffed in a suitcase.

Now, she hears a knock at her door and immediately tenses. She walks across the hardwood floor and answers it. The two detectives from yesterday stand on her doorstep.

Detective Salter says, "We're sorry to bother you, but we have a few more questions, if that's all right."

Paige swallows and feels her eyes start to tear up. Salter says gently, "I'm so sorry, but I'm sure you've heard—this is now a homicide investigation. Can we come in?"

Paige lets them into her apartment. She takes a couple of deep breaths to steady herself while her back is turned.

JAYNE REGARDS the woman across from her and Kilgour, sitting on the green velvet sofa in the sunny living room. The apartment is the first floor of a charming older home close to downtown, with high ceilings and tall, narrow windows that look out onto the street.

Paige Mason looks as if she hasn't slept. She's dressed in jeans and an old sweater. Her hair is tied behind her in a careless ponytail, still damp, and she's not wearing any makeup. She's clearly upset about Bryden, and seems apprehensive, uncomfortable at having the detectives in her home. Well, most people are.

Jayne says quietly, "Paige, we're so sorry for your loss. We understand that this must be very painful for you." Paige nods, looking down at the coffee table between them, fighting tears.

Kilgour says, "We want to get who did this." Paige looks up at them then.

Jayne is hopeful they can get more out of her today, away from the condo, and the people in it. "Paige, when we spoke to you yesterday, you said that you had known Bryden since your college days."

"Yes, that's where we met."

"Try to think. Is there anyone who might have had an interest in Bryden, from that time, or more recently? Any spurned boyfriends?"

Paige sits still, as if thinking deeply. Finally, she sighs and says, "No, not that I know of. Not that she ever mentioned."

Kilgour says, "You told us yesterday that Bryden and Sam were happy, that they had a good marriage. Do you still stand by that?"

"Of course. They were very happy."

He says, "You said that as far as you knew, neither one of them ever cheated."

"That's right."

Kilgour says, "We think you were lying."

"What? No I wasn't." She looks startled, caught out.

Jayne speaks up. "Your body language gave you away. You said, 'Neither one of them would ever cheat,' but that's not true, is it?" Jayne asks. Beside her, Detective Kilgour stares intently at Paige. Jayne asks, "So which one was cheating, Paige? Sam or Bryden?"

20

Paige looks distressed, and Jayne waits, letting the silence fill the room. When Paige still doesn't speak, Jayne says more firmly, "Paige, which one was it?"

She finally whispers her answer. "Bryden."

"Bryden was having an affair?" Jayne asks.

Paige answers reluctantly. "Yes."

"Did she tell you this?" Jayne watches Paige blink rapidly, as if to ward off more tears. Jayne wants to shake her and say, *Why didn't you tell us this yesterday?* But there is nothing to be gained from that now. She must ease this information out of her; she's obviously reluctant to part with it. But Paige appears frozen, unable to speak. Jayne tries again. "Paige, Bryden has been *murdered.* You must tell us what you know. How did you know Bryden was having an affair? Did she tell you?"

"Yes," she admits finally, meeting Jayne's eyes.

"Who was this affair with, do you know?"

"She never told me his name."

Jayne's heart falls. "Did she tell you anything about him? What he did for a living, where he lived? What he looked like?"

Paige shakes her head. "She didn't tell me anything about him, probably because she could tell I didn't approve. I was genuinely shocked by it. I thought it was an awful thing to do to Sam."

Kilgour asks, "So how did she tell you about it? How did it come up?"

"We were having a glass of wine one night, about three weeks ago. Sam wasn't home. She said, 'Can you keep a secret?' And I said, 'You know I can.' And she said, 'I've met someone. I'm having an affair.'" She stops abruptly.

"Go on," Jayne prompts.

"I said, 'How could you?' and she said, 'If you saw him, you'd understand. He's irresistible.'"

"And that's all she told you?" Jayne presses. "She didn't tell you anything else about him?"

Paige shakes her head. "No. Except how they met. She hit his car at a traffic light."

Jayne feels a surge of excitement and glances at Kilgour. She turns back to Paige. "Thank you for telling us, Paige. You've done the right thing. You've been very helpful. Did she tell you where they would meet, when she saw him?"

"No." Paige adds fretfully, "I didn't say anything yesterday because I didn't want Sam to know. It will break his heart. I guess he'll have to find out now though, won't he?"

"I'm afraid so. But Paige—didn't it occur to you yesterday, when Bryden was missing, that she might be in danger?"

She answers, her voice breaking, "I thought she might be with him, and that she'd come back. I thought she was behaving outrageously, because she was crazy about him, but that she'd come to her senses, because of Clara."

"Didn't it worry you that she didn't show up to pick up Clara from day care?"

"Yes. But Bryden would know they'd call Sam, and he would pick her up. Clara wasn't going to come to any harm. I thought she'd come back with some explanation or excuse, and Sam would believe her."

They question her at length, until it becomes clear that Paige has nothing more to tell them. Once they leave, and are out on the sidewalk, Jayne turns to Kilgour and says, "So Bryden wasn't living such a quiet, dull life after all."

"There was certainly more to her than her family or other friends knew."

"I want to talk to this Derek Gardner—we're going to pay him another visit."

IT'S ALICE'S DAY OFF. She plans to spend it sleeping in and then doing some shopping. Maybe for some new shoes. She loves shoes. One of her indulgences. And Derek loves her in heels. She has great legs, and she likes to make the most of them. And maybe she'll get something sexy for the bedroom too. She likes to keep things spicy. She doesn't want him straying.

Derek is up already. She can hear him moving around in the kitchen, operating the coffee machine. He works from home a lot. That has its advantages and disadvantages. It makes it less likely he's flirting with someone else, but it also makes him less accountable.

He appears at the bedroom door with a cup of coffee. "Are you up?" he asks. He looks very sexy this morning, she thinks; he hasn't shaved. He's wearing suit pants and a dress shirt, no tie. His rakish smile undoes her every time.

She sits up in bed, allowing the strap of her nightgown to slip off one shoulder appealingly. "Yes. And thank you." She takes the coffee from him and sips. He leans in and kisses her.

The doorbell chimes throughout the house, startling them both. "Who the hell is that?" Alice says, putting her coffee down on the nightstand.

Derek frowns, looks uncertain. "I don't know. I'll see. Why don't you stay in bed?"

She listens to him make his way to the front door, hears muted voices, but she can't tell what they're saying. She gets out of bed and hovers at the partially open bedroom door. Whoever it is, he hasn't gotten rid of them. Instead, she can hear them now moving into the living room. Her curiosity is piqued. She hears a woman's voice and goes still for a moment. Then she puts on her long silk robe, cinches the tie at her waist, checks herself in the mirror, and walks barefoot down the stairs and the long hall to the living room to see what's going on.

When she appears on the edge of the living room, she sees a tall man and a dark-haired woman in a trouser suit, neither of whom she recognizes, sitting on her sofa. Her husband is standing facing them, his back to her. The two on the sofa notice her and stare. Derek turns around and sees her. By the expression on his face, she can tell he's annoyed about something. She doesn't know if he's annoyed at the two people on his sofa, or at her appearing in her bathrobe.

"What's going on?" she asks. She doesn't like the feel of this. There's a vibe in the room; something is wrong.

"Alice, this is Detective Salter, the one I told you about. And this is her partner, Detective . . ." he turns back.

"Kilgour," the other man supplies.

"My wife, Alice," Derek says.

Alice steps into the center of the living room and studies all three of them. "Well, let's get on with it, why don't we?" she says, sitting down on the sofa across from the detectives. Her husband sits beside her and faces them as well.

"As you know, from my visit to you yesterday," Detective Salter begins, "we were investigating the disappearance of Bryden Frost. That has now turned into a homicide investigation. Her body was found last night."

"Oh dear," Alice says, making her eyes go large. "How awful."

"You didn't know?" the detective asks her.

"No," Alice says.

Derek says, "She just woke up. But I saw it on the news this morning, when I turned on my computer."

The female detective looks Alice in the eye and says, "She was murdered and left in the basement in her condominium building."

"That's terrible," Alice says. "But what does that have to do with us?"

"Your husband knew her," Detective Salter says.

"I told you, I didn't actually know her," Derek protests in a reasonable voice. "We only met twice—at the accident, and later when she paid me for the damage. That was the extent of my involvement with her."

"Yes, that's what you told me yesterday," Detective Salter says and waits a beat. Then she leans forward and says, "But now we have information that you did know her, quite well, in fact."

Alice turns and stares at her husband. She sees him flush just slightly beneath his day-old stubble. Can the detectives see it too? Alice is suddenly very angry, at the detectives and at her husband. But mostly at her husband. What has he done? What has he been up to, and not telling her about? They agreed no more secrets. He promised her no more secrets. No more misbehavior. And now this.

"What information?" Derek demands. "There can't be any information, because I'm telling you the truth." He sounds perfectly in control of himself, but she can see the vein pulsing in his temple. It does that when he's angry.

"I'm afraid I'm going to have to ask you to come down to the station to answer a few questions," the detective says.

"And what if I refuse?" Derek asks.

"That's your choice. But if you don't come willingly, we will arrest you and bring you in for questioning."

Alice watches him stare at them. He's furious now, she can tell. They don't realize what they've done.

"This is outrageous. I'm not going anywhere until I call my attorney," Derek says calmly.

"Fine," the detective says. "We'll wait."

21

Once the detectives have gone, Paige makes herself a cup of tea and sits on the sofa staring blankly at the wall, going over the interview again in her mind. She is not going in to work today. Who would expect someone to come to work when their best friend has been murdered? It's splashed all over the headlines. They have let her take some personal time. They've told her she can take vacation time too, if she needs it.

Those detectives had put her on the spot; Paige hadn't realized she'd been so transparent when they spoke to her in Bryden's condo yesterday. Whatever happens now is out of her control. She wishes this was a book she could put down; she doesn't want to know what's going to happen next.

SAM, LIZZIE, AND CLARA are back at the apartment. Detective Salter had called Sam and told him the forensics people had finished, that they could return.

Sam finds he is uncomfortable now around Lizzie. She bustles around, trying to entertain Clara. He's grateful for her help, but at the same time, he feels watched somehow. Perhaps he said too much last night.

He tells himself that she's on his side. At least she says she is, but does she have doubts? Does she think he might have killed Bryden, despite her protestations? He's caught her looking at him speculatively. It makes him think that she knows some secret about Bryden that she hasn't shared with him. What is *she* keeping back? And then it occurs to him, the possibility of betrayal—has she told the detectives something she hasn't told him?

The easy trust that existed between them when Bryden first went missing changed somehow when her body was discovered. It looks bad—his suitcase, the storage room, to which he has keys. His having no alibi. But what they haven't come up with, so far, is a motive. That's what everyone is looking for, he can feel it. The detectives terrify him. In the middle of the night, unable to sleep, he saw himself convicted and sent to prison.

Before he can think any more about that, there's a buzz on the intercom. It's his mother-and father-in-law, wanting in. When they arrive at the door moments later, he lets them in without a word. They have got themselves here by Uber.

Lizzie fusses, getting them coffee, while Sam watches, numb. Rather than being more rested after the night, everyone seems more exhausted, more depleted, more distressed. All hope gone. Except Lizzie, who seems to thrive on being needed, and appears to be running on adrenaline. She is constantly checking her phone. In a bizarre way, Lizzie almost seems to want credit for the discovery of the body. She has twice mentioned that she's glad she pushed the detectives to get the K-9 unit to search the building—that if she hadn't done that, perhaps they would still be looking.

Sam is lost in his own thoughts this morning, barely interacting with his wife's family. Still, he slowly becomes aware of his mother-in-law's eyes on him. He looks back at her and she quickly looks away. She's speculating too, Sam thinks, like Lizzie. *Does Donna think he killed Bryden?* He feels a wave of fear and sickness go through him. Have they talked about him, the three of them? They might have discussed him in Lizzie's apartment last night, before she left for the hotel, reeling from the shock of the discovery of Bryden's body. What are they thinking about him? What are they saying to the detectives? He doesn't trust them. Is this just paranoia, or is he right not to trust them? Sam realizes he must be careful what he says now, how he acts, in front of them. They are watching him. Suddenly he wants them all to leave. He wishes he could get high, just to escape all this for a while, but he doesn't have anything in the house. Perhaps he will suggest they all take Clara to the park so he can have a moment to himself. If he could just have a moment maybe he could think straight. But no one leaves, and he continues to brood.

Paige soon arrives, and this time Sam lets Lizzie answer the door. He must find out what Paige said to the detectives yesterday. She knew his wife best; if Bryden had secrets, Paige would know.

Lizzie fetches a cup of coffee for Paige, then settles Clara in the den, and they all sit awkwardly in the living room talking in low voices about Bryden, their memories of her, and about Clara, how this will affect her, and about the murder investigation. It's almost like an out-of-body experience for Sam. He is so distraught and sleep-deprived that none of it seems quite real. More like a dream. He feels uncomfortably warm, feels himself sweating. Can they tell? He didn't shower again this morning. He should have.

He surveys the people around him; he has never been less able to read a room.

. . .

DEREK GARDNER, on the advice of his attorney, is driving himself to the police station. The detectives have left ahead of them. Alice, to his annoyance, has insisted on accompanying him to the station, although he tried to dissuade her. His business attorney has recommended a criminal attorney, Joe Pagett, from their firm, Roten & Pagett, who is meeting them at the station for the interview. Derek is simmering with rage, although he doesn't think you would know it to look at him. Alice knows though. Alice knows him better than anyone. And he knows Alice better than anyone. They are alike. They understand each other. They are a team. Theirs is not a typical relationship, they both know that. They are not typical people; they are not like everybody else. They are outliers. They both feel so lucky to have found each other.

That's not to say they always trust each other. Right now, Alice doesn't seem to trust him. She clearly doesn't believe him when he says he didn't have anything to do with Bryden Frost. It's not like he can offer to take a lie-detector test for her, because they both know he can beat one of those. So can she. They are both expert liars. Both members of Mensa. They tell each other that they love each other, whatever that is. They have a partnership based on sex, intellect, ambition, and joint interests. But love? They don't really know what that is.

Before they left for the police station, she'd said, "Well?" She'd folded her arms across her chest, still in her silk bathrobe, looking like a film star.

"Alice, I swear on my life, I had nothing to do with this woman. You know you're the only one for me."

She studied him, unconvinced. After all, he'd strayed before. But they'd worked that out. They are on the same team now. They can't betray each other again. They've made a commitment. They have made vows that are stronger than marriage vows. Theirs are written in blood.

"You're not lying to me, are you?" she asked. "Because if you are—"

"I'm not lying to you. I made a promise, remember? I keep my promises." He kissed her.

All the way to the station, she keeps banging away at him. "If there's anything I should know, you ought to tell me."

"There's nothing you should know."

"If you might be in any trouble, I can help," she says.

"I know, but I'm not in any trouble. Trust me."

"You didn't kill her and stuff her in a suitcase? Because if you did, just admit it. I might still be able to forgive you."

"I did not kill her," he says.

She falls silent and starts scrolling on her phone. She stares intently at something on the small screen. "You lied to me," she says, her voice chilly. She holds the phone up to his face while he's driving, and he glances at it.

"What?" he asks.

"That's her picture. She's very attractive. You said she wasn't."

"I didn't say she wasn't attractive," he answers. "I said she wasn't as attractive as you."

22

Lizzie is a nurse, and taking care of people is what she does best. She is able to put her own needs and feelings aside as required. She knows that no matter how bad things are, someone must keep functioning, keep things together. Now, in her sister's living room, she regards the rest of them and notes the grief, the lethargy, the tension. She's put Clara in front of the TV in the other room for now.

She'd watched, earlier that morning, when Sam had told her that her mother wasn't coming back, that she was in heaven now. He'd handled it sensitively, Lizzie thought. But Clara hadn't seemed to understand. "Mommy's coming back," she said.

"No, Clara, she's not. She's in heaven."

Clara shook her head. Lizzie had caught Sam's eye, seen the desperation there.

Lizzie thinks they should get some professional help for her; she'll look into that. Maybe this kind of denial is normal. But tomorrow she thinks Clara should go back to day care. A crime scene with everyone moping around waiting for developments is no place for a little girl. And she doesn't want to ask too much of Angela. Sam is going to need her.

"When will we get the autopsy results, do you think?" Lizzie asks now.

They all look at her blankly. Then Sam says, "I don't know, they didn't say, did they?"

He looks like he can't rub two thoughts together, Lizzie thinks. She turns to Paige. She's never really liked Paige. She thinks that it's probably because Paige has always seemed rather glamorous. Though she doesn't seem very glamorous now. Or maybe it's because Paige was Bryden's best friend in the world, and until Bryden went to college and met Paige, Lizzie had always considered herself to be her sister's closest friend. But perhaps that was never really true. Or maybe it's because Bryden once said carelessly that Paige was Clara's favorite babysitter, and Lizzie had always thought that she was Clara's favorite babysitter. When she'd said as much to Bryden, her sister had answered, trying to be conciliatory, *But you're her favorite aunt.* Lizzie hadn't replied. She knew perfectly well that she was Clara's only aunt.

Lizzie says, "I'm going to call them right now, for an update."

"Yes. Call them," her father says.

She has already entered Detective Salter's number into her contacts. She presses the number on her cell as they all watch. But it goes to voicemail. Lizzie disconnects without leaving a message and huffs unhappily. "I'll call back later."

Her father looks at the floor. Paige stares at her coffee mug, while Donna studies Sam when he's not looking. She seems to regard him almost with distaste. Lizzie wonders what her mother is thinking. She will ask her when they are alone.

. . .

JAYNE IS PLEASED to have a lead in the case. Paige's reluctant disclosure this morning was their first break. Now, she's eager to question Derek Gardner, who sits across from her in the interview room, in a smart suit and tie, looking poised and comfortable. Few people look poised and comfortable when being questioned in a murder investigation, so she takes note. Beside him is his very sharply dressed, and no doubt very expensive, attorney. Beside her is Detective Kilgour. The tape is running. She expects they will get a lot of *no comments*.

Jayne has to admit that Derek Gardner is a good-looking man. And there is a magnetism about him, a charisma. She remembers what Paige said, that Bryden had found him "irresistible." She can believe that Bryden felt that way. She wonders if it got her killed.

"Mr. Gardner," she begins, "could you please state your name for the tape."

"Derek Gardner," he says in a cool, deep voice. His voice is seductive too; she'd noticed it before.

"You have been read your rights and are here with your attorney, Joe Pagett, to answer questions in our inquiry into the murder of Bryden Frost." She takes him through how they met once again—the car accident, the date it happened, how he messaged her and met her at the coffee shop to get the money she owed him for repairs. Then she asks, "Did you have any contact with Bryden Frost other than those occasions you have told us about?"

"No, I did not."

"That's interesting," Jayne says, "because we have a witness who says that you were having an affair with her."

He manages to look genuinely scornful. She has to hand it to him, he can act. Perhaps he trusted Bryden not to say anything. And now it's backfired on him.

"I don't know how that's possible, when it isn't true," he says smoothly.

"Well, we only have your word for it, don't we, since Bryden is dead and we can't ask her," Jayne says, unruffled. She takes another tack. "Have you ever cheated on your wife before?"

"I don't see how my marriage is any of your business," Derek says.

"Everything is my business in a murder investigation," she tells him. "Please answer the question."

"No comment."

"Does your wife know that you've cheated on her in the past? Because I have to tell you, Derek, the way she was looking at you this morning in your house—well, she didn't seem all that surprised at the suggestion."

Derek gives her a cold look but doesn't say anything.

Jayne asks, "Where were you on Tuesday, between noon and five o'clock?"

"I was at home, working, all afternoon."

"Do you have anyone who can verify that for you?"

"No, I'm afraid not."

"I see. Have you ever been to the condominium building at 100 Constitution Drive in Buckingham Lake?" she continues.

"No. I've told you this. I've never been there."

"Are you quite sure?" None of the footage shows Derek in the building. But he might have known that he could go in and out through the underground garage without being seen, if Bryden had told him.

"Yes, quite sure."

"Has Bryden Frost ever been in your home? I understand you work from home quite frequently. It would be a convenient place for a tryst, wouldn't it, while your wife is at work?"

He glares at her, the first indication that she's getting to him. "She's never been in my home. As I have told you, I barely knew her."

"So if we get a search warrant and go over your house with a fine-tooth comb, that wouldn't worry you at all?"

He turns to his attorney as if he's had enough. "We're done here. I'm leaving."

His expensive attorney speaks up. "Where did you get this information you say you have about my client?"

"From a reliable source."

The attorney smirks. "You're fishing. You have nothing on my client. You don't have sufficient grounds to get a search warrant for his residence and you know it." He adds, "And even though he's entirely innocent, I'm not going to let him give you consent to search his house, because he doesn't need the media seeing that. He's a respectable businessman. This sort of thing could ruin him." The attorney stands up and says, "Unless you're arresting my client, which I very much doubt, we're leaving."

Jayne stands too. She ends the tape and watches them exit the room, Derek Gardner leaving a very faint scent of expensive cologne behind him. She turns to Kilgour and mutters, "Fucker."

23

izzie's mother gets up stiffly from the sofa. She looks so old, Lizzie thinks, she even moves differently. Her mother gives her a subtle glance, signaling Lizzie to follow her. She does it in such a way that Lizzie knows she wants to make it seem natural. She waits for her mother to reach the kitchen. Then Lizzie makes a show of noticing her coffee cup is empty and gets up. "I'm going to get more coffee, anybody want some?"

Sam and Jim shake their heads. Paige looks up at her and shakes her head too. When Lizzie reaches the kitchen, her mother is waiting for her and steps in close. "We need to talk," she mouths.

Lizzie feels a clutch of fear. Does her mother know something? Has she been keeping something from them? Lizzie nods silently and starts making more coffee to provide some covering noise. She turns on the tap to fill the carafe.

"What if Sam did it?" her mother whispers quietly. Her face is strained, and her tired eyes are full of horrible possibility.

So, her mother is considering it, Lizzie thinks. She's not that surprised. It's an obvious question, really. She swallows, unsure how to respond. This signals a shift in family dynamics that Lizzie doesn't think she's ready for. She can't think of anything to say; her mother seems to take that as agreement.

"You think he did!" her mother says accusingly, wide-eyed.

She turns off the tap. "No! I don't know," Lizzie whispers back. This is not what she wants. "I can't believe that. Sam couldn't have done it. He loved her."

"He doesn't have an alibi," her mother points out quietly. "Don't you think that's strange? Why wasn't he at work? Does he always take such long lunches? Maybe we don't know him as well as we thought. Maybe Bryden was keeping things from us." Her mother begins to tremble, and Lizzie instinctively reaches out and holds her in an embrace. She smells her mother's powdery skin, absorbs her grief, her pain. Her mother begins to sob brokenly against her shoulder. "I should have been there for her," her mother weeps. "It's all my fault."

Lizzie is suddenly aware of someone else with them in the kitchen. She lifts her head and turns. It's Paige; she's crept up on them, caught them unawares. How much has she heard?

"It's not your fault," Paige says to Lizzie's mother in a low, sympathetic voice. "You mustn't think that." She adds firmly, "You must never think that."

JAYNE STANDS AT the front of the incident room, glancing behind her at the whiteboard. Beside the enlarged photographs of Bryden Frost and Sam Frost, there is now also one of Derek Gardner. She turns back to face the others in the room.

"Derek Gardner is a smooth character; he's got a sharp attorney and he's not going to be easy to crack. So we need to find everything we can on him. He says he was home all Tuesday afternoon. Keep checking the CCTV on the roads around the condo building and the surrounding area. He drives a black Tesla Model Y; we've got the plate number. Go all the way back to the date they met at the coffee shop, January 26, and forward from there. Maybe we'll catch him going into the garage before the cameras broke down, but I doubt it. I think he's too smart for that. They probably met somewhere else. Look into his background, his business, his marriage. He says he was home alone, working, at the time Bryden Frost was killed. Let's see if we can poke holes in that, through CCTV, witnesses—did any neighbors see him leave the house that day? At this point, he and the husband, Sam Frost, are our main suspects. If she was cheating, that gives the husband a motive as well. We may have an ugly love triangle here." She pauses.

"It could be either one of them," Jayne says. "We've learned from the building manager that sometimes the door to the storage area is left propped open by the residents. That means whoever killed her and left her in that open locker didn't necessarily have to have keys to the storage area. It could have been Derek Gardner. Has there been any progress on verifying the husband's alibi?"

An officer speaks up. "We spoke to the food truck owner—Gino Morelli—where Sam got his lunch. He confirmed it, and it's on Sam's credit card. We're going back to the park now to talk to people over the lunch hour to see if we can find anyone who saw him after that."

"What about his car?"

"There's no CCTV coverage where he says he parked it."

Jayne says, "Okay, so let's say it's him. He picks up lunch, drives home—it's only about a seven-minute drive from Washington Park to the condo. He knows his wife is working from home that day. He gets her to buzz him in so there's no record he's there. He goes up to the apartment, kills her, removes her clothes, puts her in the suitcase." She pauses. "What does he do with the clothes? We haven't found them anywhere. He takes her in the suitcase down to the storage locker. He took a risk that someone might see him with a large suitcase and recognize him after the fact," Jayne says.

"It might have been much less of a risk if he took the stairs," Kilgour suggests. "He might not have run into anyone. And if he'd heard someone above or below, he could have waited till they were out of sight or ducked back onto one of the floors."

Jayne nods. "She weighed a hundred and twenty pounds, but it would be doable. And there were wheels on the suitcase. Let's try that. Martin, you're pretty fit, go over there at one o'clock and take the stairs from the eighth floor down to the storage room. Do it a few times and see if you run into anyone or not and report back to me."

There's a chuckle of sympathy around the room for Martin, fit or not.

She continues. "He uses his keys, or not, if it's open, to get into the storage locker area. He leaves the suitcase in the open locker, hidden behind boxes, then what? He gets back in his car, with her clothes. What's he carrying those in? He has to get rid of them. But he has to go back to work. Where did he get rid of the clothes? You've already reviewed any CCTV footage we can get on the routes to and from his office, right?"

"Yes. We've already done that. There aren't many cameras. We haven't spotted him," an officer replies.

Kilgour says, "But he would have had time, on his way back to work, if he hurried. He picked up the BLT at twelve fifteen. Bryden did her last computer backup at twelve forty-two. He arrives after that, kills her, undresses her, puts her in the suitcase. How long would that take? Fifteen minutes? He might have needed another fifteen minutes to hide the suitcase. By now it's one fifteen. It's about a fifteen-minute drive to his office. He got there at about two. He had time to get rid of the evidence—almost half an hour. And we don't have any CCTV coverage of that route to see where he went, and he hasn't turned up anywhere else—we've looked."

Jayne nods. "What about on the way to the day care?" she asks.

"Judging by the timelines, he went directly to the day care that afternoon when he left the office, and then he went directly home again."

"Most likely on the way back to work then," Jayne says. "And he wouldn't want his three-year-old to see him throwing something away. He could have dumped the clothes anywhere," Jayne says. "A dumpster, the river—without CCTV to know where he might have gone, it's like looking for a needle in a haystack." She sighs.

Kilgour asks, "Why did he move the body at all? Why risk being seen with the suitcase? Why not just leave her there?"

Jayne suggests, "Maybe he didn't want his daughter to see the body. He would have known the day care would call him when Bryden didn't show up, that he'd have to go there directly to pick her up and bring her home."

Some nods in the room. It makes sense.

Kilgour offers, "Derek Gardner might have known that the cameras in the underground parking garage weren't working—Bryden might have told him. She might have invited him over that day, while she was working from home. Or he might have just shown up and she buzzed him in. He might have killed her, on the spur of the moment— maybe she threatened to tell his wife—put her in the suitcase, and left her in the storage locker—if the door was propped open. He doesn't have much of an alibi either."

Jayne nods slowly. "This one isn't going to be easy," she says. "So far, we have no physical evidence." She stands up straighter, signaling the meeting is over. "Kilgour and I are off to the Coroner's Office for the autopsy results."

The officers start moving back to their desks—to hop on their computers, their phones. She has a good team. If there is anything to find, they will find it.

24

Jayne and Kilgour leave the police station and get into an unmarked car. Kilgour drives. It doesn't take long to arrive at the Coroner's Office, and they make their way across the pavement and through the heavy glass doors without speaking. Jayne knows that autopsies are not most people's favorite thing about being a homicide detective, but Jayne doesn't mind. Not anymore. She's become used to it. She doesn't know if that's a good thing or a bad thing. She doesn't want to become hardened, inured to all the suffering she comes across, but how the hell else can she do this job year in and year out? She thinks briefly of Michael as their footsteps click on the shiny linoleum along the empty hall. Michael keeps her human. He keeps her from dwelling too much on the dark side of human nature. He wants to get married and maybe have a baby someday. She's not at all sure she would be able to reconcile those completely different sides of her life. She's not even sure she should try.

She pulls open the door and the familiar sights and smells greet her.

The antiseptic steel tables, the body-length refrigerated drawers. The bright overhead lights. The steel instruments, the bone saws, the sinks, the scales, the viewing area up above. Jayne doesn't like to observe from the viewing area, she prefers to be down here on the floor, with the body, able to ask the forensic pathologist questions as they strike her. She doesn't want to be at a remove—that isn't what makes a good detective. She wants to be close to the victim, to study her intimately.

But they are not here to observe an autopsy today; it has already been carried out. They are here for the results.

"Hi, Ginny," Jayne says, greeting the longtime forensic pathologist. Ginny Furness is in her late fifties, almost a generation older than Jayne, but they have always got on well. They are both no-nonsense and go about their work with curiosity and persistence. Jayne knows Ginny has children, grown now, and makes a mental note to ask her, over a drink some evening, how she managed it.

"There you are," Ginny says pleasantly. "I've finished with her." She walks over to a gurney with a sheeted body, and Jayne and Kilgour follow. Ginny pulls the sheet down from the top of the head to rest below the feet, without speaking. She gives them a moment.

Jayne looks down at the woman on the gurney, cold and lifeless. It always strikes Jayne how different someone looks in death compared to how they looked in life. She's never thought they look like they're just sleeping. The animating force is missing, and it's everything. This isn't Bryden Frost anymore. Bryden Frost is gone. The long blond hair is pulled away from her face, her eyes are open. Her body looks untouched to Jayne's eyes, apart from the large, grisly, Y incision that was done to conduct the autopsy. There are no visible marks around the neck or throat, as she was expecting. No apparent sign of a head wound. No stab wounds, although she wasn't expecting those, if Bryden was killed in the apartment, because it was pristine. She looks at Ginny questioningly. "Cause of death?" she asks.

"This wasn't an easy one, but I'd say asphyxiation. There is some facial congestion, some petechial hemorrhaging."

"Method?"

"Again, tricky. She obviously wasn't strangled or choked. The hyoid bone is intact, and as you can see, there are no signs of pressure on the neck. I found no fibers around her mouth or nose, so it is unlikely that she was smothered with a pillow, for example. If I had to guess, I'd say she had a plastic bag held over her head until she died. Most likely, someone put it over her head from behind and held it tightly to her face."

"A plastic bag," Jayne repeats thoughtfully. She imagines it, the plastic sticking to the woman's gasping face, her terror as she realizes what's happening.

"Best guess," Ginny says.

"Any sign of sexual assault?"

"No, not at all."

"Did you find anything else?"

Ginny shakes her head regretfully. "I'm afraid not. No signs of being drugged, no puncture marks. Tox screen will take longer, but not really expecting anything there. Given how she was probably killed, I suspect she fought back, and there is some bruising on the back of her forearms, indicating a struggle. But we found nothing under her nails; they were clean. That might make sense if she was surprised from behind. No foreign hairs on the body. And strangely, very few fibers. We'd expect more from her own clothing, which I understand is missing?"

"Yes," Jayne answers.

"So we don't have them to make a comparison."

Jayne nods. "The clothes her husband described her as wearing that day have not been found. Black yoga pants and a gray sweatshirt.

I've just issued an appeal through the media in the hopes that if anyone finds them they'll come forward."

Ginny nods and continues. "Her clothes were probably stripped off her after, possibly to make it easier to fit her inside the suitcase, or more likely to get rid of any possible transfer evidence. Whoever it was had to be fairly strong, to overpower her and then to get her in that suitcase."

"Time of death?"

"I'd say between noon and five p.m.—I can't be any more exact than that."

Jayne nods absently. "What do you think—crime of passion?" she asks.

"Maybe. Lack of sexual assault doesn't mean it isn't. A crime of passion isn't necessarily about sex, it can be about rage."

Jayne nods. "Thanks, Ginny." She looks at Kilgour. "We'd better get to the Forensics lab."

As she's leaving, Jayne turns back and suggests spontaneously, "You wouldn't want to meet me some night for a drink, would you, Ginny?"

The pathologist is clearly surprised at the invitation. But she smiles and nods. "Sure, anytime. My kids have all flown the nest. I've got time."

PAIGE WANTS TO SCREAM. The grief and tension in the condo are so heavy it's unbearable. But she's Bryden's best friend, and Sam asked her to come, and she has nowhere else to be right now. She can't think of a good excuse to leave. She is uncomfortable, being here with the family at such a terrible time, in such circumstances. When she knows something they don't.

She thinks about that weird conclave in the kitchen a short while ago, when she overheard Lizzie and her mother. She'd suspected they'd crept out to talk, so she'd pretended she wanted some more coffee after all. And now she knows they suspect Sam. At least Donna does—she's not sure about Lizzie.

Sam hasn't showered since Bryden went missing, that's obvious. He's usually so well groomed. Right now, he looks unkempt and distraught—pretty much how you'd expect him to look, given the circumstances. She knows she doesn't look too great herself.

She must step in and help where she can. She must help Sam with Clara. She is Clara's godmother after all. She wonders how Lizzie will feel about that. Lizzie has always been a little jealous of Clara's affection for Paige; she might want to take over. Lizzie has a tendency to do that. And it looks like Sam is letting her. But it's early days yet; he may find his feet.

She can't put off talking privately to Sam any longer; she must tell him what she told the detectives. She gives him a glance, rises, and says, "I'm going to check on Clara." The little girl has been watching TV in the den.

"I'll come with you," Sam offers and stands up stiffly as well.

Paige heads anxiously toward the den, feels Sam following her. Clara is cuddled in the corner of the sofa, sucking her thumb, watching cartoons. Paige sits down beside her and puts an arm around her affectionately. The little girl curls into her. But they can't talk in front of Clara.

And now, finding herself almost alone with Sam for the first time since Bryden went missing, Clara burrowing into her, she doesn't know how to be.

"We need to talk," Sam says, his voice low.

She gives him a sharp look. "Not here. We can go down the hall," she says quietly. She pulls Clara away to face her. "Are you okay, sweetie?" Clara nods at her gravely. "Are you okay to watch television for a bit longer? And then maybe I can take you out to the park?" Clara nods again. "Good girl." Paige kisses the top of her head, then gets up and goes quietly into the hall, Sam close behind her. She walks farther away from the living room, close to the bathroom around the corner, where they won't be seen or heard. She turns around to face him. He's right in front of her, his face close to hers.

He doesn't kiss her. She doesn't know what she was expecting.

He asks, his voice low and tense, "What did you say to the detectives?"

She's taken aback; he's looking at her as if he doesn't trust her, as if he's afraid that she said something she shouldn't to the detectives. She would never do that. She will protect him, of course she will.

"Nothing," she lies. She amends her answer. "I didn't tell them about us. I wouldn't do that. I know how that would look." She adds, "And I don't want my name in the newspapers either."

He looks relieved.

She keeps an eye over his shoulder, to watch for anyone coming down the hall. She looks at him uneasily and says, "But there's something you should know."

25

Jayne and Kilgour look down at the suitcase they'd last seen in the storage locker. They're in the lab, and Jonathan Fell, the head of the Forensic Investigation Unit, is staring at it with them. The suitcase is a burgundy, hard-sided Samsonite. It's completely plain, except for a small, partially scraped-off sticker on one side, though there's still a bit of red and yellow remaining.

Fell says, "Of course the husband's fingerprints are all over it, as it's his suitcase. The wife's prints are there too. And a whole host of others, as you might expect, considering how much luggage is handled. It's going to take time to process them all. We might get some to check against a suspect, if we're lucky. But I wouldn't hold your breath; the killer probably wore gloves."

Jayne nods.

Fell continues, "We haven't found anything else on or in the suitcase, or anything useful from the storage locker area—lots of prints to process and eliminate, but again, I'm guessing the killer wore gloves. We weren't able to recover any usable footprints from the cement floor either. The apartment—same thing. Lots of fingerprints—we're processing them and then we'll have to compare them to the victim, husband, the family, and friends—and eliminate anyone who could legitimately have been in the apartment and see if there's anyone left. Same with hair and fibers." He adds, "It was an exceptionally clean murder." He pauses and says, "Almost as if the body and the suitcase were carefully vacuumed. We're checking the contents of the vacuum cleaner bag, of course."

"Ginny says she was probably smothered with a plastic bag."

He nods. "There was no obvious plastic bag left on the scene. There was a drawer of used plastic bags in the kitchen, and we're going through those looking for any signs of mucous or skin cells—in case the killer used the bag and then stuffed it back in the kitchen drawer, but I think whoever did this was too smart for that. Probably took it with them. That, and the clothes."

Jayne can't help but be disappointed.

"The suitcase is on wheels, which makes it relatively easy to transport, but it would have taken someone of considerable strength to overcome her and lift a dead body and fold her into that suitcase. It's harder than it looks." He adds, "It could have been either a man or a woman, as long as they were strong enough. My guess is a man, though. Dumping her like that? So dismissive."

Jayne nods. "Someone took her out of that apartment and down to the storage locker. We've got to hope somebody saw the killer with that suitcase. But so far, no one has admitted to seeing anything. And it's cold outside, so no one would have thought it was odd, seeing someone wearing gloves." She adds, "Anything else?"

He muses, "It's almost like it was done professionally."

"What do you mean?" Jayne asks.

"I mean—it's the perfect crime. They've left no evidence behind. Whoever did this was either very clever or very lucky."

As they leave, Jayne finds herself mulling over that line. "Either very clever or very lucky—what do you think, Kilgour?"

"Maybe both."

It's true, Jayne thinks. Even the cleverest murderer needs to have luck on his side if he's to get away with it. Was this one so lucky that no one saw him in the building with the suitcase? In Jayne's experience, luck always runs out.

DEREK GARDNER SITS in his office at home in front of three large computer monitors. The atmosphere at home has been tense ever since those damn detectives showed up unannounced at their door this morning. Derek is quietly furious at them. Furious at the situation. He's even rather furious with his lovely wife, who doesn't seem to believe him when he tells her he had nothing to do with the death of this woman.

The interview had been an inconvenience. He thinks he performed well. He always does. He's often thought that he could have been an actor. He's got the looks. But he couldn't abide the appalling lack of privacy that successful actors have to live with. He couldn't do that. He prefers to live a little under the radar.

When he'd come out of the interview, he'd thanked his attorney, taken Alice by the arm in a sanguine fashion, and directed her to the car without a word. Once they were inside the Tesla, she turned to him with her big eyes and said, "Well?"

"We have nothing to worry about," he said. "They only wanted to question me because I'd met her recently, and we'd exchanged contact information, that's all." He added, "Waste of time."

She narrowed her eyes at him. "Why did that detective think you'd been involved with her? Because she certainly did seem to think that."

"She *said* she had information, but the attorney says she was just fishing, making shit up. You know as well as I do that police are allowed to tell lies in interviews. They do it all the time."

"So that's the end of it?" Alice said.

"I hope so," he'd replied.

But she'd banged around the house in a sulk for a while until she announced that she was going to go shopping and that he'd better prepare himself for a large Visa bill.

"Fine," he said agreeably and kissed her goodbye. He doesn't mind a large Visa bill. If he knows his wife, she will be out buying shoes, and lingerie for makeup sex tonight—he certainly can't complain about that.

He tries to focus on the work in front of him on his computer. But he finds it difficult—as much as he'd like to, he can't stop thinking about that detective. Something about her makes him think of a pit bull. He dislikes pit bulls.

ALICE TRIES on a lot of shoes. She's wearing a short skirt that shows off her legs, and she poses in front of the mirror in the shop, this way and that, admiring the various shoes, considering how they make her feel. In the end she buys three pairs of high heels. Her favorite are the red patent leather. She already has red patent leather, but oh well.

She stops for a coffee to reenergize, and as she sips her cappuccino, her expensive purchases piled on the chair beside her, she thinks about her husband. *What has he been up to?* she wonders. Perhaps nothing. Or perhaps he's been having an affair with this woman, and perhaps he killed her. On the bright side, at least that means it's over. On the other hand, it means he's lying to her, and he promised her he would never lie to her again. Not after last time.

She can't help it. She pulls out her phone and looks online again for the photograph of Bryden Frost. She *is* very beautiful. Or at least she was. She isn't anymore. But Alice is still here, very much alive, and after she finishes her coffee, she's going to go buy some new lingerie that will drive Derek mad with lust.

But should she have to do that? It makes her a little angry. She loves lingerie, and she loves sex, but she'd prefer not to feel this constant pressure to do things to *keep* him. It shouldn't have to take so much effort. When she's with him she feels completely confident; she knows that she is all he wants, that she has absolute control over him. But when she's not with him, when he's out of her sight, she's not so sure. Maybe there's some other woman who thinks *she* is all he wants. He has a way of making you feel that way in the moment.

She's a control freak, she knows that. They've talked about that, about her issues. Well, everyone has issues, she's not the only one. He has issues too. But it's not like they can go for professional counseling. She smiles a little at the idea. What would a psychologist make of them?

The thing is, he's out of her sight quite a lot. Enough that he was able to meet this woman—at a fender bender, not at a party or a bar, and the accident wasn't his fault—and to get her contact information and meet her again. What might have happened from there? He might have never seen her again, like he says. Or he might have asked if he could buy her a drink. There might have been chemistry. He might have leaned over and kissed her, instantly sweeping her off her feet. She knows what his kisses are like.

Did Bryden Frost wear heels? Alice wonders. Impossible to tell when all she has to go on is one headshot from the news. Maybe she'll ask him, Alice thinks acidly. She continues with her musings. He might have asked the dead woman over to their house, that day they met at the coffee shop. It's a spectacular house, and no one can fail to be impressed by it. He is a bit of a show-off.

She might have said yes. It's not far from the coffee shop he said they met at. There are no cameras on their house, he hadn't wanted to bother, and now she asks herself why. Wasn't that a bit odd for someone who works in cybersecurity? She'd thought maybe it was worth getting one of those doorbell cameras because of all the packages that arrive, but he put her off. Why? Did he have women coming to the house?

She hadn't thought so. The one she knows about he took to a hotel. Alice has a pretty good nose—surely she would know if he'd brought her to the house. And he wouldn't have another woman in their bed. He wouldn't dare. He's not stupid. But there's the guest suite downstairs. He could fuck whoever he wanted down there, and she wouldn't know. She decides that when she gets home, she will tear that bed apart to make sure he's telling the truth. He can't do this to her.

They have a deal.

He wouldn't be where he is today if it wasn't for her. He owes her.

She won't be putting up with any more fucking around.

26

Jayne decides to speak to Bryden Frost's doctor. They'd found her contact information in Bryden's phone. Kilgour drives them to the medical practice in midtown. When they arrive, Jayne identifies herself quietly to the harried receptionist at the front desk and asks to speak to Dr. Bonnie Sheppard. The waiting room is full.

"I'll tell her you're here. It shouldn't be long," the woman says.

A few minutes later, Jayne and Kilgour are escorted into an examining room, and then a couple of minutes after that, the door is opened by a woman in her forties, her hair tied back in a neat ponytail. She looks rather exhausted.

"Hi, I'm Dr. Sheppard," she says.

"I'm Detective Jayne Salter and this is Detective Kilgour," Jayne says. "You had a patient by the name of Bryden Frost?"

A shadow falls over the other woman's face. "Yes, I was her family physician." She adds, "I had been her doctor for several years "It's terrible what happened to her."

"We're trying to find out more about her. Did you have any— concerns about her?"

The doctor sighs unhappily and admits, "Yes." She pauses. "Normally, patient confidentiality would prevent me from disclosing patient information, but it's different now that she's dead. In New York, as doctors, in the case of suspected spousal abuse, we are advised to direct a patient toward all sorts of resources. We don't have a duty to report except in the case of child abuse. And in this case, Bryden denied it."

"She was being abused?" Jayne asks.

"I can't be certain, but I believe so." She takes a breath. "She came in with a cracked rib."

"When was that?" Jayne asks.

"About a month ago," the doctor replies. "She'd tried to ignore it, but the pain from a cracked rib is significant. She ended up coming to me for some painkillers. She said she'd fallen on some stairs. But her injuries didn't look consistent with that explanation to me. I told her it looked to me more like she'd been kicked in the ribs. We've had a pretty good relationship over the years, so I asked her point-blank if her husband was hurting her." She pauses.

"And?" Jayne prods.

The doctor sighs, resigned. "And she denied it. Like they so often do, at least in the beginning. I tried to give her pamphlets with organizations she could call, told her she was a smart, strong woman with a little girl, told her she had options, but she got defensive and left pretty quickly. I never saw her again." She looks back at Jayne, her eyes full of regret. "Of course, I can't be sure."

"Thank you, Dr. Sheppard. You've been very helpful."

"It's so awful. Her poor child."

Jayne thanks the doctor again as she walks them out.

SAM HELPS CLARA do up her little pink jacket before grabbing his own coat while Paige puts hers on. They are taking Clara to the park.

Everyone seems to agree that Clara shouldn't be parked in front of the television all day, but no one seems to have the energy to give her the attention she needs. Even Lizzie seems tired now, Sam thinks.

As if reading his thoughts, Lizzie says to him quietly, as they're about to leave, "I think maybe tomorrow Clara should go back to day care. Maybe going back to her routine will be good for her."

Clara had been kept home today because it seemed inappropriate to take her the day after her mother was found dead. And they were afraid of what she might overhear.

"I think that's a good idea," Sam agrees. He's Clara's father, he knows he should be more proactive. Lizzie seemed so natural taking over as caregiver, but that can't go on forever. At some point he must step up. He must do all the parenting now without Bryden. But the thought of that is overwhelming.

Sam can't wait to get out of the apartment. There's something Paige wants to tell him, and she didn't want to tell him inside. What the hell is it? It's making him nervous. He's not sure he wants to hear it. At the park, they will be able to talk freely, while Clara runs around out of earshot.

The tension between them is thick as they ride down in the elevator. Mercifully, the elevator doesn't stop for anyone else to get on. Once outside, they make it past the clutch of media who mostly leave them alone, probably because they have Clara with them.

The park is right across the street from the condo. It has a playground with climbing apparatus, swings, slides, and seesaws. There are only a couple of women there, mothers or nannies with young children. Sam and Paige ignore them. It all looks so innocent, from another time, Sam thinks. He and Bryden used to bring Clara here together on weekend mornings, coffees in their hands. Now, he and Paige coax Clara forward, and she ambles toward the sandbox on her own while they stand on the adult perimeter, Sam waiting for Paige to say something. But she seems reluctant to speak.

"Well?" Sam says at last, turning to her, with half an eye still on his daughter as she plays with the toys littered in the sandbox. "What do you have to tell me?"

He watches Paige's eyes slide away from his.

"This is going to be hard, but I think you should know," Paige says. "The police know and they're going to tell you at some point."

"Know what, for Christ's sake?"

She looks at him now and says reluctantly, "Bryden was having an affair."

"What?" He feels his body turn cold.

"I'm sorry," Paige says earnestly.

He turns away and watches Clara using a yellow bucket to make a sandcastle. He doesn't know what to say. What should he say? Finally, he manages, "How do you know?"

"She told me."

"When?"

"About three weeks ago."

"And you're just telling me this now?"

"She was my best friend, Sam!" She adds, "I knew you'd be upset."

"Of course I'm upset! For fuck's sake, Paige!" He reminds himself to lower his voice. He asks, after a long beat, "Who was it?"

"It was that guy she hit in the Tesla."

He turns to face her now. "Seriously?" He feels himself clenching his jaw. "How do the police know? Did you tell them?"

She nods miserably, her eyes watching Clara. "I'm sorry. I didn't know what to do. They kept pushing me and pushing me, and I didn't want to tell them about us." She adds, "I—I thought it would deflect them."

He's very upset now and doesn't bother to hide it. He hisses, "But now they'll think I had a motive to kill her. They'll think I *knew* she was having an affair. Did you think of that?"

"I told them you didn't know about it."

"They won't believe that, Paige!"

She moves closer to him and waits for him to focus on her, his gaze furious. "If I'd told them about us, they'd think you had a motive too," she says defensively.

In the silence that follows, Sam turns to watch his daughter play by herself in the sand. His mind is racing. Now they will have another suspect, Bryden's lover. He lets out a long exhale. But they will be looking more closely at him, too, and Paige could hurt him. He realizes he will have to be careful with her.

Sleeping with his wife's best friend has been a mistake. A terrible mistake.

27

Sam is not even sure how it happened. Paige is an attractive woman; he's always been aware of it. But so was his wife, and he'd remained faithful to her. Through pregnancy and child-birth, through the aftermath, through the exhaustion of raising a small child, through the programmed sex scheduled through the fertile parts of her cycle as they tried for months to conceive another child. But it hadn't happened. The doctors said there was nothing wrong, it would happen, it would just take time. But the fun had gone out of trying, for both of them. Perhaps that was what had made him receptive to Paige.

Bryden had routinely gone out of town overnight once a month or so on business. Paige had started coming over in the evenings when Bryden was away, to keep him company and spend time with Clara. The first time, he'd told Bryden, and she thought that it was nice, that they'd had fun while she was away. The second time Paige invited herself over when Bryden was away, he hadn't told his wife. He wasn't sure why. There had been something between him and Paige that night, some new, delicious tension. They'd watched a movie together after they put Clara to bed. Paige didn't have a partner in her life at the time. She'd complained lightly about the quality of the men out there, said all the good ones were taken. He knew she was lonely. He kept his distance.

The third time, he was on the cusp of telling her that maybe she shouldn't come over every time Bryden was away. That he really could manage his toddler on his own. But he didn't. And that night, after Clara was asleep in bed, and they sat down to watch TV with a glass of wine—that had been a mistake, the glass of wine—somehow, she'd kissed him. And he hadn't been able to resist the easy pleasure of it. By the time they were half undressed, he'd pulled her into the bedroom, and she'd spent most of the night.

"We've crossed a line," she said, clinging naked to him afterward, running her finger down his chest.

He was feeling sated, pleasantly relaxed. "Bryden must never know," he whispered to her, looking directly into her eyes.

"No, never," she agreed. "We must never hurt her."

And so it had become an ongoing thing these last few months, that every time Bryden went away on business, he'd had sex in the marital bed with his wife's best friend. Paige always left early in the morning, before Clara woke up. At some point, he knew, Paige would start dating someone else, and it would be over.

Now Sam glances at Paige uneasily, her long brown hair blowing around her face in the breeze, wondering how much this revelation about Bryden's affair will hurt him. The detectives already seem to think he killed his wife. Well, he's not Husband of the Year.

IN THE CHILLY PARK, with the cold March wind, Paige observes Sam, the way he's clenching his jaw as he watches his daughter, and feels a matching anxiety course through her. He's right. If the detectives knew he was cheating, or if they think he knew Bryden was cheating on him, it gives him motive. He's obviously scared. But it also gives them someone else to focus on.

She stands beside him, wanting to pull him into a hug, but she can't do that in front of Clara. Not in public, she wouldn't dare. And certainly not with all the media around. They will have to be more careful than ever.

She's worried for herself and Sam both. The police obviously suspect him. She doesn't want to see herself dragged through the mud by the media. She can imagine what they'd say about her, the *best friend*.

The sex has been casual, but great. She doesn't really know how he feels about her. And now Bryden is dead, and that might change everything.

DONNA IS RELIEVED when Sam and Paige leave with Clara. They need to talk—she and Jim and Lizzie.

Once they've gone, Donna glances at Lizzie and then says to her husband, "Jim." He lifts his head and looks back at her uneasily.

They'd been so overwhelmed with grief last night at the discovery of the body, the thread of hope snapped, that they'd been unable to speak. This morning, Donna had kept her doubts about Sam from her husband. She doesn't really know what he thinks; he's been so shut down. But now it's time, Donna thinks, in the living room of the condo, to be honest. "I know we've all been supportive of Sam, but we have to consider the possibility—" She can't finish.

"What are you suggesting?" Jim asks uneasily. But he knows. "That Sam did this? That he murdered our girl? That's impossible," he insists, shaking his head. "I can't believe it."

"Because you don't *want* to believe it," Donna says, trembling, holding her ground.

"I *can't* believe it! That he could do that! To the mother of his child—kill her and . . . and . . . do that to her body." He seems to recoil from the very idea, leaning back further against the sofa, his face twisting. "Think of what you're saying!"

"Husbands kill their wives all the time," Donna says, "in horrible ways."

"I can't believe it either," Lizzie says, speaking up.

Donna is taken aback. "I thought—"

"You don't know Sam as well as I do. He's not capable of something like this," Lizzie insists. "Whoever did this must be—" She can't seem to finish the thought. She adds stubbornly, "I just can't see it. He loved her."

Donna looks back at the two of them. "I'm not necessarily saying he *did* it. I'm saying it's possible, and maybe we should just stop blindly believing everything he says."

"It's for the police to figure out," Jim says wearily.

"He has no alibi," Donna points out. "Am I the only one here who finds that odd? A two-hour blank in the workday?" The other two stare back at her. "We don't know what was going on in their marriage."

"Bryden and I were close, Mom," Lizzie says. "If things were bad, she would have told me. I would have noticed. There was nothing wrong, I'm sure of it."

Donna doesn't agree. She's not sure Bryden would have told her sister if there were problems, if she would have told anyone. She knows Bryden and Lizzie had a complicated relationship, were sometimes at odds. "He's not acting like an innocent man," Donna says.

"How do you mean?" Lizzie asks. "How would you expect him to act under the circumstances?"

"I don't know, but there's something about him. I think he's hiding something. He's not like he used to be. Something about him has changed."

Lizzie says, exasperated, "How could he *not* be changed?"

A short time later, when Sam and Paige return from the park with Clara, Donna studies Sam, his tight, worried expression, and thinks, her stomach cramping, *He looks guilty.*

28

Jayne has asked Sam Frost to come back in for further questioning. It's late Thursday afternoon, and her team has been busy. Sam is on his way. She wonders if this time he will want an attorney. They now know about the wife's affair with Derek Gardner, and that it's likely that he was physically abusive to his wife. Sam had said that their marriage was perfect. She's about to punch a big hole in that idea.

She checks in with the team in the incident room first. The officers have reported back that no one they've spoken to can confirm Sam was in Washington Park on Tuesday. The officer who took the stairs from the eighth floor to where Bryden's body was found had run into no one. They are interviewing everyone who lives or works in the condo building again, chasing down any visitors, hoping to find someone who might have seen somebody with the suitcase. They are looking into Derek Gardner too. But right now, she wants to focus her attention on the husband.

When Sam is waiting for them in the interview room, she and Kilgour enter together. She tells him that he is here to answer questions voluntarily to help in their investigation and that he can leave at any time. She tells him this to make him relax, in the hopes of getting more out of him. The truth is, if he decides he doesn't want to be here and gets up to leave, she will tell him he's no longer here voluntarily and have Kilgour read him his rights. He might then opt for an attorney, but at least he's alone for now. She asks Sam to identify himself for the tape.

"Sam," she begins, her voice deliberately sympathetic, "how are you holding up?"

"I'm okay," he says, not looking okay at all. His face has hollowed in the short time since his wife was reported missing. He looks like he's barely slept and there's a faint whiff of sweat coming from him. She notes that he's wearing the same jeans and T-shirt he was wearing the day before.

"And how is Clara?" she asks, out of genuine concern. She lay awake last night thinking about the little girl, what it will be like for her growing up without a mother. What it will be like for her if it turns out her father is the one who killed her. What it will be like for her when she's old enough to learn the details.

"I don't really know," he admits. "It's hard to know how all this will affect her. She's so young." His voice catches.

"Children are resilient," Jayne says gently.

"I've heard that," Sam says, looking as if he has his doubts.

Maybe he lies awake at night too, Jayne thinks, worrying about his daughter. Or maybe he lies awake worrying about himself. It's her job to find out if this man is a murderer. She must discover the truth, for Clara's sake.

"Tell me about the rest of the family," Jayne says. "Are you close to Donna and Jim? Are they able to help with Clara?"

"Yes, we're close. I'm sure they'll help where they can, but they live in Florida."

"What about Lizzie? Is she likely to lend a hand going forward?"

He nods. "Yes. She adores Clara."

"She and her sister were very close, I understand."

He gives her a look. "Is that what Lizzie told you?"

"Yes. Why, do you not think so?"

"I wouldn't call them *close*. To be honest, I think they had a bit of a difficult relationship."

"Difficult how?" Jayne asks, interested. Lizzie certainly hadn't said anything like this, and when asked, the parents had said the girls had a "normal sibling relationship."

"I think Lizzie is—was—a bit jealous of Bryden. She always felt like she was in Bryden's shadow. Bryden was always careful to try to not make her feel that way. Lizzie would take offense easily. Mostly they got along. There were good times, but there was conflict."

"I see," Jayne says, filing that information in her mind. "Sam, we've had the results of the autopsy," Jayne says quietly. She allows a short pause. "Your wife was asphyxiated, probably by some kind of plastic bag held over her head."

Sam licks his visibly dry lips. "That's terrible," he whispers.

"It is," Jayne agrees. "There was no sexual assault." She waits another beat and adds, "Which makes it somewhat less likely that it was a stranger, and more likely it was someone she knew." He says nothing, just swallows nervously. "Since we spoke last night," Jayne says, "we've learned some new information that I want to talk to you about."

He looks back at her, his eyes glazed. "What information?"

"We spoke to Bryden's physician. She suspects that your wife was a victim of domestic violence." Jayne can tell by the shock on Sam's face that he wasn't expecting this.

"That's bullshit," Sam says. "I loved my wife. I never laid a hand on her."

"I've got her medical records. A cracked rib, about a month ago—remember that? She saw her physician because she needed something for the pain. Her doctor says it looked like she'd been kicked in the ribs. Is that how you treated the wife you loved so much, Sam?" Jayne can barely keep the hostility out of her voice.

Sam has gone completely still and silent. Jayne carries on. "You still deny you physically assaulted your wife?"

"Yes, of course I deny it. I never laid a finger on her."

Jayne glances at Kilgour, signaling him to continue.

Kilgour says, "We've also learned that your wife had been having an affair."

Jayne watches Sam closely. Sees his glazed eyes flicker, then blink. Is he surprised? She can't tell.

"I don't believe it," Sam says.

"I'm afraid it's true," Kilgour says neutrally. "Her best friend, Paige, told us about it."

"Bryden wouldn't cheat," he says bluntly. "We have a three-year-old daughter. Her family was everything to her. She wouldn't jeopardize that."

Jayne says, "She was sleeping with Derek Gardner, the man she had the minor car accident with several weeks ago." She watches him clench his hands on the surface of the table between them.

"No."

"Are you saying you didn't know that she was having an affair?" Kilgour asks.

"Of course I didn't know!" Sam swallows and asks, "Did *he* kill her?"

Kilgour ignores the question. "You were never suspicious of her?" he asks. Sam shakes his head. "Didn't check up on her?"

He stops shaking his head. He looks at Kilgour. "What do you mean? Like hiring a private investigator to follow her?" he scoffs. "No."

"No," Kilgour answers. "I mean, did you ever call her employer to confirm that she had business meetings in Buffalo on"—he looks down at the folder on the desk in front of him, opens it, and scans a page—"January eighteenth and February twenty-second?"

They've got him, and he knows it. Jayne watches the color drain from Sam's face. Watches his Adam's apple bob up and down as he swallows. She waits for him to answer. When he doesn't, she repeats the question. "Did you call her employer to try to confirm that she was in fact away on business on these two dates?"

"I want an attorney," Sam says, his voice breaking.

29

Sam is scared out of his wits. He sweats in his chair, the smell rank, alone in the interview room, waiting. The videotape had been turned off when the interview was suspended, but he doesn't know if there are other cameras on the room, watching him. Other people in this room—people like him, suspected of murder— have probably been at risk for suicide.

He'd called the largest law firm in Albany and asked them to send their best criminal attorney. He waits for the attorney to arrive, trying to order his chaotic thoughts. They're all over the place. He tries to remember what Paige said. The immediate problem is what he knew about his wife. He told Paige he didn't know anything. He was afraid it would come to this. Afraid they would find out about the phone call. He didn't know about the guy with the Tesla. But he *had* checked up on her.

The attorney finally arrives, and they are granted some time alone to consult. The attorney, Laura Szabo, a woman of about fifty, listens attentively to what Sam tells her. And then she advises him to answer all further questions with "No comment."

The detectives return to the room and resume the interview. Sam can feel his heart beating too fast. His attorney doesn't seem too sympathetic. Why did they send him a female attorney, Sam frets, when he's probably going to be charged with murdering his wife? He begins to feel dizzy and lightheaded; there's a pounding in his ears.

Detective Salter says, looking closely at him, "Are you all right, Sam?"

Her voice seems distant, fading in and out. But he nods. He wonders if he's going to have a heart attack.

The detective says, "Did you call your wife's employer to try to confirm that she had upcoming business meetings in Buffalo on January eighteenth and February twenty-second of this year?"

"No comment." His chest is feeling increasingly tight. It's the vise again, like before, in the apartment. He's having another panic attack. He tries to remember what Lizzie told him to do. But he can't think, and his breath is coming in ragged pants, and he instinctively clutches at his chest.

Detective Salter asks, "Are you all right? Do you need us to call 911?"

He shakes his head, manages to say, "No. I'm fine."

He hears the detective say, *Interview suspended at 6:46 p.m.*

Slowly, the panic subsides. He's able to breathe again, as the vise that holds him gradually loosens its grip. He sits in a pool of sweat and fear. He doesn't want to tell them it was a panic attack, but they seem to know.

Laura Szabo addresses the detectives. "Are you holding my client, or can he go home?"

"He can go," Detective Salter says, "for now."

Sam is relieved to hear that they're letting him go but he knows what they think. They think he's guilty as hell.

. . .

DEREK GARDNER HEARS his wife come in the front door, recognizes the familiar rustling of shopping bags. It sounds like she's had a productive day. He leaves his office and goes out to join her. "A good day, I see," he says, eyeing her purchases.

"Yes. I decided to treat myself," she says, "because you have been causing me stress."

"You know I don't mean to," he says, approaching her.

"But you do anyway."

His voice becomes a little sharp. "I had nothing to do with that woman, Alice."

"So you say."

He knows she doesn't trust him. He doesn't trust her either. They are both completely self-interested, and they both know it, but they do better together than apart, and they both know that too. Sometimes their relationship becomes tiresome. But mostly it's exciting. He knows she worries about him straying, because of that time she caught him. She doesn't know about the times she hadn't caught him, before that. Still, that one time, there had been hysterics, and flying shoes that narrowly missed his head, and threats. He thinks of this now as she shows off her new purchases in the living room, while he sinks into the sofa, pretending to pay attention.

He'd made a promise to her after that, to stay away from other women. He thinks she cheated on him after, just once, to even the score, because that's what he would do if he was her, but he's willing to let that go. He's never been as jealous, as possessive, as she is. And he owes her. She's right about that.

His cybersecurity firm is making them good money, but it took money to get it off the ground. Money he didn't have. She'd gotten it for him. She hadn't told him what she was planning, only presented it to him afterward, a fait accompli, a gift. He wonders now, if she had told him what she was going to do, would he have stopped her? Probably not. He's as cold-blooded as she is.

He supposes most other husbands would have been horrified. But she didn't choose another husband; she chose him. And he was grateful, and actually rather impressed. Neither one of them had liked her mother anyway. She was a trivial woman. Always nervous around them, looking at them as if she were afraid of what they might do next. Her timidity always annoyed Alice, provoked her.

He looks at Alice now in the sexy red patent-leather stilettos, and his thoughts about her mother disappear. Derek likes to think of the two of them as special, as people unhampered by the same restraints that hamper other people.

"What do you think?" she purrs, posing with a hand on one hip, one heel coyly raised. She arches her back a little.

"They're perfect," he says, his voice growing husky. "You're perfect."

She walks slowly up to him, swaying her hips, crawls into his lap, straddling him, and fastens her mouth on his. He can feel himself become instantly aroused. She must feel it too.

"I am, aren't I?" she whispers after the kiss. "You don't deserve me."

"No, I don't," he whispers back, unbuttoning her blouse.

30

———

izzie doesn't like the look of Sam when he returns to the condo from the police station. His eyes are wild as he collapses into an armchair. Fortunately, Clara is at Angela's and Paige left some time ago. "What did they say?" Lizzie asks, concerned. He gazes back at her vacantly and doesn't answer. His hands are shaking. She asks more sharply, "What happened, Sam?"

He swallows nervously. "They told me Bryden was having an affair," he says.

"What?" Lizzie says, taken completely off guard. "Surely that can't be true."

Her parents look completely unprepared for this news. She can tell that they don't want to believe it either.

Sam continues, his voice strained, "They said she was having an affair with Derek Gardner, that man she had the car accident with."

The silence in the room is profound. "No way," Lizzie protests after a long pause. Then, "How do they know?"

"She confided in Paige, and Paige told them," Sam says. Then he breaks down into sobs and covers his face with his hands.

Lizzie freezes. Paige knew about this? And told the police about it? Without a word to any of them? Lizzie considers going to Sam and putting a comforting hand on his shoulder, but something stops her. Perhaps it is her mother, sitting in clear judgment of her son-in-law, her face an open book. Her mother's expression suddenly makes Lizzie wonder if Sam knew about the affair. She catches her mother's eye and knows she's thinking the same thing. Lizzie then glances at her father, sees the wheels inside his mind turning, the fresh dismay on his lined face. And Lizzie finds she is angry that her sister didn't confide in her but confided in Paige instead.

"Did you know about this?" Lizzie's mother asks Sam, her voice accusing.

Sam uncovers his face and addresses his mother-in-law. "No! I had no idea. Not a clue. I trusted her completely." He adds, after a moment, "It must have been this Derek Gardner who killed her. It seems obvious. But the detectives think it gives me a motive." His voice shaking. "I didn't even know, I swear!"

It's as if a bomb has gone off in the living room; everyone is waiting for the dust to settle, for their senses to return to normal, to take stock of this new reality.

Lizzie observes Sam in the silence. "Did they say anything else?" she asks finally.

He seems to be trying to gather his thoughts for a moment and says, "They have the autopsy results." He chokes out, "Someone— someone held a plastic bag over her head."

Lizzie sees her mother's hand fly silently to her mouth in horror. Her father makes a guttural sound in his throat. She turns back to Sam. "What else?"

"She wasn't sexually assaulted, and that makes them think it was someone she knew." He says into the disturbed silence, "I got an attorney."

Lizzie can read the room, and she can tell that her parents want to leave—*their son-in-law has hired an attorney*—and that Sam wants them gone. The atmosphere is intolerable. Lizzie stands up. "Mom and Dad are exhausted. I'm going to take them home now, make them a proper meal."

She's tired too, and she needs to be alone. She wants to be in her own room tonight.

"Of course," Sam says wearily. "You go. We'll be fine. I've got Angela if I need her."

HOURS LATER, after she's tried to get her parents to eat, and cleaned up, and her mother and father have retired to the spare room for the night, possibly even more shattered than the night before, Lizzie retreats to her own bedroom and quietly closes the door. She's been itching to get online properly all day, but being stuck at her sister's place, with no privacy, she's had to be satisfied with sneaking hurried looks at her phone and making only brief posts. She's dying to immerse herself in what the Facebook group is saying about her sister's murder. Now her guilty secret, her addiction to online true crime groups, has an intensely personal dimension.

She logs in under her Emma Porter profile and quickly scans the new posts about her sister. There are quite a lot of them, and she finds that gratifying. She goes back and rereads what she posted from her apartment the night before, after Bryden's body had been found, with the same picture of the front of Bryden's condominium building.

Some of you have heard about what's going on at the condo at 100 Constitution Drive. Warning: Long post! The missing woman's body has been found in a suitcase tonight in a storage locker in the basement of the building. This is what I know so far. Her name was Bryden Frost. She was thirty-five years old, married with one child. She'd been missing since yesterday, when she didn't turn up to pick up her child from day care. She'd been working from home and her laptop was open on the dining room table. Her purse, phone, and keys were still in the apartment. The police searched the building yesterday evening but didn't find her. But today they came back with a dog from the K-9 unit and the dog was able to locate her remains. That's all information that has already been in the news if you've been paying attention. But I happen to know a few things that haven't been in the news. Fact one: The suitcase she was found in was taken from the closet of the apartment Bryden lived in. Fact two: The storage locker she was found in was unlocked and open. The storage area is usually kept locked, but it's possible that sometimes it is left propped open by the tenants, so in my opinion, the killer didn't necessarily have to have keys. Fact three: There is no CCTV coverage in the elevators or on the individual floors, only on the front and back doors on the ground level, and the CCTV cameras on the parking garage were not working. Fact four: The police—the investigation is being led by Detective Jayne Salter, of the Albany Police Department—took the husband in for questioning tonight after the body was discovered. Here are my thoughts:

The police are going to focus on the husband, just because he's the husband. I think they lack imagination. We can do better.

She went missing from the apartment in the early afternoon on Tuesday, March 7. She was working from home that day and it looked as if she'd just stepped out for a minute. Think about it—anyone could have knocked on her door. She might have opened it and been overpowered and killed. It didn't necessarily have to be someone she knew; it didn't have to be her husband. The killer might then have looked around the apartment for something to dispose of the body and found the suitcase. He could have taken her down to the storage locker in it and left her there.

So many questions! Why not just leave her there, in the apartment? Why put her in a suitcase and move her to the storage locker at all? I figure it could have been anyone who lives in the building or works there or visits regularly. Then, if they're caught on video entering or exiting the building the police won't have any reason to suspect them. Once in the building, there were no cameras to catch the killer going from Bryden's apartment to the storage lockers with the suitcase.

It could also have been someone who came in through the garage, but they'd need a key card to get in, unless the victim buzzed them in, which I suppose is possible.

The police seem to think it was the husband, but I think they're not casting their net as widely as they should. Anyone else have any insights, thoughts, ideas, information? Let's get the true crime hive working on this one!

31

izzie sits back in her chair. She's certain that anyone involved in the investigation knows that it was the husband's suitcase. Things leak. Ditto about the open storage locker and the lax security. She'd divulged nothing that reveals that she is a member of the family, or that she even knows them, or how she knows any of this.

People have been commenting, and as she reads the comments, she feels a thrill.

Mark Mammolotti
Fascinating! How do you know all this?

Chris Belliveau
Do you live in that building?

Farah Spence
Are you police?/paramedic?/journalist?/friend?/
neighbor?

Jen McKague
Oh . . . this reminds me a bit of the Elisa Lam case!
She went missing in a building and no one could find
her! Until they did, in the water tank. Ew.

Karen Hennin
I wouldn't be so quick to dismiss the husband. It
usually is the husband in real life.

Maya Vukovic
Intriguing case! Poor woman.

Brittany Clement
Do you know how she was killed? Murder
weapon?

Jordan Ross
Any sexual assault? Police aren't saying.

Brittany Clement
Police aren't saying much, as usual.

On it goes, and Lizzie immerses herself in it. Alone late at night with her online friends, Lizzie feels happy that her sister is getting so much attention. Lizzie feels right at the very center of things for a change, and she likes it. She thinks about what to write now for her update. Her fingers hover over the keyboard. She makes a new post, reusing the picture of the front of the condo with its address showing. It's her signature photo.

> The husband was released last night after questioning.
> Looks like he was down at the police station again late
> today for further questioning but was again released.
> I think they're barking up the wrong tree. I think
> sometimes police are too single-minded, and don't look
> at all the possibilities, they're too focused on solving the
> crime quickly. I mean, *maybe* he did it, but I don't think
> we should leap to that conclusion.

Lizzie pauses, realizing that there's so much she can't say on here, for fear of giving herself away. About how Bryden was killed with a plastic bag. About the lack of sexual assault. *About her lover, Derek Gardner.* But it would give her so much cred if she was the one to break the news about Derek Gardner, about all of this. It will be in the news soon enough anyway won't it? They will have to investigate Gardner; they won't be able to keep it quiet forever. She has read all the online news coverage of the case that she can find and there has been no mention of him so far. The detectives seem to be keeping her sister's affair to themselves for now. They've told Sam, and he told the family. But she's afraid of it being traced back to her. She has sometimes wondered if the police monitor these groups.

Her parents would be horrified to know what she's doing, that she spends most of her free time hanging out with these people. That she's using her sister's murder as a way to belong. They would think it tacky, tasteless, abhorrent. She doesn't need their judgment. She still hovers over the keyboard, undecided. But she can't quite bring herself to put what she knows out there.

She sees a new comment appear below her own post:

> **Susan Day**
> I heard one of them was having an affair.

She answers quickly.

> **Emma Porter**
> Susan Day Where did you hear that?

JAYNE LEANS HER HEAD back against Michael's shoulder on her sofa and cradles a glass of red wine in her hand. She's glad he's here. The solidity, the goodness of him after such a long day is a balm. It's getting late, but she can't quiet her mind, can't stop thinking about the case. She feels for the family, for the little girl. She thinks about today's interviews with the husband and the lover.

They've found little on Derek Gardner. He's not on social media at all. There's a website for his business, of course, which looks professional. His company appears to be quite successful.

She shifts a little to look up at Michael. "You're a psychologist. Hypothetically, what kind of person would hold a plastic bag over a woman's head from behind until she was dead, then dispose of her body that way?" He shrugs noncommittally. She presses. "What does your gut tell you?" she asks. His face becomes serious, as he considers her question.

Finally he says, "It strikes me as very cold. If the bag over the head was held from behind, then he's not . . . confronting her, as he would be if he was strangling her with his hands, face-to-face, for example. It's efficient, convenient, not messy. The suitcase and storage locker too. Like she needs to be gotten rid of with a minimum of fuss and bother."

"That's interesting," she says. "Ginny—the pathologist—thought it might be a crime of passion, of rage. Fell thought the suitcase and the locker were dismissive, as if the message the killer was sending, unconsciously, is that she was to be discarded, thrown away, as if she were garbage. That seems like rage to me."

"Maybe. But to me it seems more like whoever did it was solving a problem."

DONNA SLEEPS FITFULLY for a while but then wakes with a jolt. She was dreaming of a plastic bag being held over her face, and now finds herself sitting up in bed, gasping. Jim, beside her, wakes too and reaches for her with concern. "Are you all right?"

She takes a deep breath. "I had a nightmare."

He gently pulls her back down into the bed and hugs her close. He doesn't ask her what the nightmare was, and she's glad. She clings to him. He and Lizzie are all she has left. And there's Clara too, of course. As her husband holds her tight, she thinks about Clara, about what the future might hold for her. It's so uncertain. Because it's possible that her father might be the one who murdered her mother. The more she thinks of it, the more Donna thinks it might be true. The police seem to think so, and they probably know what they're doing. And now they know he might have had a motive.

Bryden was having an affair. It's a hard thing to swallow. It's possible this other man, her lover, killed her. She thought she knew her daughter, but truly, what did she know about her daughter's private life? Maybe she should talk to Paige. Apparently Paige—Bryden's best friend—knows more about what was going on in her daughter's life than anybody else. Maybe she knew why Bryden was having the affair. Maybe she knew details of their marriage. If she knew something else that made Sam look guilty, would she tell the police? Or would she protect him? Maybe she's already told the detectives other things that they are keeping back, that the family doesn't know about. Maybe Sam hasn't told them everything. She definitely picked up on some tension between Sam and Paige today, when they brought Clara back from the park.

And if Sam did kill Bryden? What then? If he's convicted, she and Jim can try to get custody of Clara and bring her up as their own. But what if they can't prove it? What if he did it, but they can't convict him? Then he will never let them have her.

And Clara will grow up with a monster.

32

S am tosses and turns, unable to sleep, his mind panicking. The
police know. He denied it, but they know how he treated Bryden sometimes.

He knew how to hurt her when he wanted to. Which wasn't very
often, but sometimes. Sometimes he didn't know who he was, or why
he did the things he did. Sometimes a mood came over him and he
needed someone to bear the brunt of his anger and stress. Someone to
insult or ignore. Someone to slap or kick. Everyone always thought they
were the perfect couple, he reflects now, but that wasn't true.

He thought no one else knew what went on between him and his
wife behind closed doors when he lost his temper. He thought Bryden
would have been too embarrassed, too ashamed, to confide in anyone.
He thought if she'd confided in anyone it would have been Paige, and
she obviously has no idea, or she wouldn't still like him. But she'd been
to her doctor, without telling him. It feels like a betrayal.

It's confusing, even to him, why Bryden put up with it. Why do women allow themselves to be abused? Why are they so accommodating to men's anger and their need to control? Did she love him that much? She loved him enough to forgive him—or at least he thought so. He doesn't think he deserved her love. He doesn't even like himself, not at all. If only she'd been stronger and stood up to him. Told him she wasn't going to take any of his shit. He wishes that she had. Then maybe things wouldn't have turned out the way they did. He realizes he's blaming her for his bad behavior, but still, he thinks, it's true. If she'd stood up to him, he would have stopped. She made it too easy for him to give in to his darker impulses. But maybe he's just lying to himself.

One of his earliest memories is of how as a small child, he used to lash out at his mother when he was angry. And she took it. She never hit him back or yelled at him to stop. It infuriated him and confused him, even then, as a part of him wanted her to take control of all his overwhelming, angry feelings. It made him feel even more out of control, and it made him ashamed of himself.

But he grew out of it somehow. The first years of marriage were fine. Until the stress of raising a small child, and the stress of a high-pressure job began to get to him.

And instead of standing up to him, like he needed, like he wanted, Bryden took it, just like his mother had. She suffered in silence. And then she met Derek Gardner and became his lover. What was she thinking? That she would leave him for this other, better man? That she would take Clara with her? From what he understands, this man is already married. And now something else occurs to him: Did she know he was cheating on her? Did she intuit it in some way? She couldn't have known it was her best friend he was sleeping with, because she wouldn't have stood for that, would she?

But maybe she did know. Maybe that's why she told Paige about her lover, hoping it would get back to him, across their pillow. Had she been playing some kind of game with him? It would be such a passive-aggressive thing for her to do, to secretly sleep with someone else, he thinks, instead of standing up to him.

He never left any marks. He was careful that way. He was not the kind of man to give his wife a black eye. He couldn't have anyone asking questions. They were both educated professionals—he was not some lowlife. He thought she'd never been to see a doctor. But she had. And now the detectives know.

He sweats with fear and shame in the dark, soaking his sheets through.

AFTER ALL that great sex—kinky lingerie and kinky shoes—Derek is out cold. Alice rises up on one elbow and studies him in the moonlight coming through the bedroom skylight. He's movie-star handsome. And he smells and feels as good as he looks. She's rather spoiled by him. She doesn't think anyone else will ever do. Which is why she doesn't want to lose him. She slips out of bed. He doesn't even stir.

She pads in bare feet across the bedroom and down the stairs and then down the hall to the stairs that lead to the basement suite. It's not a typical basement—it's huge, and there are large glass doors leading outside, so there's a lot of light. It looks out onto a large, lush yard. It's not dark in the daytime, like you'd expect a basement to be. With all the windows and skylights, nothing in this house is dark, except for the inhabitants.

Now she stands in the center of the basement suite and looks outside. There's moonlight filtering in here too. The blinds are wide open. After a moment, she presses a button and the motorized blinds close. She doesn't want anyone looking in.

She enters the bedroom and approaches the bed. It looks properly made, but she knows that he would cover his tracks. She pulls back the coverlet. The bed does not look slept in, or used, at all. After careful examination, she's satisfied. She remakes the bed and checks the linen cupboard. She supposes he could have washed the sheets and replaced them, but would he go to that much effort? Now she's starting to think that she's just paranoid. She enters the en suite bathroom. There's no need for either of them to use this bathroom, and everything is pristine, the guest soaps still wrapped in their decorative paper.

Back in the main living area, she presses the button for the blinds again, opening them, leaving everything as she found it. On her way upstairs, she begins to think that there's no way he would have brought another woman here. The neighbors could have seen them. Alice could have come home unexpectedly from work—she keeps her own hours. This other woman might have been wearing perfume. He wouldn't have risked it. He probably took her to a hotel, like the last one. That detective seemed awfully sure.

Maybe she doesn't have to do anything, and that Detective Salter will figure it out. If he slept with Bryden Frost, if he killed her, then perhaps she will know soon enough. But perhaps not—because she knows Derek is clever enough to get away with it.

She finds his wallet in his office and starts rooting through it. She pulls out all his credit cards, counts five of them. She doesn't take care of the finances, he does. He does all the banking, pays all the bills online. How is she to know if he's using one of these cards for secret trysts? She hasn't got access to his computer. She has no way of finding out if he's been paying for hotel rooms unless she asks him and makes him show her all the bills. Is she prepared to do that?

She should have kept a closer eye on him. What kind of mess has he gotten himself into?

33

———

Friday morning, when Jayne arrives early at the station, she's approached by an officer. "I've been looking into Derek Gardner," he says. "And I might have found something."

"What is it?"

"When he started his business, he had a huge infusion of cash."

"From where?"

"From his wife. She inherited it."

"Am I missing something?" Jayne asks impatiently.

He speaks more quickly. "She inherited over three million dollars from her mother, who was killed in a hit-and-run accident four years ago. It was never solved."

Jayne stares at him. She says, "Bring everything you have on it to my desk." As she walks to her office, she has more energy in her step.

Minutes later she's reading about Mary Smelt, who was killed on March 27, 2019, outside of Roxbury, New Hampshire. The woman, who was sixty-one years of age at the time, and a widow, had been walking down a lonely country road near her rural home, where she lived alone. She'd been struck by a vehicle that had left the scene. The body was found some time later by a passing motorist who saw her in the ditch. She was probably killed instantly. There were no witnesses. The victim was known to walk regularly along that road in the evenings for exercise. It might have been an accident, Jayne thinks—people often speed, especially on rural roads. It might have been getting dark; there are no streetlights in the country, she could have been hard to see. The driver might have been drinking. But he could not have been unaware that he hit her. And he fled the scene.

Or, Jayne thinks, it might have been deliberate. Someone might have known that she took her evening walk along that road at the same time every night. Jayne reads through everything in the file. The investigation seems to have been cursory. The victim's only family—the daughter, Alice Gardner, and her husband, Derek Gardner, who lived out of state in New York—were not even formally interviewed.

Jayne looks up from the file and stares at the wall in front of her, her mind whirring. Hit-and-runs are notoriously difficult to solve. If she were going to kill someone, she thinks idly, that's the method she'd use. Did Derek Gardner kill his mother-in-law for her money? It was awfully convenient. Or maybe he was just lucky, and someone else happened to do it for him.

Jayne asks an officer to find her Alice Gardner's phone number.

SAM WAKES FROM a heavy sleep to Clara looming over him on the bed.

"Daddy, when is Mommy coming home?"

"Clara, honey," he says gently, "I told you. Mommy isn't coming home. She's in heaven."

She pouts at him. "Let's get some breakfast," he says, wanting nothing more than to stay in bed. He'd finally slept. Not for long though; he'd been up half the night, and looking at the clock now he sees that it's barely seven a.m. Clara slides off the bed. He takes her by the hand and together they go silently to the kitchen in pajamas and bare feet. He settles her at the kitchen table with a bowl of cereal and puts on a pot of coffee for himself. But the adrenaline has already started, along with the nonstop voice in his head telling him he's fucked.

The police know that he abused Bryden. They know he called her office to check up on her. Such a stupid thing to do. Will they find out about Paige too? It's getting harder and harder to pretend that they had the perfect marriage.

He watches Clara, eating her cereal. If they find out about him and Paige—what would the fallout be? They'd know that he's a cheater. That he lied to the detectives.

He thinks that if they do find out, if Paige cracks under the pressure and tells them, he'll tell the truth—that it was meaningless to him. That he didn't get rid of his wife so that he could be with Paige. He sips his coffee uneasily.

And now Bryden's parents think he did it, and maybe Lizzie does too. He's not entirely sure about Lizzie.

"Daddy!" Clara says. "The buzzer."

He was so lost in his thoughts that he hadn't heard it. Now he goes to answer it. It's Lizzie. He lets her in the parking garage and waits for her to arrive.

"I promised to take Clara to day care this morning," she says when he opens the door.

"Right." He'd forgotten. He's lost all track of what day it is. "Want a coffee? I just made some."

"Sure," she says. She greets Clara in the kitchen with a big hug. "You're going to go back to see your friends today," she tells the little girl with a gentle smile.

Clara looks listless and doesn't answer, as if she doesn't care one way or the other.

"Why don't you go pick out what you want to wear," Lizzie says, "while I talk to your dad."

Clara gets up and trails off to her room, leaving Sam facing Lizzie across the kitchen table. "What are they saying?" Sam asks.

"Who?"

"Donna and Jim. They think I did it, don't they? I could tell," he says bitterly. He watches Lizzie take a deep breath.

"They think it's a possibility," Lizzie replies carefully.

"What do you think?" Sam asks bluntly.

She looks him in the eye and says, "I don't think you're a murderer, Sam." She puts her cup down carefully on the table. "But you have to admit, it doesn't look good to the police. If Bryden was having an affair—"

"I didn't know," Sam says. She nods as if she believes him. He wonders how long that will last. Will she find out about his call to Bryden's workplace? About the abuse? She probably will, he realizes. It's just a matter of time. He feels the walls closing in on him.

"Don't look so defeated," she tells him. She lowers her voice. "I can help you."

He looks at her in disbelief. "How?"

"I know people."

She says this with a conspiratorial air. And there's a strange glint in her eyes he's never seen before. It's so odd, so unlike Lizzie, that he doesn't know what to make of it. "What are you talking about?" he asks, taken aback.

"Never mind." She sits back and seems like the old Lizzie again. "Just please don't give up. We'll find out who murdered Bryden." She stands. "I'd better help Clara get ready."

Sam watches her go, wondering if his sister-in-law is losing her grip.

But then, aren't they all?

JAYNE SITS DOWN BESIDE KILGOUR, across the interview table from Alice Gardner. The woman is unusually attractive, Jayne observes, remembering her in her bathrobe at their opulent home the previous morning. It's no surprise, given the husband's looks and his apparent taste for fine things. Alice Gardner looks very well cared for, like an expensive cat. Pampered. "Thank you for coming in, Alice. Of course you're here voluntarily. We're hoping you can help us with our inquiries into the death of Bryden Frost."

"I don't see how," Alice says. "I don't know anything about Bryden Frost. And neither does my husband."

"I'm not so sure," Jayne says pleasantly. "You see, Bryden's best friend knew all about their affair. Bryden told her about it."

Alice, apparently unfazed, says, "Derek barely knew that woman."

"That's what he says, but we have information contradicting that."

"I don't believe it. Can you give me details? I'm sure I can find holes in her account," Alice says.

If Jayne's not mistaken, she senses a curiosity there. Alice seems to want to know what her husband's been up to. She doesn't trust him. Good to know. Unfortunately, Jayne is rather short on details about the affair. Paige hadn't had any to give her. Which is frustrating. She hesitates.

Alice smiles. "She didn't provide any, did she?" She tilts her head.

"You don't have any factual evidence at all. If you did, you'd tell me exactly where they met, and when. You'd show me hotel receipts."

A pampered cat, with claws, Jayne thinks.

"Well, I'm afraid I believe my husband over this friend you mention," Alice says blithely, as she rises to go.

"Sit down," Jayne says sharply.

34

Jayne regards Alice coldly; the gloves have come off.

Alice hesitates, raises her eyebrows at her. "Am I no longer free to go? Am I being detained? Shouldn't you read me my rights?"

"Why do I have a feeling you already know your rights?" Jayne says. "But yes, read her her rights, Detective Kilgour."

Kilgour does so, as Alice sits back down in her chair.

"Do you want an attorney?" Jayne asks, when he's done.

"No, of course not," Alice says coolly.

"Your husband has cheated on you before," Jayne says. She says it with confidence because they know this for a fact. They have checked all the local hotels and shown photographs of Derek Gardner and Bryden Frost. He had been seen taking a room in one particular hotel, the White Stag, on more than one occasion, with a woman who does not match the description of his wife, but does not match the photograph of Bryden Frost either. But she's not going to tell his wife that.

They are now seeking this other woman, to see what she might have to say about Derek Gardner—perhaps he likes to play asphyxiation games—but they have little to go on. No photo, no name—just a vague physical description. She could be anyone. Jayne is hoping that when they go public with Derek Gardner as a person of interest, the mystery woman will come forward.

Alice eyes her carefully but says nothing.

Jayne says, "In fact, I *can* provide details." Alice regards her stonily as she continues. "He's been seen visiting hotel rooms at the White Stag with women other than yourself." She provides the relevant dates. "One of them was Bryden Frost," she lies. "I don't know the other woman's name, unfortunately. Do you?"

Still Alice says nothing.

"Just one more thing," Jayne says, "and then you can go." She leans forward. "I'd like to talk about how your mother died."

ALICE IS SURPRISED at the mention of her mother but is careful not to show it. It makes her realize, now, that this detective is serious. That she's really going after Derek, that she thinks he slept with this woman, killed her, and stuffed her in a suitcase. Well, it's possible. "Sure," she says.

"Your mother was killed in a hit-and-run accident that was never solved," the detective says. "That must have been difficult for you."

"Very," Alice says.

"Were the two of you close?"

"Yes, we were. I was an only child. And my father died of a heart attack about ten years ago."

"What did your father do?"

"What difference does it make?"

"He left your mother rather comfortably off."

"He was a smart man. He worked in tech and made some good investments."

"And when your mother died, that money—about three million dollars, I believe—went to you."

Alice experiences an immediate, intense dislike for Detective Salter. She says blithely, "As I said, I was an only child. And both of my parents were as well. There were no other relatives."

"That's rather fortunate."

"Is it? I think I would have liked to have siblings, aunts and uncles, cousins. It was rather lonely growing up."

"But it was fortunate that, when she died, you got all her money."

"Where is this going, Detective?" Alice asks.

"What did you do with the money?" the detective asks, ignoring her question.

"Not that it's any of your business, but some of it we invested in Derek's company."

"How much did you invest in his company?"

"About half of it. The rest went into the house."

"I see," the detective says. "And I understand you and your husband were never formally interviewed by police about the hit-and-run when it happened."

"Someone came to tell us."

"But you weren't interviewed as suspects in the hit-and-run."

"No, why would we be?"

"Because you were the ones who stood to benefit from your mother's death."

Alice leans forward. "Detective, my mother was killed in New Hampshire. My husband and I were two states away, at home in Albany at the time. Of course we weren't suspects."

"And you can prove that?"

"I'm sorry? Are you seriously accusing my husband and me . . . of somehow being involved in my mother's death?"

"The case is unsolved, still open. So please answer the question. Can you prove where you both were at the time your mother was killed?"

Alice smiles. "I don't know how. Derek and I were at home together. I remember it well, because the next morning, very early, the police came to the door and informed us of what had happened."

The detective leans in closer and says, "I understand that you feel you need to protect him, Alice. But think about what he might have done. Was he really home with you the night of the hit-and-run, or are you just giving him an alibi? Did he tell you he was somewhere else, and you believed him? Because Alice, as hard as you might find it to believe, if you're covering up for him, it's possible he is the one who killed your mother. And he might have killed Bryden Frost. Do you really want to live with a man like that?"

Alice doesn't dignify that with an answer. When the detective says she may go, Alice gets up and walks out with all the poise she can muster. She's raging inside, but you wouldn't know it to look at her. She knows she appears unruffled, because she catches sight of her reflection in a window on the way out. She's worked on cultivating that unflappable exterior her whole life. She knows how important appearances are. She can't let people know what's going on inside, what she's really thinking—she learned that early.

That detective—Alice hates her. She wants something terrible to happen to her. She thinks it would be nice if Detective Salter were hit by a bus on the way home tonight. She hopes that her partner, if she has one, is nasty and abusive and decides that tonight is the night to finish her off. If only Detective Salter were out of the picture.

She thinks about that as she gets in her car and drives home. She must talk to Derek.

. . .

LIZZIE DROPS CLARA at day care and then drives home to her own apartment. She wants to spend all day online, but her parents are there. She wishes they would go to a hotel. That's uncharitable of her, she knows, but she's finding it a strain to host them, especially in the current circumstances. They're all emotionally raw. But she can't help wondering if they would be hurting quite as much if it were Lizzie who'd been found dead in a storage locker. She's always been the disappointing daughter—not as pretty, not as accomplished. She hasn't set the world on fire, she hasn't married and provided grandchildren, which seems to be a ridiculous expectation in this day and age, but nonetheless her parents seem to expect it. And now she's almost getting too old. She tries to push these thoughts aside, but when her parents are staying with her, these are the thoughts that crowd her. Somehow, when she's around her parents she slips into old thought patterns and behaviors that she'd hoped she'd left behind.

Lizzie loved her sister. She misses her already. But their relationship had always been complicated, conflicted. Bryden was always prettier, more lovable, got better grades in school. She did everything right, without even seeming to try. Lizzie wasn't valedictorian. Lizzie didn't get a date for the prom. Lizzie didn't get a scholarship to college. Lizzie didn't marry a wonderful husband and produce a lovely child. Lizzie always felt lesser-than.

Lizzie can't deny that she feels a certain freedom now that Bryden is gone. Is that wrong? Is it wrong to enjoy the fact that maybe Bryden wasn't so perfect after all, and that maybe now her parents are starting to realize it? Now her parents think Sam might have killed her. Maybe for once, they think their favorite daughter might have made a *mistake*. And she had an *affair*! What do her parents think of their perfect daughter now?

She feels the urge to hole up in her bedroom and get online; it's pulling her, but she has to ignore it for now. She has to make do with scrolling on her phone, reading the posts on the Facebook group with her parents hovering, oblivious.

She hadn't learned anything further from Sam this morning. She'd hoped he might tell her more about his latest police interview when they were alone, which had been the whole point of her offering to go over this morning and take Clara to day care for him. But he'd given her nothing new.

She remembers his reaction when she'd said she could help, that she knew people. He'd pulled back from her, given her an odd look. Had she revealed too much? Should she have toned it down? She feels uneasy about it now. The truth is, her online sleuthing *is* an obsession. It has been for some time now. But she should be more careful. No more slipups.

Bryden wasn't the only one hiding a part of her life from everyone else.

35

Paige Mason has been alone in her apartment all morning. She hasn't wanted to see anyone. She wonders if she should go back to work soon, to keep her mind off things, because her brain is cycling ruinously. She needs to think about something else.

She hears a knock at her door and freezes. *Who the hell is that?* She's so jumpy. Her first thought is the detectives—are they back again? As she hesitates, the knock comes again. She hurries to the door and opens it. She is completely surprised to see who's standing there.

"Paige," Donna Houser says. "Can I come in?"

Donna is alone, and so bowed down with grief that it hurts Paige to look at her. "Yes, of course," she says, opening the door wide. "I've just made some tea. Do you want some?"

"That would be nice, thank you," Donna says tiredly.

Paige finds herself in her small kitchen, sipping tea across from Bryden's mother at the table by the window. Donna seems reluctant to start. "How are you holding up?" Paige asks at last.

The older woman says, "I'm not, really."

Paige nods sadly back at her, at a loss for what to say. She doesn't know what she can do for her.

As if she's just read her mind, Donna clears her throat and says, "I was hoping, as Bryden's best friend, you might be able to tell me more about her life before she died."

Paige is both taken aback and immediately uncomfortable. She thinks about how she'd had sex with Sam whenever Bryden was away on business, and flushes.

Donna seems to notice and says, "You knew she was having an affair—with this man she had the accident with."

Trapped, all Paige can do is nod.

"I just find it so hard to understand," the older woman says. "I thought Bryden was happy with Sam. It's like everything I believed about my daughter's life is a lie. I was hoping you could tell me what was really going on."

"I know. It's so hard to understand," Paige agrees, swallowing. "I thought they were happy too. I was stunned when she told me about Derek. It was—I thought it was so out of character for her."

Donna leans in over her tea. "But there must have been a reason. Bryden wouldn't risk her marriage, her family, that way. Was she unhappy? Was Sam not good to her?"

Paige feels ashamed, sitting across from Bryden's mother, who doesn't know what she was doing with Bryden's husband in the marital bed. She says, "She didn't say they weren't happy, just that she'd started seeing this other man, and that Sam didn't know."

"You're sure he didn't know? Because the detectives seem to think he did."

"He didn't. Bryden was so sure he didn't."

Donna sighs and slumps in her chair. "I'm not sure I believe that. Maybe Bryden thought he didn't know, but he could have." She pauses and adds fretfully, "I'm so worried about Clara. They have to solve this quickly. We have to know the truth. What if Sam did do this to her?" She whispers, "What if he gets away with it and Clara has to grow up with him?"

Paige sees the naked horror on the other woman's face. She reaches out and puts her hand on top of Donna's and says, "I honestly don't think Sam could have done it. He loved her so much, Donna. He isn't a violent man."

"I'm not so sure," Donna says. She gets up slowly. "I'd better get back to Jim. We're going to look at funeral homes."

DEREK GARDNER IS WORKING in his home office when Alice storms into the house. He comes out to greet her, takes one look, and says, "What's wrong? Where have you been?"

"I have been to see Detective fucking Salter," she says.

"What? Why?" Derek is instantly uneasy. He didn't know about this. What the hell was she doing, going off to talk to the detectives without telling him?

"She called my cell this morning, when I was in the car on my way to work, and asked me to come to the station. So I went."

"Why didn't you tell me, for Christ's sake?" He's angry.

"Oh, I don't know. You don't tell *me* everything, do you?" It's a jab, and it pisses him off even more.

"Let's not play games, Alice. This is serious. Don't fuck around."

"It wouldn't *be* serious if *you* didn't fuck around," she points out acidly. She's pissed off too.

He needs to dial it down a notch. He has to think about damage control. They are standing across from each other in the living room, both too tense to sit down. Derek eases his voice off the throttle. "Just tell me what happened." He hopes she hasn't done him any harm. He knows she's smart. He knows that she is an accomplished liar and dis-sembler, and that she can usually keep her cool. But not always.

"She wanted to know about you and that Bryden woman."

"What did you say?"

"I told them you had nothing to do with her, other than that ac-cident."

"Good," he says, beginning to relax a little.

"Is it true?" she asks.

"Yes, it's true. I didn't sleep with her, and I didn't kill her. For fuck's sake, Alice!"

She looks back at him coldly. "She said that you were seen at a hotel with her. Taking a room."

"That's bullshit! She's lying to you."

"That's not all they said." But then, like the diva she is, she doesn't tell him what else they said. Instead, she walks to the window at the front of the room and looks out onto the street, her back to him.

He runs one hand through his hair in frustration. "Are you going to tell me or not?"

She turns around to face him. "They also know about the other woman. The one whose name you refuse to tell me."

Shit. No wonder she's so angry, he thinks. They've waved this in her face and hurt her ego. He never thought he'd get caught. But Alice was too smart for him. "You know why I can't tell you her name," he says. They've been over this. He can't tell her because Alice might do something to harm her. Alice has a nasty streak. He takes a deep breath. "Tell me what they know."

"They know that you took her to the White Stag Hotel."

He narrows his eyes at her. He doesn't want to protest too much, so he keeps his mouth shut. But it's not good that they know he has cheated on his wife. And he fears they will use it to drive a wedge be-tween them.

"But," his wife says, "we might have a bigger problem than Bryden Frost."

"And what's that?" Derek asks sharply. Sometimes he finds his wife a bit trying.

"They were asking me about Mom."

His adrenaline spikes. "What about her?" But he knows. There's only one reason the detective would bring that up.

"Salter's been looking into you, and she found out that I—we—inherited her estate when she died. And she found out about the hit-and-run that hasn't been solved."

"Fuck," he mutters.

"Yes, a bit worrying, isn't it?" Alice says. "She wanted to know how much of the inheritance went into your business."

"The nosy bitch."

"She was also surprised to learn that neither of us were interviewed as suspects."

"*Fuck*," Derek repeats, running a hand through his hair again. He looks across the room at her. This isn't good at all. "Was she just fishing? Or was she genuinely suspicious?"

"I think she's genuinely suspicious," Alice answers, "of you. She thinks you killed Bryden Frost, and now she also thinks you killed my mother."

"She thinks *I* killed her?"

Alice approaches him and smiles at the irony of it. "That's what she said. She wanted to know where you were that night. I said we were at home together. She accused me of covering up for you. Asked me if I really wanted to live with a man who probably murdered a woman and stuffed her in a suitcase, and who ran over my mother for her money."

"But we both know that you killed your mother, Alice."

"I know that, and you know that, but the detectives don't know that."

He looks back at her beautiful face with growing unease. "This isn't good."

"No shit."

"You shouldn't have spoken to her," Derek says angrily.

"Like I had a choice? She was always going to bring me in, and you know it. They even read me my rights."

"We need to think," Derek says. "We may not be able to *prove* where we were that night, but if we always back each other up, they'll never be able to prove you did it."

"If we always back each other up, they'll never be able to prove you did it either."

"What the fuck are you saying, Alice?"

"I'm saying it's your fault we're in this mess! If you hadn't been fucking Bryden Frost, they wouldn't be looking at what happened to my mother."

He bites his tongue.

36

On Wednesday evening Tracy's husband had come home from work, almost jaunty, reporting that another detective had been at the dealership that day trying to find holes in his alibi. "But he couldn't, because there aren't any. Everybody vouched for me. There's even CCTV. They won't be bothering us anymore," he'd said to her. He'd brought home a bottle of wine to celebrate. She'd smiled and congratulated him. It *was* a relief. But he irritated her. How could he ignore the elephant in the room? He'd had no alibi the first time—had he forgotten?

Then Bryden's body had been discovered that same night. She'd been so upset by it that she hadn't been able to go in to work again the next day. But she's back at work today. Tracy is a copywriter for a legal publishing company. The days are often slow, and she has lots of time to think. Now, she thinks about her neighbor, Bryden Frost. It's horrifying what happened to her. Sickening what happens to women. It could happen to any of us, she thinks. She has lots of time to scroll, and has been following all the news about Bryden online, imagining her hideous final moments.

She also thinks about Kayly Medoff, the woman who accused her husband. Previously she has tried *not* to think about her. Medoff claimed to have been taken against her will into a van by a masked man, bound, raped, terrorized, and ultimately released. She'd named Tracy's husband. The horrible publicity had all but destroyed them. When he was released without charge, somehow that had not warranted the same splashy attention from the media. It's something that she's still bitter about.

Now, with just a moment's hesitation, Tracy googles Kayly Medoff and Henry Kemp on her computer and is rewarded with a flood of articles, some with accompanying photographs. Revisiting them makes her feel ill, and she has to close her eyes for a moment. But then she opens them again and takes a deep breath. She's alone in her quiet office, and she reads them all with close attention. Not everything had made the news. She knows things that aren't in here.

The only way she will ever know for sure is if she talks to Kayly Medoff herself. She can no longer go through life fearing another knock on their door. Tracy's photograph had never made it into the news, so Kayly won't know what she looks like. How will Tracy find her? Is she even still living in the same city? Tracy had wanted to leave Albany and make a fresh start somewhere else, but Henry had had too much money sunk into the dealership to move. She knows Kayly doesn't work at Dunkin' Donuts anymore. Henry told her.

Maybe she's on Facebook?

To Tracy's surprise, it doesn't take long to find her.

JAYNE SITS AT her desk in her office, staring at the wall across from her, savoring a piece of dark chocolate and reflecting on the interview with Alice Gardner. On the wall, there is a large, framed print of an iceberg showing the tip of it above water and the bulk of it underneath. Jayne looks at it often, to remind herself that the dangerous part is hidden beneath the surface, and that what we see is just a small part of the picture.

Detective Kilgour steps in with two cups of coffee and sits down heavily across from her. Jayne reaches for the coffee and says, "Thanks." She offers him some chocolate and takes a sip. "The hit-and-run is out of our jurisdiction of course, but let's talk with the officers who handled the case in New Hampshire. And let's name Derek Gardner as a person of interest. Make him sweat a little. He's a handsome man—the reporters will jump to the obvious conclusion."

LIZZIE WAS MORE THAN HAPPY to loan her parents her car. Her mother had come to her after she'd returned from taking Clara to day care and asked if they could borrow it to visit some funeral homes. They wanted a private ceremony, as soon as possible. Lizzie asked if they wanted her to come and was surprised when her mother said it wasn't necessary. But that was fine with her. She wasn't really in the mood to visit funeral homes and cemeteries. She has things to do.

The minute her parents are out the door with her car keys, Lizzie logs on to the Facebook group. There's a slew of new entries since she left off in the middle of the previous night. Interest in the case is picking up since it's all over the news. The number of members in this group has shot up from 66 to 119. She focuses on the comments to her last post.

> **Andi Rosen**
> You're right about cops and tunnel vision. But it's also true that the murderer is usually someone the victim knew. And it's very often the husband.

> **Jilly Malek**
> I love a good body in a suitcase murder. Remember that one in Delray Beach?

> **Skylar Vasey**
> Usually they're dismembered beforehand to make them fit. The more gruesome the better I like it.

Lizzie finds herself recoiling at some of the comments. She scrolls back through, looking for the earlier comment from Susan Day. Ah, there it is, from the night before. She rereads it:

> **Susan Day**
> I heard one of them was having an affair.

Lizzie had replied, as Emma Porter:

> **Emma Porter**
> Susan Day Where did you hear that?

Now there's an answer.

> **Susan Day**
> Emma Porter Idk. Seems obvious. Haven't you seen her picture? She was gorgeous. She was probably getting some on the side.

Lizzie feels irritated by this. She doesn't need to be reminded that her sister was gorgeous. She finds it distasteful, disrespectful to Bryden. She replies.

> **Emma Porter**
> Susan Day That doesn't mean she wasn't a faithful wife and a good mother.

Susan Day
Emma Porter Okay, if you say so. The husband is
very good-looking too. Maybe he was cheating on
her. All I'm saying is, somebody might have been
cheating.

Lizzie realizes this person hasn't heard anything, doesn't *know* anything. There are pictures and video clips of Sam in posts from lots of
people in the group—in the back of the police car, coming out of the
police station, even in the park with Paige and Clara. Even under
these circumstances, Lizzie can see what Susan Day means. Sam *is*
handsome. And some women actually like men accused of killing their
wives. They write to them in prison, marry them even. Lots of crazies
out there. She sees that someone named Chantelle Dubois has posted
a complete bio for Sam, and done the same for Bryden. Once they
find out about Derek Gardner, Lizzie hopes Chantelle will do the
same for him.

Lizzie is very curious about this man her sister was sleeping with.
She's googled him and found the website for his business. There's a
photo of him on the site. She goes back to it now and studies it closely,
trying to remember if she's ever seen him before.

37

The problem is," Jayne is saying, frustrated, "forensics has nothing showing that Derek Gardner was ever in that apartment. The fingerprints found in the apartment have all been accounted for. We have no physical evidence to tie him to the crime. Even if we know he was sleeping with Bryden Frost, it doesn't mean he killed her."

"True," Kilgour agrees, "but he could have motive. What if Bryden was threatening to tell his wife about them, and she's protecting him on the hit-and-run?"

An officer appears at the door. "A young woman's just come in saying she saw someone in the condo with a suitcase at the relevant time. Thought you'd want to do the interview yourself. She's in interview room three."

Jayne feels a rush of adrenaline. Together, she and Kilgour head to the interview room. The young woman is sitting at the table, waiting for them. She can't be more than twenty, Jayne thinks. She seems a little nervous, and Jayne tries to put her at ease. "Please relax," she says, smiling. "Can we get you anything? A coffee? Water?"

The young woman shakes her head. "No, thank you."

Jayne sits down and looks across the table at the other woman, trying to get the measure of her. This could be the break they've been hoping for.

"Let's start with your name," Jayne says, after introducing herself and Kilgour.

"Francine Logan," she says.

"Francine, tell us what you saw."

Her eyes move back and forth between the two detectives nervously. "I saw someone in one of the elevators with a suitcase in the building where that woman died."

"That's the condominium at 100 Constitution Drive?" Jayne clarifies.

"Yes."

"When was that?"

"On Tuesday."

"Do you live in the building?"

"No, I was visiting a friend. I went over for coffee. We both work from home now, and I don't live too far away, so we do that sometimes."

"Okay. And your friend's name?"

"Lisa Kenney? She lives with her parents in unit 402. But they go out to work during the day." She adds, "Lisa can confirm that I was there."

"And what time did you visit your friend Lisa?"

"It was around lunchtime when I got there, around noon. I'm not sure exactly what time I left. But around one thirty, give or take a few minutes."

"And when did you see this person?"

"When I left. I got on the elevator on the fourth floor to go down to the lobby and there was already someone in the elevator going down. And they had a suitcase."

Jayne knows that fits with the relevant time frame. If Bryden was killed sometime after 12:42 p.m., she might have been removed at around 1:30 or thereabouts. "Can you describe the suitcase?"

"Not really. It was big. And darkish? I'm sorry, I wasn't really paying attention. I just remember wondering if they were going somewhere and wishing I could take a vacation. It's been on my mind lately, but I can't really afford it."

"Can you describe this person?"

"I'm sorry. But I didn't really notice."

"Well, was it a man or a woman?"

"I honestly don't know," she says, embarrassed. "I was looking at my phone when the elevator opened, and I turned to face the front, but I was still looking down at my phone. I noticed the suitcase on the floor beside me but I didn't really notice the person." She adds, "I just remember wishing I had the money to go somewhere."

"So you can't describe this person at all?"

Francine shakes her head. "No," the young woman admits unhelpfully.

"Try," Jayne says, waiting. "You might have noticed something—a scent?" She tries again. "An impression?"

She shakes her head again. "Sorry. I'm not a very good witness, am I? I don't notice things, probably because I'm always staring at my phone, especially in elevators, because it's awkward, you know?" She grows flustered. "I don't mean to waste anyone's time. It's just that Lisa told me that the police were questioning everybody about seeing someone with a suitcase, and I told her what I saw, and she told me I had to tell the police even though I couldn't remember much, so I came in."

"Well, we're glad you did, Francine," Jayne says. "This person in the elevator. Did they get off at the lobby too?"

"No, they stayed on."

"Are you sure you can't remember anything else? This is important." The young woman flushes and shakes her head. "Well, thank
you for coming in," Jayne says. She hands her a card. "And please give
us a call if anything else comes to mind, okay?"

"Sure," she says, and gets up, her face faintly pink as she leaves.

"What do you make of that?" Kilgour asks Jayne after she's gone.

"I don't know," Jayne says. "She was exceptionally vague. The tim-
ing is bang on, so she could be telling the truth. Or she might be
making it all up. Enjoying her fifteen minutes. But I don't think so."
She sighs. "Check in with the team at the condo—see if they've heard
of anyone else in the building going somewhere that day with a suitcase. If there's no one to account for it, Francine Logan *may* have been
in the elevator with our killer."

DEREK GARDNER IS coldly furious as he drives downtown. He's
agitated, and he doesn't like the feeling. He's usually quite cool, unruffled. He likes to be in control. He's got a problem now, and he's not
sure how to handle it. He wasn't that worried about Bryden Frost, not
really, not till that bitch of a detective had brought up Alice's mother.

He drives into the downtown core. He wanted to get away from
Alice, who'd decided not to go into work after all. He was going to
hide out at his office downtown. He'll have to face everyone there at
some point anyway. Better to carry on like business as usual, get in
front of things, reassure everyone that they might hear things about
him, but it's all bullshit. He has a business to run. He must hold his
nerve till all this blows over.

But his thoughts take him down an uncomfortable path. He has this
business because of his wife's money. The cool, hip offices with the
good address, the smart employees, the top-of-the-line equipment—all

bought with her inheritance. The high-end clients he got himself, but still. She gave him his start.

Alice loves him, as well as she can love anyone. But can he trust her? He knows what she's capable of. She killed her own mother in cold blood. And then came home and told him about it, as if she were a cat dropping the gift of a dead mouse at his feet.

He pulls into the underground parking garage beneath his office building. He circles around to his level and finds his own space. There's someone parked next to it. A car he doesn't recognize, a black Range Rover. It's parked too close, so that when he goes to get out of his car, he barely has enough room to open his door to exit his vehicle. It annoys him. *Who the hell does this guy think he is?* He resists the impulse to smash his own car door into the side of the Range Rover. *Fucking asshole.*

He squeezes out of his car awkwardly, sucking in his breath. Once he's out he closes his own door and stares malevolently at the other car. He reaches into his trouser pocket for his keys. He glances around him, but there's nobody there; he's quite alone. He knows where the cameras are. Derek takes his keys in his right hand, singles out one, and walks around the back of the Range Rover to the other side of it and digs the point into the Rover's new paint near the front fender. Then he drags the key with great force along the entire side of the vehicle, leaving a bold, ugly scar across the length of it.

"I SPOKE TO THE PEOPLE in charge of the hit-and-run investigation in New Hampshire," Jayne says to Kilgour in her office later in the afternoon. "They did a shoddy job, if you ask me. There wasn't much of an investigation. They didn't find any witnesses,"

"Maybe there weren't any," Kilgour points out.

"Well, I suppose. Apparently, it's a rural area—very little traffic on that road. But what better place to run over your mother-in-law?" She muses, "There's a very poor solve rate for hit-and-runs, only about ten percent." She sighs. "Maybe I should cut them some slack. Anyway," she continues, "they decided that it was a simple hit-and-run, not a murder." She sighs heavily. "You saw how I tried to rattle Alice. I practically told her that if she's lying to give her husband an alibi, and if he killed her mother, and Bryden Frost, she might be next."

"It didn't seem to faze her."

"No, it didn't. She seems almost as cold-blooded as he is. Maybe they're meant for each other."

38

Alice waits for her husband to come back from work. She got a text from him saying that he was at the office. But she has also seen his picture in the news. She's dismayed that he's been named a person of interest, that the suggestion of his affair with Bryden is public.

Alice is furious. She even threw an expensive glass against the kitchen wall and watched it shatter. After a while, she cleaned it up. Then she started making a beef bourguignon—chopping up the vegetables with energy. Cooking relaxes her.

It's his fault this is happening. If he'd stayed away from that woman, if he'd managed to *keep it in his pants*, if he'd managed to *keep his promise*, they wouldn't be looking into her mother's accident. She still thinks of it that way; she always refers to it as her mother's hit-and-run accident, if anyone should bring it up. She never calls it her mother's murder.

Even though that's exactly what it was.

Alice had been rather clever about it. Her mother was a slave to routine; it was one of the many things about her that drove Alice crazy. Alice prefers to be spontaneous. But not always. When it came to murdering her mother, she thought about it for a long time and planned it carefully. It was going to be a surprise—to her mother, obviously, but also to Derek.

She did it for him. But if she's honest, she did it for herself too. She wanted Derek to have the money to start his business with a splash, and she wanted a glamorous home, and nice things, and she didn't want to wait. And—if she's *completely* honest—she wanted Derek to be grateful, and proud of her, and to know what she was capable of. It helped that she really didn't like her mother, and visiting her on holidays was getting to be tiresome. She wouldn't have visited at all if it weren't for the inheritance, but she'd had enough of playing the dutiful daughter. They were always so painful, those duty visits, her mother with her nervous eyes flicking back and forth between her and Derek, as if expecting one of them to demand money, or to suddenly rise up and choke her.

The funny thing is, her mother always seemed to think that Derek was the dangerous one, when really, it was Alice she should have been afraid of.

She knew her mother always walked along that lonely side road at 6:30, after supper, to get her daily exercise. There was never anybody on that road, not that Alice ever saw. Earlier that day, she drove from Albany, through Vermont to New Hampshire, in her husband's car. It was leased by the company, and it was new, and no one around her mother's place had seen it before so there was no chance of it being recognized.

She arrived unannounced. Her mother hadn't seemed particularly happy to see her, Alice thought. She'd wanted to know why she was there without Derek. She'd asked if they'd split up, seeming almost hopeful. It irritated Alice. She didn't know why her mother was so down on Derek. He was the best thing that had ever happened to her. But her mother had once told her in private, quite earnestly, that she thought there might be something wrong with him, that he might be a sociopath. Alice had laughed. Well, it *was* funny.

Alice hadn't stayed long on that last visit. She left sometime before her mother's daily walk, taking the spare house key, and drove Derek's newly leased car into a nearby hiding spot she'd scouted out beforehand. An opening into a field shielded by trees. Then she walked the short distance back to her mother's place and hid behind a shed, waiting for her to leave the house. After she'd gone, Alice put on some gloves, let herself back into the house, and took her mother's car keys off the kitchen counter. She climbed into her mother's pickup truck, started the engine, and carefully checking first to see that there was no one around, turned down the road. When she saw her mother walking in the distance, she smiled. When she got close enough, she hit the gas. The truck made a lot of noise when it accelerated so suddenly. Her mother whirled around, recognized her own truck, her own daughter, bearing down on her in the short seconds before she was hit. The look on her face! Then there was a tremendous thud, and she went flying in an arc and landed in the ditch. Alice carried on at a normal speed to the next intersection and turned around. She drove the truck back to her mother's house, slowing to observe the spot where her mother's body must be. She parked the truck where she'd found it, checking for damage. It was a large, sturdy truck, a Dodge Ram, and there was only a small dent on the right front. No blood, because her mother was wearing her long, thick coat, as Alice expected. She'd made sure there was no dashcam.

She returned the keys and washed up the coffee mugs they'd used earlier and put them away, still wearing her gloves. She locked the door from the inside and walked back down the lonely road ready to take cover if anyone should come along, but no one did. When she reached the site of the accident, Alice stood on the edge of the ditch and watched her mother. It was dark, and she had to use a flashlight, but even from there she could tell that her mother was clearly dead, her eyes wide open.

Alice returned to the leased car and drove home, arriving at about eleven o'clock.

When she got in, Derek kissed her and asked, "It's really late. Where have you been? I texted but you didn't answer."

She didn't answer because she'd deliberately left her cell phone at home, in the drawer of her nightstand. "I've been to visit my mother," she answered.

"And how's your mother?"

And she'd said, "Dead."

She'd told him all about it, feeling rather gleeful. He'd looked back at her as if he didn't quite know what to make of her. "No one knows I went to visit her," Alice told him. "You must say that I was here with you from about five o'clock. That we were here together all evening."

"Okay," he agreed.

"And we need to delete those texts, right now."

"Okay."

She went to retrieve her cell phone, and they deleted the incriminating messages together.

Alice said, "They'll never find the vehicle that hit her because it was her own truck, and they'll never even look at it. I mean, is that genius, or what?"

He had to agree, it was genius.

"And now all that lovely money will come to us," she said, her hands clasped behind his neck. "We won't have to wait much longer." They had talked about her mother's money on numerous occasions, about not wanting to wait for it. And now she'd taken care of it for them. He seemed pretty happy about that. He'd swept her off to bed.

And it was perfect, really. Someone came to deliver the bad news the next morning, and they behaved suitably shocked and upset. They got the money a year and a half later, no questions asked. As far as she knew, they'd never examined her mother's truck. Why would they? And things had been almost perfect ever since.

Until Derek met Bryden Frost.

Now Alice's thoughts turn to what happens next. What should she do? She's so angry at Derek that she could almost kill *him*. But then she wouldn't have him anymore, and she can't face that. How would she ever replace him?

Alice has to remind herself that Derek might be a murderer now too. How does she feel about that? She gives it a moment's thought. She's okay with it, she decides. As long as he doesn't try anything on her.

The only upside to all this is that maybe this focus on the murder of Bryden Frost will scare him into behaving from now on. Maybe he won't stray anymore. Alice thinks she should be enough for him. He's lucky to have her. She'll figure some way out of this mess he's made.

Her thoughts turn to that bitch of a detective, Jayne Salter.

39

A new post to the Facebook group features side-by-side photos of Derek Gardner and Sam Frost, along with the bold question:

> Are you Team Derek or Team Sam?

Lizzie quickly scans the comments. There's a long stream of Team Sams and Team Dereks. It looks about neck and neck. She's not sure if Team Sam means you think Sam killed Bryden or you think he's innocent. She reads more closely, and it becomes clear that if you're Team Sam it means you think Sam is a murderer.

> **Anonymous member**
> It might not be either of them. You shouldn't leap to conclusions about people. It destroys lives.

Brittany Clement
Can't decide. Might be either. They both look like
killers to me.

Lizzie feels she has to reply.

Emma Porter
Brittany Clement I don't know how you can tell
that from a photo. You don't even know them.

Brittany Clement
Emma Porter Seriously? Look at their eyes. You
can see it if you pay attention.

Lizzie thinks about that. Can you? If you know what you're looking for, is it possible to tell if someone is a killer by looking at their eyes? Surely not, or the police would catch them every time. What BS.

Brittany Clement makes a new post.

Maybe one of these guys has killed before. I hope the
police check their backgrounds thoroughly.

Farah Spence
Of course they will. That's their job.

Chris Belliveau
I've been looking into both of them and haven't found
anything, and I'm pretty good.

Deep Diver
I live near that building, and I've been looking online
almost nonstop for anyone who lives there that might
be suspicious. So far, I've found two possibles. One
guy likes kiddie porn. I let the authorities know.

> **Farah Spence**
> Deep Diver Good for you!

Lots of likes on that one.

Lizzie sits back in her chair and thinks about Clara, living in an apartment in the same building as a man who likes kiddie porn. She hopes they arrest him. She's grateful to Deep Diver. It's awful what you find when you start turning over rocks and looking underneath.

> **Deep Diver**
> And even more intriguing, there's another guy, *who lives on the same floor as Bryden Frost,* who was arrested for false imprisonment and rape a couple of years ago, but never charged, for lack of evidence. Hello!!! I can't give his name or unit number on here. Wonder what the police are doing about him?

Lizzie can't resist.

> **Emma Porter**
> Deep Diver The police have dismissed him as a suspect. He has an alibi.

> **Deep Diver**
> Emma Porter Well I hope they know what they're doing. And how do you know?

She ignores Deep Diver's question. Lizzie enjoys being the one who knows something that the others don't know.

Impulsively, she posts a close-up of her sister's face from her phone; one that is recognizable as Bryden but that no one else has ever seen. Accompanying the photo, she writes:

> I know how she died.

A whole string of *hows* quickly shows up on her screen. She savors it for a moment.

She hovers over her keyboard and begins another new post; this time she goes back to her standard photo of the front of the building.

> She was asphyxiated. A plastic bag was held over her face.

> **Karen Hennin**
> How do you know that? And where did you get that photo of her?

> **Emma Porter**
> Karen Hennin I know someone in the police. I hear things.

> **Brittany Clement**
> Emma Porter What else have you heard?

Then there's a whole chorus of replies from others demanding to know more too.

Lizzie feels a surge of excitement. Why didn't she think of this before? She can hide behind this lie, pretend she knows someone in the police. It's believable. Of course there could be leaks. She makes another post.

> There was no sexual assault.

> **Brittany Clement**
> Tell us more.

> **Farah Spence**
> Then why was she naked? The police said that her clothes are missing. They're looking for them.

Lizzie posts again.

> She had bra and panties on. Just her yoga pants and
> sweatshirt are missing.

> **Brittany Clement**
> That's what I heard too, she was in bra and panties.

> **Emma Porter**
> Brittany Clement How did you hear it?

> **Brittany Clement**
> Emma Porter I know people too.

That gives Lizzie pause. Who could this be? A journalist maybe, snooping around the police for information, snooping here too? Or someone from the police? She wonders again whether the police check out these groups. She shouldn't have posted that photo of Bryden from her phone. Lizzie picks up her cell phone, searches for the photo, and deletes it. She looks at Brittany Clement's profile but there's no information about her at all. Just a blank. She taps out a new post.

> The lack of sexual assault makes them think it's more
> likely that it wasn't a stranger. But I don't agree. I don't
> think it was someone she knew.

> **Karen Hennin**
> You seem VERY worried that they might think it
> was someone she knew. Are you one of those
> people?

Lizzie feels her heart begin to pound. She will stick to her story of having a friend in the police. She just has to brazen it out.

> **Emma Porter**
> Karen Hennin No. I didn't know her.

> **Brittany Clement**
> Emma Porter Maybe I did.

Lizzie stares at the words on her screen. Who the fuck is this? Is someone playing with her?

> **Emma Porter**
> Brittany Clement Did you know her or not? And if so, tell us how.

But Brittany Clement doesn't answer.

Lizzie sits for a moment, perfectly still, waiting for Brittany Clement. But it becomes clear that she's not going to reply. Plenty of other people want to interact with her, however. Lizzie spends more time discussing the case online with the people in the group. She thinks she's become someone they are turning to, as an authority on this case that they're all so engrossed in. It's because they think she's got a friend in the police. Lizzie has never felt so important, so *noticed*, even though she is anonymous. She glows inside. She posts again.

> I might even be responsible, in an indirect way, for finding her. They'd already searched the building thoroughly on the day she disappeared but couldn't find her. I suggested to my police friend that they bring in a cadaver dog, and they finally did. It was the dog that found her in the storage locker.

Well, she did suggest it to the detective. Lizzie takes a deep breath, finds herself trembling. Has she gone too far? She's going out on a limb now, but she can't help it. It's addictive, this sharing. This belonging. And when it's anonymous, it feels safe somehow, even if maybe it isn't. It's intoxicating.

That last post gets a lot of reaction. She's so absorbed in what she's doing that she's completely startled by the knocking on her bedroom door.

She hears her mother calling, "Lizzie, it's time for supper. What are you doing in there?"

40

Donna watches her daughter Lizzie throughout supper. They're eating a bucket of takeout fried chicken, the three of them, in Lizzie's apartment. Donna hasn't mentioned anything about her visit to Paige earlier today.

There is no thought of going over to Sam's anymore. Donna has made it clear to Jim and Lizzie that she thinks that Sam may have killed her older daughter. She can tell Jim is struggling to process this too. But not Lizzie. Lizzie seems stubborn in her refusal to even consider the possibility that Bryden may have been murdered by her own husband, even though he is the most obvious suspect. And he's hired himself an attorney.

Donna tries to make allowances for Lizzie. It's hard to stomach, after all. Maybe she just can't face it. She's always liked Sam, looked up to him. She's in denial. She's so innocent, really. She's never been married; perhaps she idealizes the marital state. Donna doesn't know.

She likes to think that if Lizzie does, it's because she's been witness to the happy and stable marriage of her parents. Donna had always thought that bringing up her daughters in a happy home would protect them from the kind of tragedy that seems to have befallen Bryden. How wrong she was. If Sam killed her . . . How could Bryden have chosen so badly? Did growing up in a happy home backfire? Was she too naïve about how things might be, too trusting? Maybe girls from dysfunctional homes are wiser, choose better? Fare better? And maybe Bryden felt she couldn't tell her mother about the problems in her marriage because she didn't feel she'd lived up to her parents' example. Donna doesn't know. She'll never know.

Thinking about all this makes Donna profoundly depressed. Maybe Bryden had reasons for finding comfort with someone else. But maybe that other man was the one who killed her. Oh, her poor, sweet Bryden.

Donna slides a look at Lizzie. She seems different tonight, somehow, humming with an unusual energy, her earlier exhaustion gone. She has an almost feverish brightness in her eyes. What was she doing in her room earlier? She'd had her door closed when she and Jim got back from the funeral homes. Donna had wanted to allow Lizzie some downtime after everything she has done lately, so she left her undisturbed all afternoon and went about getting supper herself. She'd thought Lizzie was napping, but now she wonders if she was on the computer.

Does Lizzie have a secret boyfriend online that she hasn't told them about? Donna hopes not. She doesn't like how everyone seems to meet their partners online these days, with Tinder and all sorts of ridiculous apps. That's no way to meet a life partner. But it seems as if that's all people ever do anymore. No wonder her younger daughter is still single.

Now Lizzie asks, as she helps herself to more coleslaw, "How did the funeral home visits go?"

Donna says, "I think we found a suitable one," but she's dispirited and doesn't say anything more.

Her husband glances at her in concern and says, "We think we'll go with the Montgomery one—it seemed nice. They can arrange a small, private ceremony for next Wednesday."

"Is that what Sam wants?" Lizzie asks.

That lands like a lead balloon. Donna says, "I don't know. I suppose you can ask him, but that's what we're doing. We're her parents."

Neither of them had ever considered burying their daughter before. You don't think about your child dying before you. She and Jim haven't even gone about making funeral arrangements for themselves yet. Donna feels another surge of grief. It's like waves, crashing up against the shore, some waves bigger and stronger than others, but relentless. Or like contractions, during childbirth—you think some of them will kill you. It's like that. This might kill her.

But Lizzie already seems to have lost interest in the funeral arrangements. There's that odd look in her eye again, an unusual excitement. Maybe she's secretly in love. Or maybe her daughter is taking drugs. Her stomach suddenly seems to fall out at the bottom. Dear God, she can't deal with that too. Not now. Should she ask her? But she can't. She can't, right now, ask her surviving daughter if she's abusing drugs. But her mind races headlong. Lizzie's a nurse, maybe it's easy for her to get them. Donna knows that drug abuse is rampant among all walks of life these days. It's a scourge. People trying to escape their pain—physical, emotional, spiritual. It's an epidemic. She couldn't survive if her only remaining daughter became victim to that.

She tells herself she has to stop catastrophizing like this, imagining the worst. She thought the worst had already happened, but she still has one daughter to lose. Donna takes a breath and asks, "Lizzie, are you managing all right?"

Lizzie looks back at her. "Yes. Why wouldn't I be?"

It's a strange thing to say, Donna thinks, glancing at her husband. He seems to think so too.

DEREK LETS HIMSELF into the house. He can smell something good cooking. Alice is an excellent cook. But it usually means she's upset. He makes his way uneasily in the direction of the kitchen.

"Hi," he says, as if he's a perfectly normal man, speaking to his perfectly normal wife, at the end of a perfectly normal day.

"How was your day?" Alice asks, holding out a wooden spoon with something hot and fragrant on it. He sips tentatively, so that he doesn't burn his tongue. "Delicious," he says truthfully. "Beef bourguignon."

And now he knows something is up. He's the one in the doghouse, so why is she making his favorite meal? He proceeds carefully. "It was okay," he says. He wants to reassure her. "Alice, those detectives have nothing, no evidence, so there's nothing to be worried about. Besides, I didn't kill her."

"Of course you didn't," she agrees, as if she's merely humoring him, and she's willing to let bygones be bygones.

What a pair they make, he thinks. He was so lucky to find her. They were so lucky to find each other. They were made for each other.

"But it's unpleasant, the attention," she complains. "The news suggesting that you were her lover, that you might have killed her. People talking about it."

"Yes," he agrees, "it's unpleasant." It had been awkward at the office today, having to reassure his staff that it was all bullshit, that he didn't even know the murdered woman except from their car accident. More awkward still, talking to clients. This will be bad for business.

"Do you think it will all blow over?" his wife asks him.

"I think so. We can rise above it. Her husband probably killed her, like you said."

"Well, I hope they convict him, whether he did it or not."

And that's Alice in a nutshell, Derek thinks. She's always on his side, no matter what he's done.

"And then there's my mother," she says.

"But is there really anything to worry about?" Derek asks, coming up to her and massaging her shoulders. "As long as we stick to our story, there really isn't anything they can do. There's no evidence there either." It was almost four years ago. Everything belonging to her mother—the truck, the house, every trace of her life, had been sold off or given away. He says, "Even if they were able to track down the truck, there's no way to connect that tiny dent to something that happened years ago. They could never prove it."

"I suppose," she says, stirring the pot.

IT'S FRIDAY NIGHT, and Jayne goes home relatively early, for the middle of a murder investigation. Michael is coming over. They'll order in, he'll bring a bottle of wine. She's only a call away if there are any developments.

She's really looking forward to spending some downtime with Michael. She feels she's hardly seen him since this all kicked off three days ago with Bryden Frost's disappearance. She remembers Tuesday—it was their anniversary.

Now Michael rubs her feet on the sofa while they wait for their Thai food to arrive. She watches him and remembers that she needs to have that drink with Ginny. About how to do it all—give a family the love and attention they deserve while you're in the trenches every day seeing terrible things as a homicide detective. An image of

Bryden's body squeezed into the suitcase comes unbidden to her mind's eye.

She doesn't, as a rule, discuss her cases with Michael. But sometimes it's as if he can sense she's not fully there with him, that her mind is thinking about work.

Michael reaches over and tops up her wineglass from the bottle sitting beside them on the coffee table. "What are you thinking?" he asks her.

Jayne answers thoughtfully. "You know, it's never like they say it is, at the beginning. At first, everyone said that the Frosts were perfectly happy. No problems. Neither of them would ever cheat. The perfect little family. And then you start to look beneath the surface, and it all starts to come out—all the ugliness." She thinks of the affair, the abuse, the murder.

"People are complicated," Michael says. "They give in to all sorts of unconscious impulses and desires that mess up their lives. I see it too, as a psychologist."

"I know you do."

"We're not so far removed from animals, you know, not as far as we think. We lived like animals for much longer than we've been wearing clothes and living in cities. But the animal is still there, underneath the clothes." He has a sip of wine. "Whoever killed this woman, Bryden, they stepped outside the bounds of civilized society for a moment. And that's a tragedy. For her, for her family, even for the perpetrator." He sighs and stops rubbing her feet for a moment and looks at her. "But what's even more concerning is when it's not just the individual who steps outside the norms of civilized society, who breaks the unwritten rules we somehow all agreed to be bound by when we decided to live as civilized beings."

"I know," she agrees, reflecting on everything frightening that's going on in the world these days. "It's scary."

"Yes. When millions of people believe fantasy over fact, choose emotion over reason, society can break down pretty quickly. It happens all the time."

Jayne looks back at him, more doubtful than ever. What hope is there for any of them? Does it even make any sense to bring another child into this world?

He leans in and kisses her. "But we can always choose to be good," he says.

And she loves him for it. She will carry his words with her tomorrow when she goes back to work.

41

Saturday morning dawns, gray and drizzly. Lizzie's parents hover around her, cramping her style. They have nowhere to go. She's afraid to close herself in her bedroom on the computer in case her mother barges in and sees what she's doing. There's no lock on her door. She's restless, frustrated. She lounges in the living room and checks the news about Bryden's case on her phone constantly, but there's nothing new. Lizzie craves information. Information she can share. This stasis, this boredom, is awful.

"What are you up to today?" Lizzie asks her parents, hoping this will prod them into doing something.

They look blankly back at her. "Nothing," her mother says listlessly.

She realizes her parents are just waiting. Waiting for the funeral so that they can lay Bryden to rest. Waiting for someone to be arrested. Waiting for the truth. For closure. It seems impossible that Bryden went missing just four days ago, that they will bury her in four more.

Lizzie wants the funeral to be done and over with so that her parents will go home. They can't be planning on staying in town indefinitely, as long as the investigation lasts. If so, they can't stay here. She'll go out of her mind. It could be weeks, months. "I think I'll go out," Lizzie says.

"Where?" her mother asks.

She hesitates, but then decides to tell the truth. "To Sam's." Her mother looks back at her, her face set, but before she can say anything Lizzie preempts her. "I know what you're thinking, but I don't think he killed her. And I know you don't want me to see him, but I want to see Clara. I want to make sure she's okay."

Her mother nods, chastened.

"Can you bring her over here? For a visit?" Jim asks.

"If he'll let me. He might not."

It's as if suddenly they all realize how it might be. The grandparents might never see their only grandchild again. Sam knows they suspect him of murder—he's not going to let his little girl come over here and have her head filled with poison. As if any of them would do that, Lizzie thinks. Her mother wouldn't say anything to a three-year-old against her father, would she? Suddenly she's not sure.

"What *are* we going to do about Clara?" Lizzie asks her parents. The ensuing silence tells her how loaded this question is.

Donna says, a little stridently, "We're not losing Clara too."

Lizzie chooses her words carefully. "Sam is her father. If you persist in acting like you believe he killed Bryden, he's not going to let you see her. You must know that."

Jim speaks up calmly. "She has a point, Donna."

Donna replies, "If he did kill her, they'll arrest him. They'll convict him. He'll spend the rest of his life in prison. And we'll apply for custody."

"You want to raise her? Are you sure?" Lizzie asks. She's not sure how she feels about that. But she's not prepared to raise Clara herself.

"Of course we want to raise her. Unless you want to do it."

But Lizzie doesn't want to do it, and her parents seem to know that. "I still think you're wrong about Sam," Lizzie says evasively.

"Maybe," her mother says. "I hope so. Maybe it was that man she was seeing. I hope they find out who did it, and, for Clara's sake, that it wasn't her father." She breaks down and begins to weep. Her husband stands watching her, his hands twitching helplessly and his lower lip trembling.

Lizzie speaks quietly. "Look, Sam still trusts me. He'll let me see her whenever I want, I'm sure. I'll let you know how she is, how she's doing. But if I don't see Sam, then we might lose Clara altogether."

Her mother nods miserably through her tears.

Lizzie wonders if he's got Paige over there helping him with her. She thinks to herself, *her favorite babysitter.*

SAM LOOKS AT the text message from Lizzie. *Can I come over?*

He would like to see her—he needs a friendly face. He's going crazy in the condo on Saturday morning, trying to entertain Clara by himself. There are reporters outside the building; he can see them from the windows. He feels trapped. At least Lizzie doesn't think he's a murderer. He'd considered asking Paige to come over but had second thoughts. And Angela has gone out. He texts Lizzie back gratefully. *Yes, come over. Clara and I would love to see you.*

Lizzie had texted him the day before that her parents had gone out looking at funeral homes, and that they wanted a very small, private funeral, as soon as possible. They hadn't asked him what he wanted for the funeral, or to come along. He'd been relieved, although it spoke volumes about what they think of him. He suspects they can't bear to be around him anymore.

He tells Clara in a bright voice that her Aunt Lizzie is coming over, and the little girl perks up a little. He feels guilty that he doesn't want to take her to the park, not with all those vultures out there, ready to shout at him and call him a murderer. Not after last time. Maybe Lizzie could take her to the park for him.

He thinks about Lizzie, remembers what she was like last time he saw her, that weird intensity, what she said about knowing people. What was that all about? Maybe he'll ask her.

Lizzie arrives, and Clara holds up her arms to be picked up. Lizzie carries her into the kitchen, following him. He puts on a fresh pot of coffee. They can't really talk with Clara there. They interact with Clara for a while, have a snack with her, then settle her in another room with a puzzle so they can speak privately in the kitchen.

"Have you spoken to the detectives lately?" Lizzie asks.

"Not since Thursday evening, at the police station," he says.

He's afraid, and he needs someone on his side. Everyone will think he killed her. He can't bear the thought of prison. He clutches her arm across the kitchen table.

"Lizzie, you must believe me. I didn't kill her." He tries to read her eyes, but he can't be sure she believes him. "I didn't know she was cheating," he says. "You must believe me, Lizzie. I didn't kill her."

"I know," she says, after a long moment. "I believe you." He sags in relief. "But I can't say the same about my parents."

He's not surprised. He shrugs.

She looks at him with those intense eyes of hers. "Is there anything else I should know? Anything else the police might find out?" she asks.

He shakes his head, lowering his eyes. "No. Nothing. I swear."

42

Lizzie spends some more time with Clara, but she's troubled, not able to focus on her niece the way she usually would. She wants to take her to the park, but she's intimidated by the crowd of reporters outside the front of the building. She'd been able to bypass them, driving in through the underground parking garage. Now she stands at the window, staring down at them. Someone out there sees her and waves. Lizzie is taken aback, steps quickly away from the window.

Everyone knows which windows belong to unit 804. Everyone knows a woman was murdered here. Lizzie wonders if that will make it easier or more difficult for Sam to sell the condo when the time comes. She should check to see if it's already been added to that site that keeps track of homes where murders have occurred. Housecreep, she thinks it's called. Maybe she'll do that tonight.

She realizes how tired she is of being cooped up. "I think I'll take Clara out to the park after all," she calls to Sam. "Is that all right?"

"Sure. Okay if I don't come with you? I mean, they'd be swarming around me, but I think they'll leave you alone."

"You think? They know what I look like, what Clara looks like."

He seems to consider it. Then he says, "Clara needs some fresh air. If they harass you, come right back. And I'll complain to the detectives, maybe they can do something about them."

"Okay." She bundles Clara up quickly, takes her by the hand, and together they leave the apartment and take the elevator down to the lobby.

As they exit the condo's glass front doors, they are met with the crowd of media. They don't rush her and Clara, but they stand in clusters and watch them. The reporters know who they are. Lizzie says nothing, keeps her head down, and tries to make her way to the park across the street, tugging Clara by the hand. She is aware of their photographs being taken, and she doesn't like it. She stops in her tracks. "Please," she says. "No photographs. Respect our privacy. She's only three years old." And then she keeps walking. It doesn't stop the photographers, but what did she expect? And worse, she seems to have opened up a dialogue with them, because now they're calling out questions, with no regard for Clara at all.

Does the family support Sam?

Haven't seen Bryden's parents over here for a while. Why's that?

Who do you think killed your sister, Lizzie?

She's quickened the pace. This was a mistake. She can turn back now and run the gauntlet again or keep going. She decides to keep going, clutching Clara's hand tightly, hurrying her along. Thankfully, the bastards don't cross the street to the park to follow them. Instead, discouraged, they return to the front of the building. They'll have a long wait if they expect Sam to come out the front door, she thinks.

It's a cool, blustery day, and there are few families in the playground. Lizzie pushes Clara on the swings for a while, singing to her, then lifts her out and sits on a bench with her back to the condominium, and sends Clara off to play in the sandbox. She's watching Clara, lost in thought, when she becomes aware of someone sitting down beside her. It startles her. She hadn't seen anyone approach, hadn't been paying attention. It's a woman with auburn hair. There are other, empty benches this woman could have chosen, Lizzie notices, annoyed. Lizzie almost gets up.

"Hi," the other woman says, smiling. "I'm Alice."

Lizzie isn't sure what to make of her, but she seems friendly, not threatening, like the press. Ballsy, anyway. Is she sympathetic?

"Are you with the media?" Lizzie asks suspiciously.

"Oh no, I *hate* the media," Alice says. "They're crucifying my husband."

"Who's your husband?" Lizzie asks.

"Derek Gardner."

Lizzie stares at her. This is a surprise. "Your husband was sleeping with my sister," Lizzie says in a low voice.

"Probably," Alice agrees.

"He probably killed her," Lizzie hisses.

"Oh, I don't know about that," Alice replies. "I think her husband killed her."

"Well, I don't."

"Of course you don't. We never want to believe the worst of those close to us, do we? But I think the detectives will find what they need to put her husband away."

"What are you talking about?" Lizzie suspects she should grab Clara and go. But something makes her stay. "What are you doing here?" she asks uneasily.

"I wanted to meet you, and I want you to give Sam a message."

Lizzie feels her stomach curdle. "What message?"

Alice leans in closer to her. "Tell him he's not going to get away with it."

Then she rises gracefully from the bench, leans down, and whispers, "*I'm Team Sam.*"

She walks away without looking back, leaving a trace of her perfume behind her.

43

―――――

Lizzie remains glued to the park bench, her heart racing. She's so rattled that she forgets to watch Clara. *I'm Team Sam.* She's just spoken to the wife of Derek Gardner, the man who was sleeping with her sister. Was she threatening Sam with that message? What does she know? It unnerves her that this woman, Alice, has sought her out, that she must know, somehow, that Lizzie's on the Facebook group. Does she know she is posting as Emma Porter? How could she? Had she been standing, watching, beneath Sam's windows, waiting for her to come out? Lizzie shudders involuntarily. She feels like she's been exposed.

The sun moves behind a cloud, and suddenly she's chilled. She gets up off the bench and moves closer to where Clara is wandering around the playground. After twenty minutes, she calls Clara to her and says it's time to go. She takes her hand and prepares to walk back through the media and into the condo. They take more photos but let them pass mostly unmolested. Someone calls out, *Who were you talking to?* She keeps her mouth shut.

"You weren't gone that long," Sam says, once they're back inside the apartment. "Everything all right?"

"It was cold," Lizzie answers, helping Clara remove her jacket. She suggests to Clara that she go work on her puzzle again. Once she's gone into the other room, Lizzie tells Sam about Alice and her warning, *Tell him he's not going to get away with it.* She doesn't mention the bit about Team Sam.

"What the fuck?" he says. "How dare she approach you! We should tell the police."

"Should we?" Lizzie asks uncertainly.

"She's harassing us! She's obviously afraid her husband did it. If she wasn't worried, why would she use you to deliver that message? You have to tell the detectives."

Lizzie's not so sure. She's worried that Alice might know something; she'd seemed so confident. *He's not going to get away with it.*

But she *would* like to talk to the detectives again.

WHEN JAYNE IS INFORMED that Lizzie Houser is here to see her, she summons Kilgour and together they meet Lizzie and take her into an empty interview room. Does she have something she's decided she now wants to say? It's always helpful when the family surrounding a suspect starts to crumble. But what comes next is entirely unexpected.

Lizzie says, "Alice Gardner accosted me in the park outside the condo this morning. She knew who I was. "She was . . . threatening."

"How do you mean?"

"She told me she had a warning for Sam."

"Go on," Jayne urges.

"She told me to tell him 'He's not going to get away with it.'"

"Did she say anything else?" Jayne asks.

"No." Lizzie asks, "Don't you think it's suspicious? I mean, is that the way the wife of an innocent man would act?"

Jayne glances at Kilgour, beside her, wondering what he makes of it. She answers, "I don't know what's going through her mind."

"Well, can you talk to her? Tell her to leave us alone?"

"I'll see what I can do," Jayne says, and rises to show her out. But Lizzie remains stubbornly seated.

"My parents and I want to know how the investigation is going," Lizzie says. "We're entitled to that. Bryden was my sister. My parents are going out of their minds. You must tell us if you're making any progress."

But Jayne won't be telling this woman anything. Anything she tells Lizzie will make it right back to Sam. "We're doing everything we can. We're making progress. I can't tell you more than that."

Lizzie gives her a contemptuous look, one Jayne hasn't seen from her before. Lizzie stands up. "Thanks for nothing." On her way out the door she turns back and says, "You know, if it weren't for me, you probably wouldn't even have found her by now."

"Excuse me?" Jayne says.

"I'm the one who asked you to get the cadaver dog, remember?" Then Lizzie asks, "Are you close to making an arrest?"

Jayne regards her. "As I said, we're still conducting our investigation."

"What about Derek Gardner?" Lizzie persists. When Jayne remains silent, she continues. "What about other people in the building? Have you found anything? Do you have any DNA from the crime scene?"

Jayne studies the younger woman curiously. "I have nothing more to say." Once she's gone, Jayne turns back to Kilgour and raises her eyebrows at him. "She's pretty intense, don't you think?"

Kilgour says, "I remember her wanting the K-9 unit. I don't recall her suggesting a cadaver dog, in particular."

"It's an odd thing to say though."

He shrugs. "She's pissed off at us, thinks we're not doing our jobs. It was just a parting shot."

"She acts like she thinks she knows how to do our jobs better than we do."

DONNA IS WAITING on pins and needles when Lizzie arrives back home, anxious to hear news about her granddaughter. She sees immediately that Lizzie is in a mood. It's in the way she tosses off her jacket, kicks off her shoes. It's in the expression on her face. She's angry about something. Donna's nerves almost fail. Is Sam not going to let them see Clara anymore? Did they have an argument? "What's wrong?" she asks her daughter.

Lizzie flings herself into an armchair and says, "Those detectives are useless. I stopped by the police station on the way home and they still wouldn't tell me anything."

Donna takes a deep breath. She knows her daughter is anxious for information, they all are, but this is how the police work. "You have to let them do their jobs," she says.

"Are they?" Lizzie asks. "Doing their jobs? How do we even know?"

Donna says, "We have to assume they know what they're doing."

"Why? The world is full of incompetent people barely doing their jobs. Why should the police be any different?"

Before Donna can say anything else, Lizzie gets up and storms into her bedroom, slamming her door. Donna watches after her, worried.

Jim, who'd heard it all, comes up behind her and says, "She's just upset. It's a lot to deal with."

She never even got a chance to ask her about Clara. Lizzie will calm down, Donna tells herself. She'll ask her about Clara later.

But she's worried about Lizzie. She seems . . . different. Not herself at all.

44

_____

What Paige feels the most, on Saturday afternoon, more than grief, is loneliness. She misses Bryden. And she misses Sam, and Clara. She knows it would be wiser to stay away.

She remembers the way Sam had been the last time she saw him, on Thursday in the park outside the condo with Clara. Maybe now he's had time to calm down, to come to grips with his new reality. He might be starting to cope, trying to see a way forward. She wants to be there for him, and for Clara. Bryden was her best friend.

She decides not to text him first in case he tells her not to come. She gets in her car for the short, familiar drive to Sam's condo. She arrives at the entrance to the underground parking and uses the keypad to call his apartment.

"It's Paige," she says. She senses a hesitation, but then he buzzes her in.

On her way up in the elevator to the eighth floor she tries not to think about what happened to Bryden. She does enough of that late at night, waiting for sleep to come.

She knocks on the door, and Sam opens it. For a moment he stares at her. She suddenly wants to kiss him, but she knows Clara is probably here somewhere. He lets her into the apartment and closes the door.

"Clara's at Angela's," he says.

She nods, studying him. He's showered and put on fresh clothes—jeans and a casual, buttoned shirt. He's even shaved. It's a good sign. She reaches out and gently caresses his cheek, meaning to comfort. His hand reaches up to clasp hers.

"Don't," he says.

"It's going to be okay," she whispers.

"Is it?" he says, his voice low.

SAM STARES BACK AT PAIGE. Her eyes are large, her hand is still on his cheek. It's intoxicating, her wanting him. She's like Bryden used to be, before she learned what he could be like.

She leans forward and kisses him on the mouth. And it's like before, he hesitates for a fraction of a second, and then he gives in to it, relaxes into her mouth, pushing her up against the door, wanting to lose himself in pleasure, to forget everything that's happened. It's a long, sensual, probing kiss, and when they break apart, they are both out of breath. He stares into her eyes, sees the longing and arousal there. He takes her by the hand and leads her to the bedroom, avoiding the windows so that they can't be seen. Once they're in the bedroom, he closes the door.

They start tearing off each other's clothes. "We have to be quiet," he breathes into her ear, "in case Angela comes to the door." She nods and undoes his jeans. And somehow, it's even better this time, as they make love in near silence. He's missed her, missed this. It's the first time since what happened to Bryden that Sam has been able to put everything out of his mind, and it's bliss.

But right after, Sam gets out of bed and begins dressing, his back to her.

"What are you doing?" Paige asks.

"Get dressed," he says. "Angela might bring Clara back soon."

She climbs out of the bed, reaching for her clothes strewn across the floor as Sam slips out of the room, closing the door behind him.

What the hell is he doing? He can't be having sex with his wife's best friend days after she's been murdered. With his daughter at the neighbor's down the hall. He must be out of his mind. He goes into the kitchen and drinks a glass of water, trying to pull himself together. When he returns to the bedroom, Paige is dressed and brushing her hair in front of Bryden's mirror, with Bryden's hairbrush. He starts making the bed. Once that's done, he says, "Let's go out to the kitchen."

He makes them coffee and they sit at the table. He has to say something about this, make things clear. "Paige—"

But she reaches out and places a finger against his lips. She says, "I know what you're going to say. And you're right. We have to be careful."

"What if Angela had brought Clara back, and I had to answer the door doing up my pants, and you're here?" He can't believe how reckless he's been. But that's what he is. Reckless. He's someone who gives in to his impulses. That's always been the problem.

"She didn't. Nobody knows but us. Bryden was my best friend." Her eyes begin to well up. "I'm Clara's godmother. It's perfectly reasonable that I spend time with the both of you. Especially now."

He looks back at her. He doesn't love her. She could never replace Bryden. He'd been worried that the detectives would find out about their affair, but she's not going to say anything.

He says, "We have to be very careful."

. . .

JAYNE HAS BEEN THINKING about Alice. Why would she approach Lizzie? What's to be gained from it? It might suggest she's more worried about Derek possibly having killed Bryden than she's let on. People can be protective of their partners, even if their behavior seems unforgivable to anyone else.

Jayne stares again at the picture of the iceberg on the wall across from her. What is she missing? Maybe Alice already knew about the affair between Bryden and her husband. Maybe she'd followed him one day, seen them together. Alice strikes Jayne as that kind of woman. She can imagine it playing out.

Maybe she's been looking at the Gardners all wrong. Is it possible that *Alice* killed Bryden, and now she's toying with them all?

45

izzie has stuck a chair up under the handle of her bedroom door to prevent her mother from coming in unexpectedly and seeing what she's doing. She sits at her desk, turns on her computer, and puts on headphones to play music in the background. Without even reading to catch up on everything that's been posted, she starts typing a new post as Emma Porter, again using her photo of the front of the building.

> It's been three days since Bryden Frost's body was found at 100 Constitution Drive. Why haven't they made an arrest? They're not saying much publicly, as usual. What do *we* think?

She hits post.

With that off her chest, she reads what people have posted since she was last online, late the night before. There are many more people in this group than there were. There are more comments to her posts now, too, and some of them are a bit disturbing.

> **Mel Schep**
> I think she deserved it. It's wrong to sleep with another man when you're already married.

> **Ange O'Neil**
> Mel Schep Oh fuck off. No woman deserves to be murdered.

> **Mel Schep**
> Ange O'Neil She got exactly what she deserved!

Now something new comes in. Deep Diver has posted a picture of a uniformed officer outside a Dunkin' Donuts shop and accompanying text.

> While the cops have been slacking, or having donuts or whatever, I've been busy looking further into Derek Gardner, and his wife, Alice Gardner. And guess what?? I found something VERY interesting! She inherited MILLIONS from her mother when she was killed four years ago in a—wait for it—HIT-AND-RUN. WHICH HAS NEVER BEEN SOLVED. This case just gets more and more interesting! Maybe Sam Frost killed his wife, I don't know. But if she was sleeping with Derek Gardner—think about it. Maybe he's killed before. Maybe he deliberately ran down his mother-in-law with a car and left the scene so he and his wife would get all her money. And this one happened on a lonely rural road in New Hampshire, outside of a tiny town called Roxbury. I've looked into this, and it looks like they weren't even considered suspects, because the police said they had no suspects. But what if he got away with it? And what if he killed Bryden? I'm switching my vote from TEAM SAM to TEAM DEREK. I think he's a killer. It takes someone very

cold-blooded to run over an old lady. And it takes someone very cold-blooded to hold a plastic bag over a woman's face till she's dead and stuff her body in a suitcase.

Brittany Clement
Wow! How many million?

Deep Diver
Brittany Clement Three million

Brittany Clement
Deep Diver That's money worth killing for!

Deep Diver
Brittany Clement Right?

Brittany Clement
Deep Diver If he did it, his wife must know what he did.

Deep Diver
Brittany Clement Ya think?

Brittany Clement
Deep Diver What do you know about her?

Deep Diver
Brittany Clement See new post

There's a new post from Deep Diver, and Lizzie quickly looks at it. A photograph of a familiar woman with auburn hair, with the following text.

Here's a pic. She's a looker. Only child, wealthy parents. Neither she nor her husband, Derek, are on social media,

> which makes them weird in my book. And harder to find
> out about. But he has his own cybersecurity firm and she
> works at the University at Albany. I've attached a photo
> of a short news article about the accident.

Lizzie reads all this breathlessly. Reads the posted newspaper article too. This makes Derek look very much like a killer. No wonder his
wife is worried.

She remembers Alice, sitting with her on the bench. *I'm Team
Sam.* Alice knows that Lizzie is on here, or she never would have said
that to her. So which one is she? Does she know that Lizzie is Emma
Porter? And if so, how? Has she seen through her "friend in the police" story?

Alice might suspect, but she can't be sure. Lizzie's not going to stop
because of Alice Gardner.

She sits at her computer, her fingers hovering over the keyboard, de-
ciding how to respond in a comment to Deep Diver's post.

> **Emma Porter**
> You're right. I already knew about the hit-and-run
> because of my contact in the police. But they've
> been keeping it quiet.

> **Deep Diver**
> Emma Porter Maybe it's time to apply pressure
> to the police so they take this seriously. I'll send
> this info to the news media in Albany, and they
> can dig deeper. Let's see what happens! I love to
> help catch killers. That's what we're all about,
> right?

> **Emma Porter**
> Deep Diver And maybe they could reopen
> the case?

> **Deep Diver**
> **Emma Porter** It's still open. But it's in another jurisdiction. I'll see what more I can find out.

Lizzie feels frustrated that she's been upstaged by Deep Diver. She doesn't like it. She doesn't feel that high she felt yesterday, when she had so much to report, when everyone was hanging on her every word. She misses it. But she has something she *can* say.

> I was at the condo today, hanging around, trying to eavesdrop on the journalists outside the building. And guess what I saw? Bryden's sister, Lizzie, and Bryden's little girl—I forget her name—they came out of the building and went across the street to the park. I saw a woman go up and sit beside her on a park bench and talk to her. And now, looking at this picture from Deep Diver, I realize who it was. It was Alice Gardner. Why would Alice Gardner be talking to Bryden's sister?

DONNA WAITS for her daughter to come out of her room. She waits for hours. What is she doing in there? She wants to ask her about Clara. Finally, she approaches her bedroom door, taps on it, and calls out, "Lizzie? Are you busy? Can you come out for a minute?"

Lizzie ignores her.

She tries again. "Lizzie?" Maybe she has her headphones on, listening to music, Donna thinks. She can't wait any longer. She tries to open the door. But it's stuck. She rattles it in the frame. It won't budge. "Lizzie? Are you all right?"

She knows there's no lock on this door, but something is preventing it from opening. She is seized with alarm. Has Lizzie done something to herself? An overdose? She yells for Jim.

Jim comes quickly, grasps the situation, and begins to pound on the door, yelling, "Lizzie! Lizzie, open the door!"

Abruptly, the door opens six inches and Lizzie's face appears, pale from within the darkened room. Donna sees a chair behind her daughter as if she has just pulled it away from the door. Donna knows that chair is usually on the other side of the room. Her heart is pounding in distress. "What's going on? Are you all right?" Donna demands breathlessly.

"I'm fine," Lizzie replies, annoyed. "What do you want?"

"We want to talk to you. Why didn't you answer the door? What's wrong?"

"Nothing's wrong. I had my headphones on. I just needed some privacy."

"You've been in there—with the chair propped up against the door—for hours. What are you doing?"

"Nothing." Now she's being sullen, as if she's a teenager again, not a thirty-two-year-old adult. "I just want to be alone." And she closes the door in their faces. They can hear her shoving the chair up under the doorknob again.

Donna turns to her husband, who looks as alarmed as she is. "What's wrong with her?" Donna asks. She whispers, "Do you think she's taking drugs?"

They reluctantly move away from the bedroom door and make their way to the kitchen. Jim answers, "I don't know. Do you?"

"I don't know," Donna says. "I noticed yesterday that her eyes seemed glazed. She seems excitable, moody, different. She's a nurse, she has access to drugs."

"You don't have to be a nurse to get drugs," Jim says worriedly. "They're everywhere."

"Maybe she needs help. She's not handling Bryden's death well. None of us are."

"Is there a way to handle it well?" he asks brokenly. "How does anyone handle something like this?"

46

Jayne is in the incident room late in the afternoon when a call comes in—an officer, acting on a tip, thinks he's found Bryden's missing clothes. Jayne and Kilgour quickly climb into a car.

They arrive at a low-rise apartment building on Larch Street and drive around back, as instructed. Jayne sees two uniformed officers standing over a pile of trash that is spilling out of a small dumpster. They're both wearing gloves as if they've been picking through it. Kilgour parks the car and one of the officers approaches them as they get out.

"Might be what we're looking for," he says, and signals them to follow him.

Jayne looks down at a clear plastic bag containing what looks like a gray sweatshirt and a pair of black yoga pants, and her heart quickens. "How did you find them?"

"The janitor here called it in."

"Great. Give him my thanks, will you? I'll get the forensics team over here. They could be hers. With any luck, that's the plastic bag used to kill her."

ANGELA BRINGS CLARA BACK HOME and Paige stays with Sam and Clara in the condo until early evening. They order in a pizza—the delivery man trying to get a glimpse inside the infamous apartment, but Sam doesn't let him.

After they've eaten, Paige knows she ought to leave. She feels at home here, and her apartment is lonely, but she must go. As long as Sam is under suspicion, better that they keep some distance.

Paige is about to get up to leave when Sam gets a call on his cell. He immediately seems apprehensive. He ends the short call and tells her that they want him back at the station.

"Why?" she asks anxiously.

"I don't know."

She offers to stay with Clara while he's gone. And then she waits.

"WE HAVE SOME NEWS," Jayne says, looking at Sam. They are back in the interview room, and Sam's attorney, Laura Szabo, is present with her and Kilgour. She's brought Sam back in because she is eager to know if Sam can ID the clothes as Bryden's. And because she wants to see his reaction to the fact that they've found them. "We think we've found Bryden's missing clothing. The clothing that she was wearing the day she was murdered," Jayne says, watching him closely.

"Where?" Sam manages to say.

She ignores his question. She opens a file on the table in front of her and pulls out a couple of large photographs. She shows them to Sam. "Do these look like what Bryden was wearing that day?"

She watches Sam's face as he looks at the photographs. One shows some black and gray clothing crumpled up inside a clear plastic bag. The other shows the clothes laid out on a table. His face blanches. "They look like hers, but I can't be sure."

Jayne nods. "Forensics will confirm whether they belonged to her or not, but it will take time." She leaves the photos on the table; they seem to stare up at them accusingly, reminding them of what happened to Bryden.

Kilgour says, "Whoever murdered Bryden discarded her clothes where he thought they wouldn't be found. He might have been worried about transfer evidence, that fibers or hairs from him got onto her clothes when he held the bag over her head, so he had to get rid of them."

Sam stares back at them, clearly frightened. He's suddenly pale, as if all the blood has left his face. He starts to speak. "But—I hugged her that morning—me and Clara and Bryden did a group hug, like every morning. So there might be traces of me on her clothes."

"You never mentioned that," Jayne says.

"I forgot. I should have."

Jayne lets a long silence develop. Then she says, "We're hoping that the plastic bag in the photograph is the murder weapon. Maybe it will tell us something."

She ends the interview, turning off the recording. "You can go, for now."

SATURDAY EVENING, Derek takes Alice out to dinner at an expensive restaurant—Boccaccio's, one of her favorites. He can't shake the feeling that she's up to something, and it's making him nervous. She should just leave well enough alone. They'll be fine, as long as they sit tight, together. There have been some curious stares at the restaurant when he's been recognized—his face has been on the news as a "person of interest"—but no one has harassed them, at least.

"You look lovely tonight," he tells her.

"I know."

"I can't wait to take you home," he murmurs.

"But we haven't even had dessert yet."

He hands her the dessert menu, watches her as she studies it. She killed her mother. You would never know it to look at her. It had never bothered him before. It had made them rich. But it bothers him now. Because he knows what she's capable of, but he doesn't know what she's thinking. He's slightly afraid that he can't trust her.

"I think I'll have the profiteroles," she says, putting the menu down.

"Same."

"You'll never guess where I went this morning," she says.

He looks at her, curious, and a little worried. "I've no idea."

"I went to the condo where Bryden Frost was murdered." She leans in closer. "You remember, that woman you were fucking?"

He feels a flush of anger. He's not going to deny it again, it will just make her angrier. He tries to remain calm, but sometimes that's difficult with Alice. "Why would you go there?"

"Curiosity, I guess. I just couldn't stay away."

He waits for her to say more.

"I saw her sister come out of the building. The journalists told me who she was, but they mostly left her alone. She was with the little girl. Bryden Frost's daughter."

What is she getting at? Is she just toying with him, trying to punish him for what she thinks he's done?

"So I spoke to her."

He leans in closer to her across the table. "Why the fuck would you do that, Alice?"

"Why do I do anything? I wanted to."

He swallows. "What did you say?"

"I told her that Sam Frost killed his wife, and he wasn't going to get away with it. And she told me that she was equally sure you did it."

"Alice, I think you should stay out of this."

"It's a little late for that, don't you think?"

47

Lizzie spends most of the night on the computer in her bedroom. She's gone down the rabbit hole, and she doesn't want to come out. The real world has her parents in it, outside her bedroom door, drowning in their grief. She doesn't like them being here, watching her, worrying about her. They have always been overprotective, a little judgmental. They have always wanted more from her than she could deliver. They have always been disappointed in her.

Supper earlier that night had exploded. She'd finally come out of her room to join them for a meal her mother had prepared. They'd barely sat down when her mother started quizzing her. "Lizzie, you haven't told us what happened at Sam's this morning. How was Clara?"

Lizzie felt slightly guilty at that. She should have told them. "Clara's doing okay." She paused. "But Sam knows you suspect him. And he doesn't want you to see her."

"He can't stop us seeing our granddaughter!"

"I think he can, Mom." As her mother regarded her in distress, Lizzie said, "But he's okay with me seeing her. He trusts me. He knows I believe he's innocent. So that will have to do, for the time being."

"Maybe we can get a court order—" her mother began.

"Do you really want to do that now?" Lizzie said in exasperation. And that's what started it off.

Her mother asked, "What's wrong with you, Lizzie? Hiding in your room all day, in the dark, with a chair up against the door! What are you doing in there? Why won't you tell us?"

Lizzie snapped. "It's none of your business what I do with my life!"

"Are you doing drugs? Tell us the truth."

Lizzie found that almost laughable. For a moment she even thought, why not let them believe that, if it got them off her back? But then she realized they wouldn't get off her back—they'd get her into rehab. "No, Mom, I am not doing drugs." Then she'd left the dinner table and gone back to her room and shoved the chair up under the knob. She could hear her mother crying until she donned her headphones again.

But soon she was back online with her people.

And now, Deep Diver has a new post.

> I've spoken to a journalist with the Albany *Times Union*. They're going to run a story about the hit-and-run tomorrow morning, in the Sunday paper! Now the media will be all over it, and the police won't be able to keep it quiet. We've got to stay on them, and get this thing solved!

Lizzie is pleased, because she thinks that Derek Gardner should pay for what he did to his mother-in-law. Almost everyone on here does. There's been a storm of hate toward Derek Gardner for his cold-blooded greed. There is no doubt whatsoever in this group about him killing his mother-in-law.

But Lizzie's starting to dislike Deep Diver, getting ahead of her, getting all the attention. She's Bryden's *sister*, after all; she just can't say so. She's more important in all this than Deep Diver is. It's personal for her. She knows things nobody else does.

Lizzie's not getting much sleep, and sometimes she worries that she's losing her grip. But she feels safe enough on here, with her cover story of having a friend in the police. What can Alice Gardner do to her? And she thinks she has cleverly thrown everyone off track with her story about seeing Alice talking to Bryden's sister, Lizzie.

The blank *create post* box stares back at her; the cursor blinks.

Lizzie pauses, leans back in her chair. What can she tell them? She has nothing new to reveal. But—she could *invent* something, and no one would know any different. People make stuff up on the internet all the time. She dives deeper into the rabbit hole.

> The police are closing in on Derek Gardner. They've got CCTV of him and Bryden together at a hotel, which I cannot name. But it was in this city.

Take that, Alice, whoever you are, she thinks. It's not true, but she doesn't care. Then her mind takes off on her, and she's typing recklessly, propelled by a strange compulsion.

> But what if he didn't kill her? What if he was sleeping with her, but someone else killed her? I know a lot of you think he did it, because he murdered his mother-in-law, but hear me out. I still think it could have been someone other than Sam or Derek. It could have been anyone who lives in that condo, or visits it regularly, has a friend or family there. Because all they had to do was knock on her door, force their way in, and hold a plastic bag over her face until she was dead. Easy enough to do, if you're strong enough. If you take her by surprise. If she's not expecting it at all and turns her back on you.

And you have to ask, why move the body at all? Why not just leave her there, dead? Why bother putting her in a suitcase and taking her downstairs and risk being seen? I'll tell you why. Because the killer didn't want the little girl to come home and see her mother dead! It's so obvious. And how would the killer know she'd fit in a suitcase? Maybe they saw that thing on YouTube—*Can Adrienne Fit in a Suitcase?* It's had millions of views. And everybody has a suitcase in their closet these days. My point is, it could have been anyone! We should think outside the box!

Feverishly, she hits post.

The comments come in quickly.

Jen McKague
Googling youtube.com for *Can Adrienne Fit in a Suitcase?* right now 😊

Brittany Clement
Jen McKague OMG that's hilarious!

Karen Hennin
Maybe it was the sister. She might be worth looking into.

Farah Spence
Karen Hennin Sisters can have a real love/hate relationship. I know. I want to kill my sister all the time! 😊

Brittany Clement
Karen Hennin What do we know about her?

Lizzie watches the responses come in. She doesn't like the comments about Bryden's sister. She suddenly feels quite sick.

48

On Sunday morning, Alice looks down at the Albany *Daily Press* in dismay. On the front page toward the bottom is the headline: LOCAL MURDER CASE TAKES INTERESTING TURN.
She stands inside the front door in her bathrobe and reads the article with mounting fury.

There have been new developments in the investigation into the murder of local woman, Bryden Frost. The 35-year-old mother of one was found dead last Wednesday in the basement of the condominium building where she lived with her husband, Sam Frost, at 100 Constitution Drive, in Buckingham Lake. She had been the subject of an intense search after she vanished from her unit on Tuesday. With the help of a cadaver dog, her body was found hidden in a suitcase on the following evening. The police have ruled the death a homicide.

Sam Frost has been questioned and released by police. Another man, Derek Gardner, whom the victim knew, has also been questioned and released.

It has now come to light that Derek Gardner's mother-in-law, Mary Smelt, was killed March 27, 2019, in a hit-and-run outside of Roxbury, New Hampshire. The case remains unsolved. Alice Gardner inherited a substantial sum upon her mother's death. According to New Hampshire police, Alice and Derek Gardner maintain they were at home in Albany, together, at the time of the death.

"What the fuck?" Alice yells from the front hall.

Derek comes quickly. "What is it?"

She shoves the newspaper at him. "I can't fucking believe it!"

Derek takes the paper from her and reads, then looks up at her, his jaw tight. He clearly doesn't like it either. Still, Derek says, "That case is dead in the water. There's no way they can find any evidence now. This is just muckraking by the newspaper. We ought to sue them."

"We should. Those bastards!"

"This will blow over," Derek says. "It won't go anywhere, it can't, and they'll move on to something else."

Alice seethes. She's furious at the newspaper. Furious at Derek because this is all his fault. His calmness only stokes her rage. But he doesn't know what she's afraid of. She knows they can't get her for killing her mother. Not unless Derek turns on her and tells the truth, and he wouldn't do that. But she can't afford to have the police look any more closely into their past. Into *her* past. Because there are things hiding there that even Derek doesn't know about.

She needs to nip this in the bud.

Her cell phone buzzes in the pocket of her bathrobe. She looks at the phone and glances up at Derek. "It's Detective Salter."

JAYNE HAD READ the newspaper article too. "How did they find out?" Jayne mused to Michael at the breakfast table. "We certainly didn't say anything about the hit-and-run."

"Any good reporter could have found out about it. It wouldn't be hard."

"You're right. Anyway, it doesn't matter. If anything, it turns the heat up on them a little." She rose from the table. "I've got to go." She kissed him and drove to the station and called Alice Gardner. She wanted to speak to Alice again and now, after the newspaper article, was probably a good time.

WHEN ALICE ARRIVES, dressed more casually this time in flattering jeans, a pale-pink cashmere sweater, and high-heeled black boots, she seems to be in a mood. There's no smile on her lovely face, and after Alice sits down at the table facing her and Kilgour, she folds her arms across her chest.

"Good morning, Alice," Jayne says.

"For you, maybe," Alice says. "Have you seen today's newspaper?"

"Actually yes, I have. I'm sorry, but I don't control the press."

"Why am I here?" Alice asks.

"I want to know why you approached Sam Frost's sister, Lizzie, outside the condominium yesterday. What were you doing there?"

"I don't know. I was curious, I suppose. I went to the condo, and I saw her come out. I thought she might be fun to talk to."

"And what did you two talk about?"

"I can't remember. Turns out she wasn't that interesting."

Jayne sighs heavily. "She told us you were threatening. That you threatened Sam."

"Threatened him? How?"

"You said you wanted her to deliver a message to Sam. To tell him that he wouldn't get away with it."

"I hardly see that as a threat."

"Lizzie asked me to tell you to stay away from her, so *I'm* delivering *that* message," Jayne says. Alice merely shrugs.

There's something about Alice that makes the small hairs on the back of Jayne's neck stir. Something about her eyes; there's a coldness behind them in brief, unguarded moments. Jayne feels as if this woman is pretending to be someone she's not.

Jayne suddenly decides to go out on a limb; she hadn't planned on it, but something compels her. "We've received some new information," she says. Alice regards her coolly, waiting. "We have a witness who saw someone in the elevator on the day of the murder, at the relevant time, with a large suitcase. And we have a description."

Alice remains silent. Jayne wonders what's going through her mind. She climbs farther out on the limb and adds, "The person with the suitcase was a woman."

Alice smiles broadly at her now. "A woman. I see. And from the way you're looking at me, I'm guessing you think it might have been me?" She tilts her head at her and laughs. "Oh dear, we really are trying to throw all the spaghetti against the wall to see if anything sticks, aren't we?"

Jayne ignores her and leans in closer. "Right now, the only eyewitness we have puts a woman with a large suitcase in the elevator at approximately one thirty on the day of the murder. I'm guessing you weren't too happy about your husband's affair with Bryden Frost. Where were you last Tuesday between noon and five?"

The look that Alice gives her now makes the hairs on the back of Jayne's neck stir again. Jayne thinks she might be looking at a killer.

49

Alice regards Detective Salter with loathing. She hates her. Alice knows that she didn't kill Bryden Frost. She thinks her husband probably did though, so this information, if it's true, is encouraging. But she can't have this bitch thinking she might be a murderer. She needs her to stop looking into her at all, not looking into her with more enthusiasm. Detective Salter is still waiting for an answer.

"Well?" Salter prods.

"I have to think," Alice says, trying to remember where she was on Tuesday. The day doesn't stand out to her in any way. She only remembers hearing the news that a woman was missing and then Derek telling her that a detective had come over to ask him about her—it was the woman who'd hit his Tesla. She'd come home late, because— oh yes, she'd met friends for dinner. Before that, in the afternoon, she'd been shopping. "I was shopping."

"Shopping. Anyone with you?" Salter asks.

"No."

"Where?"

"Oh, I don't remember, exactly, all sorts of places."

"Do you have receipts?"

"I don't know. I'd have to look." She can't remember what she bought that day. She'll have to ask Derek.

"Can you do that please? And bring any receipts, if you have them, here, into the station?"

The detective smiles at her and Alice wants to slap her across the face.

As she rises to go, Salter says, with another smile, "We've found her missing clothes. And possibly the murder weapon. They're with forensics now."

"WHAT WAS THAT ABOUT?" Kilgour asks Jayne, after Alice has gone. "I thought we didn't put a lot of stock in the elevator witness. She certainly didn't say it was a woman."

"I know," Jayne agrees. "But it's possible she did see someone with a suitcase, and it might have been a woman. And if she did in fact see someone with a suitcase, it was probably the killer, because we haven't found anyone who admits to being in the building with a suitcase that day. Anyway, I wanted to rattle Alice." After a moment's pause, she asks, "Did you get a feeling from her?"

"What kind of feeling?"

"There's something about her. Something off."

PAIGE GOES OUT for a run on Sunday morning. She pounds the pavement, avoiding the puddles on the sidewalk, trying to calm herself.

She'd done her best to reassure Sam before she left the condo last night. But she, too, had been distressed when he returned from the police station and told her that they'd found Bryden's clothes. Sam seems convinced the detectives think he did it. They're obviously hoping these clothes of Bryden's will help them put him away.

She slows to a walk, panting heavily. Paige is worried. What if they do find traces of his clothing, or of him, on Bryden's clothes? He said he hugged her before he left for work that morning. She believes him. But what if the police don't? They can't prove he didn't, can they? She remembers Donna in her kitchen, the horror on her face as she accused Sam, and pushes the image away.

She doesn't want to think about that.

DEREK HEARS THE FRONT DOOR open and close and knows that Alice is back. He counts to three and then rises from his office chair to talk to her. They meet in the middle, in the living room. "Well?" he says. She shoots him an evil glance, which makes him worry. "How did it go?"

"She wanted to tell me that Lizzie complained about me 'threatening' them."

"You didn't actually threaten her, did you?" Derek asks with genuine concern. It's the sort of thing that Alice would do.

"Not really. I can't help it if she interpreted it that way."

"You know you can be a little intimidating."

She ignores that. "They've found Bryden's missing clothes." She looks at him pointedly. "Do we have anything to worry about there?"

"Not a thing," he says evenly.

She throws herself down into the deep sofa. "She might just be fucking with me, but Detective Salter told me that they have an eyewitness who saw a woman with a suitcase in the elevator at around the time of the murder."

"A woman," Derek repeats.

"And, no surprise—Detective Salter now thinks *I* killed fucking Bryden. And I'm pretty sure we both know that isn't true."

He stares back at her, holding her eyes with his.

"We have to stop her," Alice says.

He can hear the venom in his wife's voice. That's what she's like, he thinks—a viper, ready to strike. "What do you mean, stop her? Alice, we should just stay out of this," he urges her. "They're not going to be able to prove anything—about Bryden, or about your mother. You have to just leave things alone."

She looks up at him—he's now standing over her. "I can't."

"What do you mean, you can't?" He pauses. His heart sinks. "Oh Christ, Alice, what have you done?"

50

Donna hasn't slept for worry and distress. She's lost one daughter to murder, and now she's afraid she's losing another—to what she doesn't exactly know. She makes herself a piece of toast and leaves it untouched on her plate. Jim sits nearby but is too overwhelmed himself to say much.

She waits for her daughter to emerge from her bedroom. But there's no sound from within, even though Donna creeps quietly up to the door at regular intervals and listens. She doesn't dare try to open it again after the disaster of last night. But she wants to see her daughter, she wants to know that she's okay.

Finally, she says to her husband, "I'm getting dressed. I'm going to go down to the police station and see if they can direct us to some kind of Victims' Services or something. Lizzie"—she chokes on the words—"Lizzie needs help. We all do."

Jim nods. "Good idea."

"You stay here in case she comes out. Text me if she does, let me know how she is."

She gets an Uber to the station. It's not that far. She sits silently in the back seat, thinking about how she just wants to bury her daughter and go home. But she can't do that now, because she's afraid to leave Lizzie. She's not right. And there's poor Clara too.

When she gets to the police station, she'd only meant to ask at the front desk if there were any pamphlets about organizations that help those bereaved by crime, but decides to ask if Detective Salter is in. She needs to see a sympathetic face.

Detective Salter comes out to the waiting area. "Hi, Donna, what is it?"

Donna feels the tears start to roll down her cheeks, and she finds it difficult to speak.

"Come with me," Detective Salter says, and leads her into an empty room. She sits her down and brings her a cup of water.

"Do you want to talk?" the detective asks her again, gently.

Donna answers, "It's Lizzie. I don't know what to do."

"What do you mean?"

"I'm so worried about her. At first, Lizzie was coping better than the rest of us. She's a nurse and used to handling crises. But lately—she's been hiding away in her bedroom and won't come out. She puts a chair up against her door so we can't come in. She barely speaks to us. She's not eating much, and I don't think she's sleeping much either."

The detective looks back at her kindly. "I'm so sorry, Donna. Grief can hit people in different ways. She might have coped well in the beginning but perhaps now it's hitting her hard."

Donna bursts into tears. "I thought maybe she was taking drugs, but she denied it." She takes a tissue from the box that the detective slides toward her across the table. "I think she's on her computer. What else could she be doing in there? I think she's hiding from the world, that it's become too much for her." She doesn't mention her great-aunt, who ended up in a mental institution, but it's a private worry that's eating away at her. She hasn't even brought that up with her husband. "I was hoping I could get some help for her—"

"Of course," the detective says. "I can connect you with someone. There are some very good programs."

"Thank you," Donna says gratefully. She's afraid her daughter will refuse to speak to anyone. But she must try. She wipes her eyes with the tissue. "Has there been any progress in the investigation?"

"I'm sorry, I can't tell you much, other than that we *are* making progress."

She looks across at the detective, beseeching. "Do you think Sam did it?"

"I really can't say at this time."

Donna nods. "Promise me you'll solve this. We have to know the truth. Because of Clara. You understand?"

"I promise you we will do our best."

JAYNE FINDS KILGOUR in the lunchroom, getting a coffee. She grabs one too and stands beside him at the coffee station. "I just spoke to Donna Houser. She's worried about Lizzie."

"How so?" Kilgour asks, taking a careful sip of the hot coffee.

"She says she's acting strangely. Hiding in her room, propping a chair up against her door. What do you make of that?"

"It sounds paranoid," Kilgour suggests.

"That's what I thought." Jayne says thoughtfully, "Although, you know, I think Lizzie is a bit odd."

"Yup," Kilgour agrees.

"She took such an avid interest in her sister's disappearance. As if it were *exciting* for her, somehow. That keenness—it's strange."

Kilgour nods in agreement. "She wanted the dogs, and then she wanted credit for it."

Jayne says, "She wanted to accompany us on the search, remember? And her interest in true crime—she was talking to us about the Elisa Lam case like she was an expert."

"What are you thinking?"

"I'd like to know what she's up to, hiding in her bedroom, not wanting anyone to come in." She adds, "Donna mentioned her computer. I'm going to have the IT team look into any online activity about the Bryden Frost case. Usually it's a bunch of crackpots in these groups, but it's worth a look. Maybe Lizzie's on there, and it's messing with her head."

51

Alice takes her laptop from the bedroom and returns to the living room to sit in the comfy couch by the window. Derek had stormed out after their last, heated conversation, so she has the house to herself. He knows now that she's hiding something, something she's afraid that Detective Salter might discover. He badgered her to tell him what it is. But she wouldn't. She wants him to still be in love with her, and she's not entirely sure he would be if he knew.

Before he'd left, he'd looked through his desk for any receipts she might have had from Tuesday. He found a couple, one at a downtown shop at 3:03 p.m., and another for 4:11. Then there was her receipt for dinner with girlfriends at 8:37 p.m. None of them get her off the hook with Salter. She wishes she'd bought something at one fucking forty-five.

She logs on to Facebook. She clicks into the Facebook group True

Crimes in Albany NY and reviews the most recent activity on the
Bryden Frost case. She reads with interest the latest posts from Emma
Porter, who seems to know an awful lot about it. She's been wondering who Emma Porter is, wondering who is probably hiding behind
the name and claiming to have a friend in the police. She thinks it's
quite possible that it's Bryden's sister, Lizzie Houser. Who but a family member would know everything she seems to know? And she posted
that photo that no one else had seen. She remembers Lizzie's reaction
when she'd whispered, *I'm Team Sam*, to her. So she knows Lizzie is
on here somewhere, and she's not using her own name. But she might
not be Emma Porter. Emma Porter might really be someone with a
friend in the police. There's no information on her profile. There are
probably several people on here hiding their real identity behind a
fake name and a blank profile. She's on here herself, using the name
Karen Hennin. But she at least went to the effort of making up a fake
profile—using a photo of Superwoman as an avatar and adding the
description *Loves dogs, cupcakes, and political biographies.*

Alice hasn't told Derek about this Facebook group. She doesn't
want him to see the hysteria piling on about him on this page. The
legitimate media is bad enough. Team Derek has pulled well ahead
in the last couple of days, which pisses her off. Just for fun she clicks
on the YouTube video *Can Adrienne Fit in a Suitcase?*

Then she decides to challenge Emma Porter about her claim that
the police have CCTV of her husband with Bryden Frost at a local
hotel. She posts a comment under Emma's post.

> **Karen Hennin**
> Why do you say they have CCTV of Derek Gardner
> with Bryden Frost at a hotel? I'm pretty sure they
> don't. I have a friend who's a pretty plugged-in
> journalist, and he says they don't.

But Emma Porter doesn't answer. Alice agrees with Emma Porter in that they should be widening the suspect pool. Alice just doesn't want to be *in* the suspect pool. She keeps reading.

People in the group have gone on a spree, naming anyone and everyone who might have done it. Alice herself, as Karen Hennin, had suggested that Bryden's sister, Lizzie, might have done it. But Derek's wife is also suggested as a possibility. Her photo is on here now too. Obviously grabbed from the website of the university where she works. Alice reads about herself, growing more and more incensed.

> **Brittany Clement**
> Maybe Alice Gardner was jealous. Maybe she knew. Women often do know when their husbands are cheating.

> **Farah Spence**
> Brittany Clement Yeah, but not many of them murder the other woman.

> **Brittany Clement**
> Farah Spence Maybe it happens more than we realize LOL

> **Maya Vukovic**
> Maybe she was in on the murder of her mother too. Maybe they killed her together.

"For fuck's sake!" Alice blurts out loud to the empty house.

But no one seems to have heard about the eyewitness who saw a woman in the elevator, not even Emma Porter, who allegedly has the friend in the police department. So maybe it isn't true. Maybe Detective fucking Salter made it up to mess with her. She decides to throw these morons a bone. Maybe Emma Porter will confirm whether it's true or not.

Apparently there is an eyewitness. Someone who saw a person in the elevator with a suitcase at the exact time the murderer is supposed to have been there. And they have a description. But they're not sharing that just yet.

Brittany Clement
Exciting! How do you know? From your journalist friend?

Alice doesn't answer. That's all she's going to say. Let them chew on that for a while.

She is angry at Deep Diver about that newspaper article. She'd like to get back at him somehow, but she doesn't know how. His avatar is a cartoon of a scuba diver, with nothing behind that profile either. Alice knows who wrote the newspaper article though. The name is right there, on the byline. She files it away in her mind.

But right now, the person she most wants to stop, to *harm*, is Detective Salter. Alice ponders whether, if the detective were to meet with an accident, that would stop them digging into Alice. Probably not. But there can be no actual evidence that she killed Bryden. And there's no evidence that she killed her mother either.

Still, Salter's interest in her feels personal. And dangerous.

BECAUSE IT'S SUNDAY, and Jayne is in the thick of a homicide case, Michael drops by the station at lunchtime to take her out for a quick bite. Jayne is grateful because she feels like she needs a breather. It's been almost nonstop since Bryden went missing last Tuesday.

They settle themselves in a booth by the window in a diner not far from the station. They order grilled cheese sandwiches and coffee.

"You look tired," Michael observes.

"Thanks," Jayne says, smiling wryly. "If I look more tired than I did when you saw me at breakfast, it's because I feel like I just went ten rounds with a psychopath." She takes an appreciative sip of her coffee and asks, "You can't tell someone's a psychopath by just talking to them, right?"

"That's the conventional wisdom, yes."

Jayne shakes her head and lowers her voice. "I tell you, this woman, Alice, Derek Gardner's wife, she gives me the creeps. Today, just for a second, I felt like she dropped the façade, and I could see what was behind her eyes, and it was—" She pauses, thinking about how best to describe it.

"What?" Michael asks.

"Like there was nothing there. Just a darkness, an emptiness." He's looking at her curiously. "You think I'm imagining things, don't you?"

"No. But—there's such a thing as instinct."

"What do you mean?" Jayne asks.

"Some birds have the instinct to fly south in winter when it gets cold. The purpose is survival. Humans also have instincts for survival."

"So what are you saying? That on some instinctual level I may be able to tell that she's a psychopath?"

"Let's leave the psychopath label aside for a minute. It's not that helpful. But the ability to sense danger, so that we get physical symptoms— the racing heart, the feeling of the hair rising on your arms or the back of your neck—all that's coming from your prehistoric brain, which is still there at the base of your skull. We all want to survive."

Jayne registers what he's saying. "So you think that my instincts are telling me that she's dangerous?"

He nods. "I think it's more likely to be your instincts than your imagination. And I think your instincts are good, Jayne. You should trust them."

52

Derek has gone to the office downtown. It's Sunday, and nobody will be there. He can get some space from Alice and everybody else and try to think. He unlocks the sleek glass door at the end of the corridor and locks it again behind him. This is all his, he thinks, surveying the carpeted offices. The cool reception area, the stylish offices, the boardroom at the end with the large walnut table and the impressive view. All first class. All costly. He knows he owes Alice a lot. But right now, he has to fight the urge to strangle her.

No one knows his wife better than he does. No one understands her like he does, so if she's afraid of what this detective might find if she keeps digging, then it must be pretty bad. Life-in-prison bad. But Alice won't tell him what she's hiding. And that pisses him off, because he doesn't like not knowing what's going on. Alice can be dangerous. He suspects she's not telling him because she still thinks he's holding out on her about Bryden.

He's got impressive computer skills—he's in cybersecurity, after all. He can do a deep dive into his wife and see what he can find out. He's never done that before; he never had the need. Or maybe he just never had the nerve.

But he has been holding out on her too. There's his other, illegitimate business that he hasn't yet told Alice about. He's been meaning to. Maybe now is the time. If he tells her what he's been up to, maybe she'll tell him what she's been up to. A quid pro quo.

He has a small handful of powerful and wealthy clients off book. They pay him handsomely for his specialty—data manipulation. He sneaks into a target company and alters its database by adding a couple of fictitious accounts so that his clients can gain access and spy on sensitive business information without the target being any the wiser. It's a rather brilliant sideline, and he doesn't want Detective Salter looking into him. He needs her to back off. He doesn't want to appear like he's anything other than a completely respectable businessman. He thinks about his growing offshore accounts.

But if it goes south, he'd be in a lot of trouble. From the law, obviously, and possibly also from his rich, powerful, and ruthless clients. To be safe, he has a go bag all packed, ready to start a new life if necessary. A new name, a new passport, new everything. Just like in the movies. Maybe it's time for Alice to have a go bag too. That's the great thing about cybercrime, Derek thinks to himself—you can live and work from anywhere.

He sits down at his desk and logs on to his computer.

SAM HAD READ THE ARTICLE titled LOCAL MURDER CASE TAKES INTERESTING TURN on the front page of this morning's Sunday paper with a certain amount of satisfaction. It was nice to see that his rival and fellow suspect, Derek Gardner, has skeletons in his closet. Maybe he did murder his mother-in-law. Sam hopes so—he's glad to have the media focusing on someone else for a change.

He paces the living room. He's hardly left the apartment since all this began, except for his harrowing visits to the police station. He will have to take Clara to day care tomorrow though, if Lizzie or Paige doesn't offer; he doesn't relish the idea. The stares, the questions.

Paige had texted him this morning and offered to pick up some groceries for him and Clara. He's grateful; he can't imagine taking Clara out grocery shopping right now, being chased by a pack of media.

He thinks about last night, the detectives telling him about finding the clothes. How he'd scrambled to tell them that he'd hugged Bryden that morning. Why hadn't he mentioned that before? It looked like something he'd suddenly added when they found the clothes. He knows they think he killed her. But if those are Bryden's clothes—and they certainly looked like them—then he has a perfectly good explanation as to why transfer evidence from him might be on them.

He'd spoken to his attorney about it afterward outside the station in the parking lot. She hadn't seemed too worried. She said it was something that they could handle if it ever came to that. She reminded Sam that he wasn't under arrest.

But Sam can't help worrying that that might change at any moment.

ALICE DONS HER DISGUISE.

She puts on an oversize, shapeless, dark-blue jumpsuit, something Derek wears when he's working on things around the house. She rolls up the sleeves and tucks the hems of the pants into her work boots, knowing that if she is seen going into Detective Salter's apartment building, she won't be recognized. She hides her long hair up under a baseball cap. If there are cameras in Salter's building, she will spot them and govern herself accordingly.

It was easy enough to find out where Salter lived; you don't live with a cybersecurity expert without learning some tricks. It's Sunday and Alice already knows that the detective isn't home. To be sure, she'd driven by the police station half an hour ago to make sure Salter's car was in the parking lot. It was.

Derek doesn't know what she's doing. He'd gone off in a temper after their argument, probably to work at the office, as if he'd wanted time away from her. Alice gets into her car in the garage and drives to Salter's address, a historic apartment building on Willet Avenue. Six stories with an awning out front. Vintage black-and-white-checkered marble floors in the entryway. Nice enough. She'd already checked it out online. She knows Salter is single, and that she has a boyfriend, Dr. Michael Fraser. She's done her research. Like Alice, he has a job at the University at Albany, but he's a lecturer in the Psych Department. There's a chance he's in the apartment. She'll have to be careful.

First, she buzzes the apartment and doesn't get an answer. She has to assume the boyfriend isn't there. Getting into the building doesn't take long. Someone comes out via the lobby and actually holds the door for her. Once she's in, she takes the elevator to the fifth floor. Alice reaches Salter's unit, checks for cameras but doesn't spot any, and places her ear against the door to listen. Can't be too careful. She doesn't hear any sounds from within. The corridor is still empty. She pulls the nitrile gloves out of her pocket, puts them on. She makes short work of the lock. She's inside within a little more than a minute.

With the door closed, she stands perfectly still, getting her bearings. All is quiet. To the left is a small kitchen, and in front of her is the living room. It's spacious and nicely decorated, with a charming Art Deco fireplace. She may be a bitch, but at least she's got style. Her estimation of Salter goes up a notch.

She walks quietly down the hall. The bedroom door is open. She pushes it wider with a gloved finger. The room is empty, the bed made.

She checks the next room—it's small, used as an office—and the bathroom. Having done the once-over, she can now get to work. She's going to find out everything she can about Detective Salter.

She starts with the medicine cabinet. She finds a vial made out to Jayne Salter for escitalopram 20 mg. Interesting. The detective takes antidepressants, who knew? She finds birth control pills. Good-quality skin care products. She opens them, sniffs, puts them back.

She moves on to the bedroom. Opens the top drawer of the dresser and flicks through the detective's underwear drawer. Pretty standard stuff, nothing too sexy. Oh, wait—she pulls out a couple of pairs of daringly cut lace panties, one hot pink, one black. Probably a gift from the boyfriend, she thinks. She'll remember this if she's ever interviewed by Detective Salter again. *I've seen your underwear.*

She looks under the bed, and then under the mattress, but there's nothing there. On the nightstand she finds a couple of novels—*Wolf Hall* by Hilary Mantel, on top of *A Gentleman in Moscow* by Amor Towles. She puts them back down, side by side. She can't resist messing with the detective a little.

She checks all the clothes hanging in the closet, rifles through the pockets. Looks through the shoeboxes on the shelf above. She's not looking for anything in particular. She just wants to get to know her enemy better.

53

izzie lies in bed on her side. She stares at her computer across the room on her desk, without lifting her head from the pillow. She feels its pull.

It's quiet beyond her bedroom door. She heard her mother leave a while ago. She doesn't know where she went. She doesn't care. But she thinks her father is still here.

She gets up and makes her way out to the kitchen. Her father is sitting at the table reading the newspaper, which he sets aside. He smiles tentatively at her, but doesn't give her the third degree, the way her mother would.

"Hi, sweetheart," he says simply. No accusations. No frantic questions. It's a relief. She pours herself a coffee and sits down with him at the table. It's well past lunchtime.

"You want anything to eat?" he asks.

"No." She has no appetite. "Where's Mom?"

"She went out for a walk." He says, getting up, "Let me make you some toast."

She doesn't stop him. It's nice to be taken care of. He puts a plate of buttered toast in front of her and settles down across from her, picking up the newspaper again. She takes a bite of toast and realizes how hungry she is. They sit in silence while she polishes off the toast and finishes her coffee. "Thanks, I needed that," she says. He looks up and smiles at her. She can tell that he's worried about her, but he's not invasive, like her mother.

Lizzie goes back into her bedroom and turns on the computer. She can't stay away. Her obsession, her addiction pulls at her. She wants to be noticed, listened to, befriended. She wants to belong, to be part of something important, exciting. That's why she did this in the first place. She logs on and clicks into the Facebook group page.

There have been a lot of posts since she shut down her computer late last night. She smiles at the posts about Derek Gardner's wife—people are piling on about her, speculating that she might have killed Bryden, even saying that maybe she's the one who murdered her mother. Lizzie remembers the woman who sat beside her on the park bench, who told her to tell Sam that he wouldn't get away with it. So sure of herself. She's not going to like *this*, Lizzie thinks. She wonders which user name Alice is hiding behind on here, because there's no one posting as Alice Gardner.

Lizzie's about to write something when she sees a post by Karen Hennin that almost makes her heart stop.

Apparently there is an eyewitness. Someone who saw a person in the elevator with a suitcase at the exact time the murderer is supposed to have been there. And they have a description. But they're not sharing that just yet.

Lizzie stares at the post. The detectives haven't said anything about an eyewitness. A wave of anxiety knocks her back in her chair.

DONNA RETURNS HOME, walking the half hour from the station after her talk with Detective Salter. She arrives to find her daughter in the living room with her father, watching TV. Lizzie doesn't flee to her bedroom at the sight of her mother. Donna feels a slight glimmer of hope that she'll be able to get Lizzie to talk to a counselor after all. She has the information in her handbag. She smiles at her daughter. She must take a gentle approach. She must make amends for her frantic behavior last night, which was driven by fear. She's still terrified, but she can't let her fear for her daughter show.

"Where have you been, Mom?" Lizzie asks.

Donna tells the truth. "I was at the police station, talking to Detective Salter."

"Why?" Lizzie asks.

"I wanted to get some information on grief counseling."

"Oh," Lizzie says. She asks abruptly, "Did Detective Salter say anything about an eyewitness?"

"An eyewitness? No. Why?"

"I heard there was an eyewitness. Someone who saw the killer come down the elevator with the suitcase."

Donna, taken aback, stares at her daughter. She's puzzled. How is her daughter coming up with this stuff? "Where did you hear that? Detective Salter never said anything about an eyewitness. She didn't tell me anything." But Lizzie doesn't answer, hugging her knees up against her chest on the sofa. "Lizzie! Where did you hear that?" Is her daughter imagining things? Is she losing her mind? But Lizzie doesn't answer. She just looks anxious.

And then Donna suddenly understands. Despite her protests, Lizzie must be worried about Sam. She must be afraid that he might have killed Bryden, and she doesn't want to face it. That's why Lizzie's hiding in her bedroom. That's why she's having a breakdown. Poor Lizzie—her sister has been murdered, and her brother-in-law, whom she thinks the world of, probably did it. Donna just hadn't realized her younger daughter was quite so . . . fragile.

Donna takes a deep breath. "Lizzie," she says calmly, "I asked Detective Salter if there was anyone you could talk to about this. Like a counselor. And she gave me the name of somebody who is apparently very good."

"I don't want to speak to anyone," Lizzie says quickly.

This is exactly what Donna was afraid of. "Why not?" Donna asks, stifling her panic, trying to speak gently. "What's the harm?"

But Lizzie doesn't answer. She just sits with her knees drawn up to her chin and stares at the television.

54

Paige is on edge, in the living room of the condo on Sunday afternoon with Sam and Clara. She can tell that Sam is frustrated with his daughter. Sam had tried to get Angela to watch her, but she'd gone out. Clara is being demanding, refusing to watch TV, or play on the iPad, or play with her toys, or do anything on her own at all. She's tearful and cranky, and Sam is losing his patience. He looks like he wants to yell at Clara and put her in her room for a timeout.

Paige steps in and tries to soothe her. "Come here, sweetie, let me do your hair. You love it when I do your hair."

"No! I want my mommy."

Paige feels sudden tears prick behind her eyelids. "I know, honey."

"I hate you!" Clara suddenly screams. And it's not clear who she means—she's looking at both of them.

"Clara, go to your room," Sam says in a stern voice.

"No!" She says it with all the defiance of a typical three-year-old.

But Clara has never been typical—she's always been quiet, sensitive, and well behaved. Paige wonders if that will all change now, because of what's happened. Maybe she'll become a troubled little girl. Difficult. Paige hadn't really considered that before. She glances at Sam uneasily.

"Clara," Sam says, with a warning in his voice, "go to your room, right now."

"I hate you!" she screams again.

Sam rises from the sofa so quickly it takes Paige by surprise. Paige sees the sudden fear in the little girl's eyes. In two strides, he's grabbed Clara around the waist and is carrying her, kicking and screaming, toward her bedroom.

Paige has never seen Sam behave this way either. The whole scene is troubling her. Sam had been cold to her today from the moment she arrived. She thinks about slipping out. But then she remembers she promised to pick up some groceries for them. While she's thinking this, she hears Sam slam the bedroom door, and he reappears in the living room, looking angry and exhausted.

He brushes a hand across his face. "She's not handling this well."

"She's only three," Paige says, smiling tentatively. "She's lost her mother."

"It's just so fucking difficult . . ." He trails off. He doesn't need to explain.

"You know I'm here to help—you don't have to do this all on your own."

"I know. And I'm grateful."

They can both hear Clara crying her heart out in her bedroom. It's setting their nerves on edge.

"Maybe you could take her with you when you go out for groceries," Sam suggests. "I could use the break. And Clara used to love grocery shopping with Bryden."

Paige's immediate reaction is annoyance. What is she, a babysitting service? *He could use the break.* She remembers how Bryden used to complain sometimes about how she did the bulk of the household chores and the bulk of the childcare too. Paige had told Bryden she was being taken for granted. Secretly, Paige had thought it was because Bryden put up with it.

She hesitates. She doesn't want to be taken for granted. But he looks like he's at the end of his rope, and these are extenuating circumstances. "All right," she agrees.

A short time later, after Clara has calmed down and Paige has prepared a shopping list, she bundles the little girl up and takes her out to get groceries. In the car, on the way to the store, Clara is quiet, and Paige is able to think.

If she's honest with herself, she's had feelings for Sam for a long time. And now, when she thinks about the possibility of a future with Sam, she feels warm inside. Some good could come out of the tragedy of Bryden's death. She hopes that after a suitable interval, they can stop pretending. She hopes that she can eventually become Sam's wife, and mother to Clara. She tells herself that Bryden would have liked that.

She thinks he cares for her, even though he sometimes seems distant. Bryden hasn't even been dead a week. He can't accept that he has feelings for her now, so soon. She thinks about yesterday, when he pulled her into his bedroom to make love, almost the moment he saw her. He couldn't help himself, and neither could she. She thinks he could fall in love with her. And that's how it should be. Because she's already fallen in love with him.

She hadn't meant to. She held back for the longest time, because Bryden was her best friend. And then that first time—it was like magic. It was like nothing she'd ever felt before. When she was in his arms, she felt both safe and wildly excited at the same time. She was hooked. She felt guilty as hell in the beginning, but she got used to it. The guilt faded after a while.

And Clara. Her sweet goddaughter. How terrible for her to lose her mother, and in such a terrible way. But she's so young, she probably won't even remember. Some good must come of all this tragedy, Paige tells herself. She can love Clara almost as much as her real mother. And maybe Clara will have a sibling someday after all. There's all that baby stuff that Bryden had packed away, while they waited for another baby to come along.

Bryden had confided in Paige about her frustration at how long it was taking for her to conceive a second child. Clara had happened so quickly. But they'd been trying for a year, and nothing. She'd had all the baby clothes and equipment stored in the den. And Bryden told her how she'd go in and look at it, every day, handling the onesies, the cute little outfits that Clara had outgrown. Finally, she decided to move it all to the storage locker in the basement so she wouldn't have to look at it. She decided that they'd been putting too much pressure on themselves to conceive. She said she had to stop making it a priority, realize it was going to take time. Paige had helped her move everything down to the basement a few weeks ago. She thinks of that storage locker now and shudders.

She's running this errand for Sam, but it's just this once. She tells herself that as their relationship matures, she will make sure he doesn't treat her the way he treated Bryden. She will not be taken for granted. She expects better than that. She's stronger than Bryden was.

55

efreshed after her lunch with Michael, Jayne approaches members of the IT team. "Have you guys looked into any online groups about the Bryden Frost case?"

"Yes. There's the usual talk among the online sleuths. There's a Facebook group we keep an eye on. There's been a lot of posts on there about the Frost case, nothing useful. We don't know who some of these people are. Occasionally they hide behind fake profiles."

"Can you set me up so I can look through it myself?"

"Sure."

Within a few minutes, an officer has Jayne on the Facebook group True Crimes in Albany NY, and she's able to peruse all the posts about the case. She settles down to read. She starts at the beginning and reads it all.

It's unpleasant, at times, wading through so much vitriol. People show the worst of themselves online, where they can be anonymous if

they choose. Jayne thinks the internet has a lot to answer for. She remembers what Michael said, and imagines everyone in this online
group throwing off their clothes, showing who they really are underneath. Animals.

She sits up straight when she sees the post from Karen Hennin
about the eyewitness. It was posted this morning, not long after Jayne
had spoken to Alice about the eyewitness. *Is Karen Hennin Alice Gardner?* Jayne realizes that anyone can make up a fake profile if they
choose. She looks at Karen Hennin's profile: a photo of Superwoman
and the description *Loves dogs, cupcakes, and political biographies.* Then
Jayne goes back and reads every post she's made.

It makes sense, she tells herself, that Alice would be on here, even
if she has no other social media presence. She wonders if Derek is here
too. And Sam. Who the fuck are all these people? Who the fuck is
this Emma Porter, who claims to know someone in the police department and is spreading all this information? If that's true, it can't be
tolerated. She can't have people who work in the police talking to
their partners or friends about how the investigation is going and having it end up on Facebook.

Something about Emma Porter troubles her. She rereads her posts,
from the beginning. She is the one who really started this group off
on the Bryden Frost case, back on Tuesday when she first disappeared.
The excitement, the breathless tone of the posts feels familiar. She
scans faster, looking for something she'd seen the first time through.
Here it is.

*I might even be responsible, in an indirect way, for finding her. They'd
already searched the building thoroughly on the day she disappeared but
couldn't find her. I suggested to my police friend that they bring in a cadaver dog, and they finally did. It was the dog that found her in the storage locker.*

Jayne remembers Lizzie, in the station, saying much the same thing.

That's Lizzie, Jayne thinks. She's sure of it. Lizzie is Emma Porter. And she posted about Alice talking to Lizzie at the park. She returns to her strange post from late last night.

. . . all they had to do was knock on her door, force their way in, and hold a plastic bag over her face until she was dead. Easy enough to do, if you're strong enough. If you take her by surprise. If she's not expecting it at all and turns her back on you. . . . It almost sounds like she was there. *If you're strong enough . . .* Jayne knows that Lizzie is a nurse. She would be strong enough.

. . . And you have to ask, why move the body at all? Why not just leave her there, dead? Why bother putting her in a suitcase and taking her downstairs and risk being seen? I'll tell you why. Because the killer didn't want the little girl to come home and see her mother dead! It's so obvious. And how would the killer know she'd fit in a suitcase? Maybe they saw that thing on YouTube—Can Adrienne Fit in a Suitcase? It's had millions of views. And everybody has a suitcase in their closet these days. My point is, it could have been anyone! We should think outside the box!

Jayne stares at the computer. How could they have missed this?

LIZZIE REFUSES TO LET her parents come with her to the police station. She's having a hard enough time holding it together as it is. Why does Detective Salter want to see her?

She hasn't slept much the last couple of days, and she looks like crap. She has a quick shower, which makes her feel a little better, and puts on clean clothes. She forces down another piece of toast and a cup of coffee and drives to the police station. She's led to an interview room, where she has to wait for at least fifteen minutes. Finally Detective Salter enters, with Detective Kilgour. They sit down.

"Hello, Lizzie," Detective Salter begins. "Thank you for coming in. You're here voluntarily—you can leave whenever you want. We just have a few questions."

Lizzie nods, but her throat is dry. "Of course," she says.

"Tell us about your relationship with your sister," Salter says.

Lizzie is taken aback. "What do you mean?"

"Did you get along well with her?"

"Yes, of course. We were very close, as I told you before." The detective lets the silence swell, obviously waiting for more. She adds, "We had occasional arguments, like all sisters do, but we shared everything."

"You shared everything," the detective says, "and yet you had no idea she was having an affair with Derek Gardner."

"What is this?" Lizzie snaps back.

"I'm merely pointing out that your sister didn't share everything with you, the way you imagined."

"So what?"

"So I wonder if you were as close as you say. Bryden told her friend Paige about her affair."

Lizzie realizes that the detective is trying to unsettle her, and it makes her nervous.

"What was it like, growing up in your family?" the detective asks now. "Your parents seem like decent people. Were they good parents?"

"Yes."

"Just 'yes'?" Salter prods.

"They've always been good to both of us. Very supportive. Loving."

"Your parents are concerned about you," Salter says.

"They're my parents, they're always concerned about me. They know I'm struggling with what happened to Bryden. We all are."

The detective nods. "Your mother told me that lately you're spending all your time in your room, that you hardly come out."

"I'm here now, aren't I?" Lizzie answers icily.

"What have you been doing in there, Lizzie?" the detective asks. Lizzie doesn't answer. The detective continues. "I think you've been online, haven't you, Lizzie, on a Facebook group called True Crimes in Albany NY."

Lizzie feels the blood drain from her face, the dizziness rush in. She doesn't want them to see what she's posted on there. But she realizes they probably already have. That's why she's here.

Detective Salter opens a buff file folder resting on the table in front of her. She lifts a piece of paper and studies it for a moment. Then she looks at her. "Does the name Emma Porter ring a bell?"

Lizzie freezes. She can't speak.

"You know," Detective Salter continues, "I thought there was something a bit odd about you, Lizzie. You were so interested in finding your sister. But it didn't seem like the normal, healthy interest of a loving sister. You were eager to be part of the investigation. You wanted to come along on the search. You suggested the dog. That's how we know you're Emma Porter. Because you couldn't resist pointing it out to the Facebook group. And to Detective Kilgour and me too."

Lizzie just shakes her head, silent and afraid.

"You have quite an interest in true crime," Salter says. "I remember our little chat about the Elisa Lam case." She pauses, tilts her head at her. "So you went online, and started posting in the group about your sister's disappearance, and then her murder." She looks down and reads from the sheet of paper. *"A woman has just gone missing from a condominium at 100 Constitution Drive. Police are on the scene. Stay tuned for updates!"* She looks across at her. "Why did you do that, Lizzie?"

"I—I thought maybe we could help solve it."

"But you didn't tell your parents about what you were doing. Why?"

Lizzie whispers, "I thought they wouldn't approve."

Now the detective leans closer to her. "And why wouldn't they approve, Lizzie?"

56

izzie feels her face harden. "They wouldn't approve of my going online and talking about Bryden's murder. They would find it tasteless, unforgivable. They wouldn't understand."

"Why would they feel that way, if you're only trying to help?" Lizzie doesn't answer. "Is your parents' approval so important to you?"

Lizzie glares back at the detective. "No, but I don't want to hurt them unnecessarily." She adds, "They've always disapproved of true crime. They think it's—disgusting, unhealthy. 'Prurient,' my mother says. So I mostly hide it from them."

"Did your sister share your interest in true crime?" the detective asks.

Lizzie shrugs. "No, she was more like my parents. She preferred more edifying things, like visiting art museums."

"It must be especially awful for your parents, then, living through this, like something you'd see on Netflix."

Lizzie pauses. "I hadn't thought of that."

"Maybe you think they wouldn't approve of the fact that you seem to enjoy it so much, discussing your sister's murder online."

Lizzie feels her face burn. "I wouldn't say I *enjoy* it," she protests. "She was my sister. I want to know who killed her."

"I've read everything on that Facebook group," Detective Salter says. "And do you know what struck me?"

Lizzie can't bring herself to look at the detective's face. She can feel the sweat prickle in her armpits, is swamped in fear and shame.

"It struck me that maybe you were enjoying it a little *too* much."

Lizzie shakes her head. "No."

"I think you enjoyed being *in the know*. Pretending you knew someone in the police, so you could leak information without giving yourself away. Did that feel good, Lizzie?"

"No."

"I bet it did." The detective regards her, then nods at Kilgour. And now suddenly Detective Kilgour is reading her her rights, as she sits frozen in front of them. When he's finished Salter asks, "Do you want a lawyer to be here with you?"

Lizzie considers it briefly. "No."

"Okay," Detective Salter says, and continues. "I read your post from last night." Now she leans forward again and picks up the sheet of paper and reads aloud: "*all they had to do was knock on her door, force their way in, and hold a plastic bag over her face until she was dead. Easy enough to do, if you're strong enough. If you take her by surprise. If she's not expecting it at all and turns her back on you.*"

Lizzie stares back at the detective, unable to speak, to defend herself.

"It's almost like you were there," Detective Salter says. "Is that how it happened, Lizzie? Were you there?"

"What? No!" Lizzie gasps.

"You offer an explanation for why the body was moved." She reads aloud again. *"'And you have to ask, why move the body at all? Why not just leave her there, dead? Why bother putting her in a suitcase and taking her downstairs and risk being seen? I'll tell you why. Because the killer didn't want the little girl to come home and see her mother dead! It's so obvious.'"*

The detective stares at her. "Did you want the police dog because you knew your sister was there in the building? Did you know she was in the storage locker?"

"No, of course not," Lizzie whispers.

"And you wanted her found, is that it?"

"No."

"What were you doing looking at a YouTube video called *Can Adrienne Fit in a Suitcase?*"

Lizzie whispers, "I did that after—after she was found."

"Why did you write that post, Lizzie? It's a little strange."

Finally, she whispers, "I don't know."

"Do you know what I think? I think it's possible that when your sister was murdered, you were unsettled, upset, you wanted to talk about it. And you found your people, and you got carried away with the drama, the excitement of it all. With being the center of attention. I mean, that's perfectly understandable." She adds, "Even if your parents can't understand it, I can."

Lizzie feels herself nodding silently along as the detective speaks to her in her calm, quiet voice.

"We know that you and your sister didn't always get along."

"That's not true."

"Sam told us," the detective says.

"What? What did he say?"

"He said that sometimes you almost seemed to hate your sister, and that Bryden was troubled by it and didn't know what to do about it."

"That's not true. Sisters fight sometimes, that's all."

"Had you fought with your sister recently?"

"No!"

"Were you jealous of her, Lizzie? Of her luxury apartment, her handsome husband, and adorable child?" She gives her a penetrating stare. "Or—the unthinkable—did you kill your sister so that you'd have something to talk about online? Is that what happened?"

DONNA PACES THE APARTMENT nervously until Lizzie returns home. When she finally hears the door open, she starts as if a gun has gone off. Donna watches her younger daughter drop her purse and her keys and come into the living room. She looks as if she's made of glass and that she might shatter.

"What is it, Lizzie?" Donna asks. She glances at her husband, but he's staring with concern at their daughter.

Lizzie drops into an armchair. She swallows.

"Honey," Jim tries, "are you okay?"

"No." She looks back at them, her eyes large in her pale face. "They seem to think *I* killed Bryden."

Donna stares back at her younger daughter. It's as if time has been suspended. She forgets to breathe. Her mind is a perfect storm, all her fears coalescing. She can't speak.

But her husband can. "What the hell are you talking about?" His voice is strange.

"I—I'm in this Facebook group," Lizzie begins, flushing, her voice wobbling. "I've been in it for a while. I know you won't approve—it's a true crime group." She takes a deep breath and continues. "I've been posting about Bryden since she went missing." She glances up at them. "Because I wanted to find out what happened to her, that's all! It's harmless, and I thought it could actually be helpful!" Her voice rises and she speaks more quickly. "But, I don't know, Detective Salter has been reading it all, and now she's got some screwed-up idea that maybe *I* killed Bryden!"

"Why would she think that?" Jim asks, now in a controlled voice. Donna still can't seem to breathe.

"I don't know."

"You'd better show us this Facebook group."

"I don't want to."

So that's what she's been doing in her room, Donna thinks, feeling dizzy and sick. She's been online in this group, talking about her sister's murder. How vile. She finally finds her voice. "Lizzie, why would Detective Salter think you did it?"

Lizzie looks back at her, her eyes wide. "Sam told them that I hated Bryden. But you know that's not true! Why would he say that? And now Detective Salter thinks I hated her and that I killed her so that I could talk about it online!"

Donna finds herself looking back at her daughter in horror.

Jim stands up slowly, with determination, although all the color has left his face. "You're going to show us this Facebook page. Now."

57

---

erek slips back into the house quietly. It's already dark, and there aren't any lights on. He wonders where his wife is.

He's about to walk down the hall to the kitchen when he hears her voice behind him.

"Hello."

He whips around. "You startled me," he says. He sees her now, curled up on the sofa. Her laptop is closed on the coffee table in front of her. "What are you doing, sitting here in the dark?" He reaches over and turns on a table lamp. He's a little unnerved. She's so calm, watching him with her big green eyes. He sits down in an armchair near her. "Are you ever going to tell me?"

"Tell you what?"

"What you're so worried about." He sighs wearily. "Alice, I'm a cybersecurity expert. I started out as a hacker. I can usually find things. I've just spent the entire afternoon looking into you."

"And what did you find?"

She sounds more apprehensive than angry, he thinks. "Nothing." He waits.

Finally, she says, "I killed a man." She's looking away from him, into the dark. "That's what I've been keeping from you."

"Why didn't you tell me?"

"I don't know." She takes a deep breath and begins. "I was sixteen years old. I was walking home from school, and a man grabbed me and covered my mouth and dragged me into a nearby ravine. He was disgusting. Panting and slobbery and horrible. He expected me to be afraid."

She looks at him then. "I wasn't afraid. I didn't become paralyzed with fear. I certainly wasn't what he was expecting. He was trying to pull off my clothes, and I grabbed a rock and hit him over the head with it. That stopped him. Then I realized he was dead."

"Okay," he says calmly, waiting for her to continue.

"I was just going to pretend it hadn't happened, but someone saw me coming out of the ravine, someone I knew, who recognized me. So I made a big scene—call the police, hysterical tears, the whole nine yards."

"Then what happened?"

"I was arrested. My parents were horrified, thinking I'd be charged with murder. But the police realized that it was so clearly self-defense that they decided not to charge me."

"Where was this?" he asks.

"Connecticut. I was a minor, so my name was kept out of the press."

Derek isn't sure he's following. "So what are you worried about?"

"There's no statute of limitations on murder," his wife points out.

"But no one's going to come after you now."

"Salter already thinks I might have killed Bryden. I don't want her digging around."

"Even if she finds out, what can she do? You were never charged—it was self-defense! And she can't make this information public now if you were a minor at the time."

She shrugs. "Who knows what she'll do?"

"Alice, she's not like us," Derek says. "She follows the rules. You have nothing to worry about."

But he can tell that she's still keeping something back. He wants her to tell him everything, so he makes a confession of his own. "Alice, there's something I've been meaning to tell you." She looks at him, tensing. "Relax," he says. He pauses a moment and then says, "I've developed a bit of a side hustle."

"A side hustle," she repeats.

"It's not exactly legal."

"I'm listening."

"I have a very small number of clients, not on the books, who pay extremely well for my special computer skills." He pauses. "Actually, the less detail you know the better."

"Okay."

She seems to accept that. She trusts him. "How would you like to be filthy rich?" he asks.

"You know I'd like to be filthy rich," she says with a smile. She adds thoughtfully, "You don't want anyone to find out about this."

"Obviously."

"Like Detective Fucking Salter."

They lock eyes. "Especially her."

ALICE CAN'T SLEEP. She glances over at Derek, who is out cold. He doesn't overthink things. She wonders how much longer he would have held out on her about his cybercrime side gig if things hadn't reached a crisis—all because of Bryden Frost.

She'd spent all afternoon online, trying to find Susan Cleeve, her former best friend from Connecticut. Because Susan might be a problem. Most people have a profile on social media somewhere. Alice doesn't, but she's not most people—she deliberately stays off social media. She thought she'd be able to find Susan, who is much more conventional, but hadn't been able to track her down. She might have married and changed her name though.

Now, she's hoping that Susan is dead. Maybe she's moved abroad somewhere. Alice thinks Derek would be able to find her or find out what happened to her. But she doesn't want to ask him.

She remembers that day in the ravine as if it were yesterday.

And things didn't happen the way she said they had.

58

The man in the ravine hadn't been panting, slobbering, horrible. He'd been an older man that she'd been sleeping with for three months. And he didn't drag her into the ravine, with his hand clapped over her mouth so that she couldn't scream, but by now she'd told this story so often she almost believed it herself.

She was so convincing when she was talking to the detectives all those years ago. She played the part of the frightened, desperate victim perfectly. She was rather proud of herself. It made her realize that she could make people believe almost anything.

No, he didn't drag her into the ravine. He was already there, waiting for her, because she'd asked him to meet her there. She was tired of him. He was too dull, too predictable.

At first, he'd seemed exciting, forbidden, because he was so much older. And he'd found her seductive. The boys her own age or a little older were terrified of her. He wasn't intimidated, and she liked that. In retrospect, he was certainly a creep, sleeping with a sixteen-year-old girl. But he'd made sure she was sixteen, the age of consent in Connecticut, before he slept with her. He was married, and he was risking enough already, he told her.

It had all seemed so exciting in the beginning. The secret trysts. Hiding them from her parents. Having this other life that they knew nothing about. It was thrilling. They thought she was just a schoolgirl in tenth grade, a straight-A student. They had no idea. But it got old rather quickly. She liked the double life, but she began to find him too boring, too conventional. It took all the fun out of arranging secret meetings when the man you were doing it for turned out to be dull as dishwater. She'd had enough of him.

She broke it off, but he wouldn't accept it. He began to call her at home on the landline when she stopped answering his calls on her cell phone. He told her that he loved her and that he couldn't live without her. He wanted to leave his wife so that they could be together. He was delusional. She had to be blunt. "Rich," she said coldly, the second-to-last time she saw him, "I don't love you. You don't love me, you just think you do. You love your wife. Go back to her and leave me the fuck alone."

"You're just saying that," he protested. "You don't mean it." He continued to pester her. He was desperate, unhinged. So she arranged to meet him in the ravine.

And when he turned his back, she smashed him over the head with a sharp rock.

She perhaps should have stopped there, but she hit him again, and again. She waited until she was certain he was dead, and then she emerged onto the road, where she was spotted, and went into hysterics.

What happened next was nerve-racking. She told her story to the police, over and over again. She told it well, without deviation. But three things worried her. The detectives were banging on about "overkill"—apparently the first blow had been enough to kill him. And it's true that he'd dropped like a stone. They questioned her repeatedly about why she bashed his head twice more rather than run away when she could. Secondly, the man, Richard Dunbar, was a respectable businessman, with no known history of attacking women. And lastly, her best friend, Susan Cleeve, knew she'd been seeing an older man on the sly. She even had a vague description. And Alice had let her lover's first name, Rich, slip once when she was talking to Susan. So she'd told Susan that it had happened exactly the way she'd told it. He'd grabbed her and dragged her into the ravine because she'd refused to see him anymore. He told her that if he couldn't have her, he was going to kill her with his bare hands, so she had to fight back. Susan believed her and was persuaded to say nothing about their relationship.

Susan might still be out there, and it makes Alice uneasy. What if she sees the news stories about Bryden Frost, and Alice's mother? Alice doesn't like loose ends. She doesn't want to go after Susan to cover her tracks. She'd liked Susan. And she doesn't want to ask for Derek's help to find her, because Alice doesn't want to tell him that she bashed her lover's brains in when she got tired of him.

She'd much rather Detective Salter make an arrest and stop looking into her and Derek. Or else she might have to get creative.

LATE SUNDAY NIGHT, Jayne arrives home completely exhausted. All she wants is to get into her pajamas and go straight to sleep.

As she undresses in her bedroom, she has the strange sensation that something isn't quite right. She glances around her bedroom, but there's nothing specific she can put her finger on. She calls Michael to wish him good night, waking him from sleep.

"I'm sorry, I just wanted to hear your voice," she says.

"No problem. I'm glad you called," he assures her.

She talks to him as she wanders around the apartment in her pajamas. She's in the kitchen, glancing around. Something feels different, but she can't determine what it is. She pauses in her conversation.

"You all right?" Michael asks.

"Yes, I'm fine," she says, though she's a bit rattled.

She quickly sweeps her eyes around the rest of the kitchen. She has that feeling again, her hair prickling at the back of her neck. Instinct, Michael called it. An awareness of danger, in the service of survival. She returns to the bedroom, where she opens her drawers. She can't tell if anything is different. But the books on her bedside table—surely one was stacked on top of the other? Now they lie side by side.

"What are you doing?" Michael asks on the other end of the phone. "It sounds like you're cleaning or something."

She's already in the bathroom and opening her medicine cabinet. Then she knows for sure. Things have been moved, she's certain of it. "Michael, I think someone's been in my apartment."

59

On Monday morning, Kilgour greets Jayne with, "You look like you hardly slept."

Jayne gives him a tired grimace. "That's because I haven't." She confides, "I think someone broke into my apartment yesterday."

"Are you serious?"

"Nothing is missing. Just—some things were moved." She sighs wearily. "Poor Michael ended up getting out of bed and coming over." She glances at Kilgour. "He's changing the locks and putting up a security camera for me later today."

"Good idea."

Jayne pretends to be unaffected by the break-in, but the truth is, it's rattled her. Nothing like this has happened to her before. She has to ask herself, why now? Is it connected to the case? She thinks of Alice, the coldness behind her eyes, remembers Michael telling her to trust her instincts.

Jayne puts Alice out of her mind and together she and Kilgour make their way to the incident room, where she faces the team for the morning briefing.

"We have too many suspects, and so far, no evidence," she begins. "We're waiting for forensics on the clothes and the plastic bag they were found in. Maybe we'll get lucky. But if we find trace evidence on the clothes from Sam Frost, he's got an explanation—he says he hugged her that morning. And if we find evidence of Sam Frost on the plastic bag, he could argue that the plastic bag could have been taken from the kitchen drawer, and that he'd touched it previously. Of course, if we don't find anything, that doesn't mean he didn't kill her.

"We haven't been able to confirm alibis for either Sam Frost or Derek Gardner, so they remain viable suspects. Either one of them could have been buzzed into the underground garage by Bryden that day. Either one of them could have killed her and used the suitcase in the apartment and gotten away without being seen at all. The killer would almost certainly have been wearing gloves. We have the vague witness, Francine Logan, who claims to have seen someone with a suitcase in the elevator at the relevant time but has no description whatsoever. It's just as likely the killer used the stairs. Both men had motive.

"Alice Gardner also has motive—jealousy. She, too, has no alibi. But it's less likely that Bryden would have buzzed in someone from the underground parking that she didn't know and wasn't expecting, and we know Alice didn't show up on the CCTV on the ground floor."

She reviews what they've discovered on the Facebook group over the weekend. "I want to look into Lizzie Houser. She doesn't have an alibi either. I want to know everything about her. Full background—mental history, work history, everything."

. . .

PAIGE HAD GONE to Sam's condo this morning to take Clara to day care. He'd asked her to do it; he didn't want to face the people there. She got the sense that he wanted some space, so she dropped Clara at Dandylion and is now heading back to her own place. She has taken some vacation days, but she wonders if it's time she went back to work.

Now, as she drives home, she thinks unhappily about how Sam had been this morning. How he'd handed the responsibility for Clara over to her, leaving her to pack the bag of Clara's things for the day. He was distant, even when Clara was not in the room. She thinks that he can afford to be affectionate with her in private. He doesn't have to hold her at arm's length when they are alone. Maybe she needs to tell him that. They could have spent time alone together, now, while Clara's at day care. But he'd wanted to be alone.

Does he not care for her? It's so hard to tell with Sam. He doesn't talk about his feelings. She tells herself she must be patient.

But he seems to think that she will do whatever he wants, whenever he wants. She's not so sure anymore. He really should be more considerate of her, she tells herself. What she knows could hurt him.

ALICE HAS DECIDED to go in to work today.

She's looked up Dr. Michael Fraser, PhD in psychology, who lectures in the Psych Department and also, apparently, has a small private practice. He is giving a lecture at two o'clock in one of the large halls. She decides to stop in and listen; it might be fun. And she's curious.

She arrives while the students are getting settled and slips into an aisle seat a few rows from the front. It must be a first-year course, given the size of the lecture hall and the number and age of the students around her. They are children. They seem to get younger every year.

She turns her attention to the man at the podium. This is the man who sleeps with her nemesis, Detective Salter, who sees her in her racy pink and black panties. He's tall and well built, and definitely handsome, in a bookish, cerebral kind of way. Intelligence attracts her. She likes his tousled brown hair and bright blue eyes. She likes his smile. When he begins to speak, she is attracted to his voice. It's pleasant to listen to—masculine, confident, engaging. He's sexy, and she's intrigued. And oh, what luck, the lecture he's giving today is on abnormal psychology. She listens attentively, as if falling under a spell. She will have questions, after.

She'd like to meet him.

TRACY HAS SOMETHING important to do, so she has called in sick again. She's so nervous that her hands are shaking. She must calm down or she will give herself away. She drives the short distance to Kayly Medoff's workplace.

Kayly said on Facebook that she worked at Garrison Insurance Brokers. There's only one location. And now Tracy has parked outside the building and stands looking at it. Strangely, all her nerves have suddenly dissipated.

She brushes a strand of hair out of her eyes and walks into the building and up to reception and asks to see Kayly Medoff.

"Can I ask what it's regarding?" the receptionist inquires.

"It's personal," Tracy says coolly.

The receptionist makes a call and Tracy waits. A strange feeling has come over her. She can move and speak normally, but it's as if she's completely detached from what's happening.

A few moments later a young woman approaches her with a tentative smile. "Hi, I'm Kayly. Do I know you?"

She's even prettier in person, Tracy thinks. About ten years younger than Tracy herself. "No. But I hoped maybe we could talk."

Now the younger woman looks suspicious. "About what?"

"Please," Tracy implores. "Just a few minutes?"

"All right." Kayly walks her over to some leather chairs in the corner of the lobby, far enough from reception to afford them privacy. They sit.

Tracy has already decided how she's going to approach this. She begins, "You were so brave, when it happened to you."

Kayly knows immediately what she's talking about. "Were you assaulted?" There is genuine concern and compassion on her face and in her voice.

Tracy swallows, nods. "I haven't gone to the police."

"It's a big step," Kayly says. After a pause, she says gently, "You know there are support groups you can go to. I did. It helped me." She adds, "But I don't think you ever really get over it." Her eyes change and her voice trembles with emotion. "I thought he was going to kill me."

Tracy knows there's no way this woman is making up what happened to her. She swallows again and asks, "Do you regret going to the police?"

Kayly sighs heavily. "Yes and no. He was arrested but never charged because they said there wasn't enough evidence. I should have gone to the hospital or the police right away, shouldn't have showered away all the evidence. I regret that more than anything. They couldn't find the van he raped me in." She says, more bitterly, "But I know who did it. It made his life hard for a few days, but that's all. He's out there, free to do it again to someone else."

Tracy takes a deep breath and asks, "But how can you know for sure—wasn't he wearing a mask the whole time?"

"I recognized his voice. He came into Dunkin' Donuts, where I worked, almost every day. I know it was him." She pauses for a moment. "And he had this thing he did, tapping the fourth finger on his right hand. He used to do that on the counter when he was ordering coffee. And he did it in that van. But it wasn't enough for me to be able to identify him, they needed *proof.* Evidence. And I didn't have any. They knew it was him—they said they saw him tapping his finger like that in the interview room."

Tracy can't seem to catch her breath. She's suffocating. She stands up suddenly, fighting a wave of sickness. "I'm sorry," she gasps, and flees the lobby.

She makes it to her car and climbs in and locks the door. She leans her head against the steering wheel, struggling to breathe. Henry had told her that the woman claimed to recognize his voice, and that it was bullshit. But Henry had never told her about the finger tapping.

Such an annoying habit.

Her husband is a monster.

After a while she sits up. Well, now she knows.

"FRANCINE LOGAN IS HERE," one of the team says, leaning into the doorway to speak to Jayne. "She wants to talk to you."

"Maybe she's remembered something," Jayne says to Kilgour. The young woman is already sitting alone in the interview room when they enter. Jayne and Kilgour sit down across from her.

"Hello, Francine," Jayne begins. "What brings you here—have you remembered something that you want to tell us?"

Francine nods. "It's something about the suitcase. Just a small thing, but I thought I should tell you."

"Okay," Jayne says patiently.

"There was a sticker, or just the remains of a sticker, on the side. It was kind of worn off, but it was yellow and red, and it made me think of Spain, because that's somewhere that Lisa and I have talked about visiting. I know I was thinking about Spain when I was in the elevator, but I'd somehow forgotten about the sticker."

Jayne glances at Kilgour. No one knows about the half-peeled-off, red-and-yellow sticker on Sam Frost's suitcase. This is confirmation that Francine was in the elevator with the killer and the suitcase that day. Jayne feels a stirring of excitement but is careful not to show it. She asks, "Francine, is there anything more you can tell us about the person with the suitcase?"

"No, I'm sorry."

Kilgour asks, "Did you see their shoes, for example, if you were looking down?"

Francine shakes her head regretfully. "No. I was looking at my phone." She perks up. "Oh. Wait. As I was getting out of the elevator, I heard them get a call on their phone—the ringtone was a song I like."

"What song was that?" Jayne presses.

"The opening of 'Bitter Sweet Symphony,' by The Verve. I didn't hear them answer though. Whoever it was shut it off quickly."

Jayne startles. She's heard that ringtone recently. She thinks she knows who was in the elevator with that suitcase.

60

Jayne greets Paige, across from her in the interview room. She reminds her that she's here voluntarily. She begins the tape, and nods at Kilgour, seated beside her, to begin.

"So, Paige," he begins, his tone friendly. "We thought we'd follow up with you, as we haven't spoken to you in a while."

"Sure," the other woman says, her eyes darting back and forth between the two detectives.

"We'd like to talk to you about Sam. How long have you known him?"

"Pretty much since he and Bryden met, about six years ago. They became serious very quickly."

"How would you describe your relationship with Sam?" Kilgour continues.

"Well, we're friends, obviously. I spent a lot of time with him and Bryden. You know I'm Clara's godmother, right?"

"Yes. And are you in a relationship with someone now?"

"No."

Jayne now leans in. "Did you ever want to be more than just friends with Sam?" She sees Paige flush slightly, and she knows she's hit the nail on the head. "Were you and Sam having an affair?"

"No, of course not."

"Perhaps you have feelings for him," Jayne suggests.

"What? No, that's ridiculous. He was married to my best friend!"

"What about now, now that he's free?"

"That's insulting, Detective. We're friends, nothing more."

Jayne nods. "All right." She pauses for a moment. "We have some new information that's come to light." She pauses and asks Kilgour to read Paige her rights. When he's done that, she asks, "Would you like to have an attorney present?"

Paige shifts in her seat, pale but resolute. "I don't need an attorney."

Jayne proceeds. "We have a witness who got in the elevator in Bryden's building at approximately one thirty on the day of the murder. There was someone already in the elevator, with a suitcase, the same suitcase Bryden was found in." Paige doesn't visibly flinch, but Jayne thinks she sees something nervous in her eyes. "We know it was you in the elevator with the suitcase, Paige."

Paige's mouth drops open in apparent shock. "What? That's impossible. I wasn't there that day. I was home, sick. The witness is mistaken. Everyone knows how unreliable eyewitnesses can be." Jayne waits, letting the silence fill the room, until Paige adds, "I had nothing to do with Bryden's murder!"

"The witness says you received a phone call in the elevator," Jayne says. "The ringtone was the opening bars of 'Bitter Sweet Symphony' by The Verve." Kilgour presses a button on his phone. They all hear it, the distinctive opening strains of the song, coming from Paige's handbag.

"I want a lawyer," Paige says, visibly shaken.

Jayne suspends the interview.

. . .

PAIGE WAITS FOR HER ATTORNEY to arrive. She's outwardly calm, but she's quaking inside. This is all falling apart. It's the end of everything. She's been carrying all this fear inside ever since it happened— she's been almost paralyzed by it, and now she realizes none of this was worth it.

Her attorney arrives, a woman in her forties named Kate Dixon. They talk quietly together in private. When the interview resumes, they are prepared.

"We know you were in the building at 100 Constitution Drive and were in the elevator with the same suitcase that contained Bryden Frost's body at approximately one thirty last Tuesday, around the time that Bryden Frost was murdered," Detective Salter begins. "Do you want to tell us about that?"

Paige doesn't answer. She feels numb.

"Why did you kill your best friend, Paige?"

"I didn't!"

"Was it because she was in the way? Because you're in love with Sam?" When she doesn't answer, Detective Salter leans in and says, "We know it was you in the elevator, Paige. There's no getting around this."

Something inside her breaks. Her beautiful dream is falling apart. She's not going to marry Sam and be a mother to his little girl. They will find out that she left her apartment that day, and when. She remembers that hideous ride down in the elevator with the suitcase, remembers that someone got on, and got off, a young woman who'd seemed never to lift her eyes from her phone. But she'd heard her get that call.

"I didn't kill her," Paige says now, voice breaking. "Sam did."

61

Paige begins to cry. Wrenching sobs and gushing tears. The detective pushes tissues toward her, which she eventually takes and tries to pull herself together. Her attorney rests a hand comfortingly on her back.

"Go on," Detective Salter prompts.

For a moment Paige thinks of Bryden's mother, Donna, sitting in her kitchen, calling Sam a monster. At last she manages to find her voice. "He came home in the middle of the day. They had an argument, and he . . . he smothered her with a plastic bag."

"Were you there?" the detective asks.

Paige shakes her head. "No." She sniffs, wipes her eyes and nose. "He called me. I was home that day; I'd called in sick. He asked me to come to the condo. He said he needed my help."

"Did he tell you what he'd done?"

"No. He just told me he needed my help and to come quickly. He sounded frantic. I asked if I should call 911 and he said no, not to call anyone."

"What time was that?"

"It was just before one."

"Go on," the detective prods.

"I drove over, and when I got there, he let me in and—and I saw Bryden's body lying on the floor, between the foyer and the living room. I think I started to scream, but he put his hand over my mouth and told me to keep quiet. I asked him what happened. He told me that they'd had a terrible argument. That she knew . . . about us."

"So you *were* having an affair with Sam."

Paige whispers, "Yes."

"How long had the affair been going on?"

"A few months. We'd get together when she went away on business." She looks up at the detectives plaintively. "I didn't know he was going to kill her! I had no idea. I never thought anything like that would happen. He said that he hadn't meant to kill her . . . he said he just lost control."

"Then what happened?"

Paige swallows, notes that her hands are trembling. "I told him we had to call the police. But he said no, he'd go to prison for the rest of his life. He said we just had to get the body out of there and they'd never be able to prove it was him, that they'd suspect him, but they'd never be able to prove it. As long as I helped him. He wanted me to get her body out of the apartment.

"I said no, at first. I was crying, hysterical. He kept telling me to be quiet. He went to their room and got a suitcase, and I just stood there, shaking, while he took off her clothes and put her inside. He wanted me to help, but I couldn't bring myself to touch her. Then he told me to take the suitcase down to my car and get rid of it somewhere.

"But I didn't want to. I was terrified of being seen. So then he told me to just take it down to the basement and leave it there somewhere, that there were no cameras anywhere. I asked him why he couldn't do it, and he said if someone saw him, he'd be recognized, and it would be all over for him. He thought no one would notice me with a suitcase. It was less risky."

"Okay, so then what?" Salter asks.

"I gave in," she says miserably. "I was wearing gloves because it was a cold day. I left with the suitcase—it had wheels on it—and went down in the elevator to level 1B. On the way down a woman got on and got off again at the lobby. I didn't think she even looked at me, but I forgot about the phone call. I wasn't thinking straight.

"I went to where the storage lockers are. I was just going to leave the suitcase in front of the storage room door, but it was wedged open with a bit of cardboard. Then I remembered there was an open locker at the end because I'd been down there recently with Bryden, moving the baby things. So I took the suitcase inside and left it there behind some cardboard boxes."

"You say Sam called you, to get you to come over to the condo," Jayne says. "We haven't found any call to you from Sam's phone records for that time."

She answers readily. "We both had burner phones, so Bryden wouldn't see any messages. We've since gotten rid of them."

"So you drove over, and Sam buzzed you into the underground parking garage?"

She nods. "Yes." She adds, her voice bitter. "He knew the cameras weren't working, but I didn't realize then that he'd had Bryden buzz him in so there would be no record of his being there. I didn't realize that he must have planned it until . . . quite recently." She looks at the detectives imploringly. "I didn't kill her. All I did was take the body down to the basement and get rid of the clothes."

"So you disposed of the clothes?" Kilgour interjects.

"Yes, Sam asked me to. He told me to get rid of them because he had to get back to the office, because he'd been gone too long, and it would look suspicious. He said that if I cared about him, I would do this for him. And I did. And I'll regret it for the rest of my life."

"What did you do with the clothes?" he asks.

"Sam put them in the plastic bag, and I put them in my purse and then threw them in a dumpster."

"Where, exactly?" Kilgour asks.

"Behind an apartment building on Larch Street." She begins to cry again. "It all happened so fast. I couldn't think clearly. He made me promise him I wouldn't tell a soul."

"And so this whole time," Salter says, "you've been protecting Sam. You've been an accessory to murder, you do realize that?"

"Accessory after the fact," her attorney clarifies. "An important distinction."

Paige closes her eyes wearily and drags them open again. "It was wrong. I haven't been able to sleep or eat properly since it happened. Bryden was my best friend. I miss her so much." She lifts her eyes to the detectives. "I panicked. I did what he said. I didn't want him to go to prison. I thought it was an accident, that he didn't mean to kill her. It was too late for Bryden anyway, she was already dead." She adds, with a sob, "I was afraid of what would happen if I didn't help him. Afraid for Clara, growing up without a mother or father."

Salter gives her a nod, as if she almost understands.

"I'm sorry. I should have told the truth." She glances at her attorney. "And there's something else I should tell you." She hesitates.

"What's that?" Detective Salter prompts.

"Bryden wasn't having an affair with Derek Gardner or anybody else. I made that up."

"For God's sake," Salter exclaims. "Why?"

"To distract you from me and Sam. I just thought of it on the spur of the moment, when you were interviewing me, pushing me about whether one of them was having an affair, and I thought of him because I remembered that when Bryden told me about the accident, she mentioned that he was quite handsome." She adds, her voice mournful, "Bryden would never cheat."

The detective stares at her. Then Paige is arrested and taken to the cells.

BACK IN HER OFFICE, Jayne turns to Kilgour and says, "It amazes me how men can find women to do things like this for them. Let's arrest Sam and bring him in." She shakes her head. "Just think," she says, "of all the time we've wasted on Derek Gardner."

"Bad luck for him," Kilgour says. "Talk about being in the wrong place at the wrong time."

Jayne thinks about that. Paige's fib was unlucky for Derek Gardner, particularly because he and Alice seem to have something to hide. How furious he must have been—he and his cold wife—when he hadn't done anything to Bryden Frost at all. He'd never even slept with her, let alone killed her.

Maybe now he'll be able to convince his wife, Jayne thinks.

SAM HEARS THE BRISK KNOCK at the door and feels a rush of panic. No one had buzzed him to be let into the building. He doesn't want to answer. The knock comes again, and he gets up on unsteady legs.

It's the detectives, as he feared. They start telling him he's under arrest for the murder of his wife. They read him his rights, but he can't quite take any of it in. The handcuffs go on with a click and he feels like he's living someone else's life. This isn't his life. "I want to call my attorney," he manages to say, as he sways on his feet. His unsympathetic female attorney. Maybe he should get someone else.

"You can call her from the station," Detective Salter says. And then they take him away. Down the elevator, through the lobby, and out of the building, where he is subjected to the excited jostling and catcalls of the press, who watch him being taken away in handcuffs, and capture it all in images, for posterity.

Someone throws a balled-up piece of garbage at him and it hits him on the side of his face.

62

Only an hour ago, Donna had received a phone call from Detective Salter, telling her that her son-in-law has been arrested for the murder of her daughter, and that Paige Mason has also been arrested.

After she'd gotten off the phone, and blurted the news to Lizzie, Donna had run to the bathroom and thrown up. She sat on the floor tiles, heaving. Her beloved daughter had been betrayed, not only by her husband, but by her best friend. Then Jim had arrived home from the corner store. When they told him the news he'd collapsed onto the sofa and had remained there, almost catatonic.

Now Donna is driving Lizzie's car on her way to the condo to gather some things of Clara's before they pick her up from day care. Lizzie is beside her, in the passenger seat, rigid. Lizzie has keys to the condo and is on the list of people allowed to collect Clara from the day care. "I can't believe it," Lizzie says again, her voice hollow. "Not Sam."

Of course, Sam, Donna wants to say, but she holds her tongue. In spite of everything, she's relieved, because after she and Jim had read everything in that repulsive Facebook group, Lizzie's awful posts, she'd been filled with a terrible uncertainty. She had thought it was possible that Lizzie was mentally ill. And God help her, she'd thought—however briefly—that it was possible that Lizzie had murdered her own sister. She'd run to the bathroom and thrown up then too.

But now they have arrested Sam and Paige. Donna is glad to finally have an answer, to *know*. But Lizzie is having a hard time accepting the truth about Sam. Donna glances at her daughter and says, "Honey, Sam's not who you think he is."

Donna parks outside the building, as there is no one in the apartment to buzz them into the underground garage. They make their way inside. There are no reporters anymore. Presumably, Donna thinks, they saw Sam being taken away in handcuffs earlier and followed him to the police station.

As they gather up the things that Clara will need for the next few days, Donna begins to think of the daunting task ahead of her. She must keep living, although her beloved Bryden is dead. She must get through the pain and spectacle of a trial. She must officially adopt her granddaughter and bring her up, must somehow help her deal with the trauma that life has dealt her when Donna can hardly deal with it herself. And someday, she will have to tell Clara the ugly truth.

Donna must also come to terms with what Lizzie has done and find a way to support her somehow. She supposes that she and Jim will have to move back to Albany. It's not the retirement she'd imagined. She doesn't know if she can do it.

Suddenly Donna sags onto the sofa in Bryden's living room. She gazes around in horror, imagining what must have happened here, with Bryden, and Sam and Paige. She doesn't think she can go on.

"Mom?" Lizzie is kneeling down beside her, putting a hand on her shoulder. "Are you okay?"

Donna sees that there are tears in her daughter's eyes.

"You have to stay strong, Mom. Clara needs you. I need you." She adds, "And I will help."

Donna looks at Lizzie with the faintest stirring of hope, and nods.

"Let's go," Lizzie says. "I'll drive."

As they're leaving the apartment, the elevator pings, the doors slide open, and a woman steps out, holding a little girl by the hand as she starts down the corridor. She stops abruptly when she sees them.

"Angela," Lizzie says.

So this is Angela, Donna thinks, and Savanah. She'd never met them. The other woman stares back at the two of them, clearly distressed.

"Have you heard?" Lizzie asks.

Angela nods.

"Heard what, Mommy?" the little girl asks, looking up at her mother with her head tipped back.

"Nothing, Savanah." Angela opens her door and ushers her daughter inside, closing it firmly behind them, as if attempting to shut out the rest of the world.

SAM FACES THE DETECTIVES with alarm. His attorney is beside him, her face creased in concern. The stakes have changed; he has now been arrested for murder. And there must be a reason.

Detective Salter begins, "Paige has told us everything."

Sam swallows. He glances at his lawyer, takes a deep breath, closes his eyes and opens them again. "Okay, yes, I was sleeping with Paige. We agreed that we wouldn't tell you because it wouldn't look good. For me. But she means nothing to me, really."

There's a pause before the detective responds. "I don't think you understand," Detective Salter says. "Paige told us *everything*. She told us how you killed your wife."

He almost stops breathing. "What? No. No, that's not true. I didn't kill Bryden! Why would she say that?"

"She said you then called her to the scene. She said that when she arrived at the apartment, Bryden was already dead. That you told her you'd had an argument and that you'd smothered her with a plastic bag."

The detective's face swims before him; there's that tightness in his chest again, the feeling of being gripped in a vise.

The detective continues. "She said you asked her to carry the suitcase with Bryden's body in it down to the basement. That she didn't want to, but you persuaded her to do it because it was too risky for you—that you might be seen and recognized."

Sam feels his body go cold all over.

"She's lying! That never happened!" he cries. The two detectives look back at him stonily. "It's not true. I didn't kill her!" He turns in desperation to his lawyer, but she says nothing. Even his lawyer looks like she doubts him.

This can't be happening.

"She says that you told her to get rid of Bryden's clothes," Salter says.

"No, that's not true. None of this is true."

"Why would Paige say it if it weren't true?" Detective Salter asks. "She can't live with it anymore. She's going to testify against you."

Sam shakes his head, over and over, the vise on his chest getting tighter and tighter.

"What did you do with your burner phone, Sam?"

"What burner phone? I've never had a burner phone!"

The interrogation continues, and he protests his innocence again and again, but they don't believe him. He feels like he's in a dream state, that none of this is real. He'd been an awful husband, he knows that. He'd been abusive to his wife, he'd cheated on her with her best friend. And now he's going to be charged with her murder.

Oh, Christ. This is all too much. He has to stop lying to the detectives and tell them the truth. "I need a minute with my attorney," Sam says tersely.

The detective suspends the interview.

LIZZIE LOOKS DOWN at her phone, pretending to scroll casually, while her mother clasps Clara in her arms on the sofa. They've returned to her place, but they can't talk about what's happened because Clara is there, sitting on her grandma's lap. Her mother seems to have pulled herself together since earlier, at the condo. Her father, though, still seems unable to cope with the latest development.

They'd both liked Paige too.

Lizzie peeks at Facebook. The group has exploded since news of the arrests. She sees a post from Brittany Clement.

> So her husband AND her best friend have been arrested? How did we not see that coming?

> **Cynthia Rollo**
> They were in on it together. Wow, that is cold. They must have been sleeping together.

> **Deep Diver**
> I wonder how they caught them. Anyone know?

Lizzie doesn't dare post anything—her mother is watching her out of the corner of her eye. And she doesn't know anything. She's curious too. Now that she's over the initial shock about Sam, she wants to know the details.

Now there's an anonymous post.

> I know you're all focused on the arrests right now, but remember the guy on the same floor? Unlike Deep Diver, I'm not afraid to name him. It's Henry Kemp, in unit 811. He was arrested but not charged with the forcible confinement and rape of Kayly Medoff two years ago. I happen to know he did it, there just wasn't any proof.

> **Deep Diver**
> How do you know?

63

Alice hears Derek's cell phone buzz and lifts her head. They're in the kitchen, making dinner.

"It's Detective Salter," Derek says, his voice tight. Then he answers. "Hello?"

"Mr. Gardner, it's Detective Salter."

"Put it on speaker," Alice says.

Derek does as she says. "Yes? What is it?" He's looking at Alice.

"I wanted to let you know, if you haven't heard it already, that we have arrested Sam Frost and Paige Mason for the murder of Bryden Frost."

For a moment, Alice is too surprised to speak. Then she asks, "Who is Paige Mason?" loudly enough that the detective can hear her.

But the detective ignores her question. "I thought you'd both like to know," the detective continues, "that the witness who told us that Derek was having an affair with Bryden has now admitted it was a total fabrication."

Alice *is* pleasantly surprised to hear this. Despite all his denials and protestations, she'd thought for sure her husband had been sleeping with Bryden Frost. She was even half convinced he'd murdered her.

"That's what I've been telling you," Derek says to the detective, but he's still looking at his wife as he says it. "I've half a mind to sue you for harassment," Derek says.

The detective replies, "We were doing our jobs—we did absolutely nothing that would amount to harassment. In any event, I wanted to let you know, as a courtesy." She hangs up.

Alice moves closer to him and says, "I think this calls for champagne!" They always have a bottle of bubbly in the fridge in case there's cause for celebration, and this certainly counts.

Derek grins at her and takes her in his arms. "I *told* you I barely knew her. Now do you believe me?"

"Yes." She wraps her arms around him and kisses him on the mouth. Then she murmurs, "Are you really thinking of suing them? That might not be a good idea."

"No. Let's stay away from Detective Salter and the police," he answers.

As Derek wrestles with the champagne cork, Alice thinks to herself, so that's that. Danger averted. Detective Salter is going to leave them alone. She's not going to dig any deeper. Lucky for them. Lucky for the detective.

PAIGE PACES HER small jail cell in the basement of the police station. It's an enclosed room, with a small slot in the door. She can't see anything much. She has been arrested and knows that she will be charged with being an accessory to murder after the fact, and perhaps for obstruction, and that she will probably go to jail, but she hopes it won't be for too long, or maybe not at all, because she is going to help them put Sam away for murder. She weeps at the tragedy of it all—she's lost Bryden, and Sam and Clara.

She imagines Sam upstairs, being interviewed by the detectives.

She remembers how dismissive he was this morning when she'd picked up Clara to take her to day care. How he'd expected her to pick Clara up again later this afternoon. Well, she couldn't, as it turned out, and neither could he. She has realized too late how much he'd been taking her for granted. The same way he used to take Bryden for granted. And Paige isn't even married to him.

She doesn't think he loves her at all. Except for the one time they slept together since Bryden died, he's been distant, thinking only of himself.

And she's angry because she'd done so much for him. She thought that he could grow to love her. She'd put Bryden in that storage locker so that they could be together. So that she could have Bryden's life. She thought Sam was the one. If only she, and not Bryden, had met him first. It was so unfair.

She'd been so sure that Sam was the one. But he was just like all the rest of them. Unwilling to commit. Was it something about her? Was there something wrong with her? Something that men sensed, that sent them running?

If so, she has no idea what it is.

Six days ago

Bryden saves the document she's working on. It's 12:42 p.m. Time to get something to eat. Suddenly she hears the buzz of the intercom; it startles her. Someone is in the parking garage, wanting to be let in. She's not expecting anyone. She has a lot to get done today, she thinks, annoyed; she told everyone: no interruptions. She decides to ignore it, hoping someone punched in the wrong number by mistake. She rises from her chair, planning to go to the kitchen to make herself a sandwich. Her stomach grumbles.

The buzzer sounds again. Not a mistake then. Whoever it is, she will get rid of them. Now curiosity mixes with irritation. She presses the button. "Who is it?"

"Bryden? I really need to talk to you."

She listens in surprise. It's Paige, and she sounds upset. Bryden stands, thinking, by the intercom. She doesn't have time for this. But what kind of friend would she be if she turned her away? Paige knows she's working from home today; she wouldn't interrupt if it wasn't important.

"Sure, come on up." Bryden presses the button to allow Paige into the garage, worried now. What's upsetting Paige? She's going to find out soon enough. While she waits, she goes back to the dining-room table and quickly checks her phone to see if Paige had sent her texts and she'd missed them. She turns her notifications off when she's swamped with work. But there's nothing. She puts her phone back down on the table.

She hears the knock at the door and goes to open it. Paige looks odd, different. Unusually intense. Bryden feels the faint stirrings of alarm. "Paige, what is it?"

"I just—I need to talk to you." She shuts the door behind her and stands there in her coat, staring at her.

"Paige, you're scaring me a little," Bryden says. "What's happened?"

"Can you put on a pot of coffee?" Paige asks, dropping her handbag on the floor.

"Sure."

"I'm sorry to interrupt—I know you have a lot of work . . ."

"That's okay, what are friends for?" Bryden gives her a quick hug and turns her back to go to the kitchen to make the coffee. She will make a sandwich for Paige too. She feels uneasy. Why isn't Paige at work? What does she need to talk about?

She's halfway to the kitchen when she hears sudden, quick steps behind her, the sense of something coming. Before she can register what's happening, something plastic is pulled over her head, crushed hard against her face, and she is yanked backward. She gasps in shock and fear, but she can't get any air. She struggles against her attacker, thrashing her arms behind her, but the other person is taller, stronger, and Bryden flails helplessly. It's Paige behind her, Paige who has her in this deathly grip. Bryden knows it, but she can't process it. As she tries desperately to draw breath to fight, the plastic bag is sucked into her mouth. She can smell it, taste it, but she can't get any air. There is intense, crushing pressure on her nose, her face. She is suffocating in the iron hold of her assailant, drowning in her own terror. She can hear Paige's breath behind her, rasping with effort. As Bryden struggles, growing weaker and weaker, time seems to slow down, and her vision grows darker. She wonders why Paige is doing this. Her arms lose their energy, her feet kick out for the last time. As she loses consciousness, her last thoughts are of her daughter.

64

Advised that Sam and his lawyer are ready for them after half an hour on their own, Jayne and Kilgour return to the interview room. She restarts the tape.

Sam pulls himself up a little straighter and says, "I didn't kill my wife."

Jayne waits for more. There must be more.

"Paige is lying. I wasn't there. She must have killed Bryden, and she wants me to take the fall for it." He begins speaking in a rush. "She was jealous of Bryden. I think she was in love with me. But I never felt that way about her. I don't want a life with her. She's—she's obviously crazy."

"I'm afraid that doesn't help us very much," Jayne says.

Sam says abruptly, "I wasn't in the park that day like I said."

Jayne raises an eyebrow. She thinks of the man-hours that went into trying to confirm his alibi. "And where exactly were you, Sam?" She's expecting another lie, a desperate attempt from a desperate man.

He hesitates, then confesses, "I have a drug problem."

"What kind of a drug problem?" Jayne asks.

Sam glances at his attorney for reassurance, and she gives him a quick nod. He takes a deep breath, lets it out. "I have a high-pressure job. I work in investments. There's a lot of stress. And yes, sometimes I took it out on Bryden, physically." He pauses.

"Go on."

"Some of the guys at work do a bit of coke; everyone looks the other way. I tried that, but then I found oxy." He sighs heavily. "After a while, I needed more, so I—I started crushing it, and—" His face flushes and she sees that this is difficult for him to admit, that he's ashamed. "Bryden didn't know. Paige doesn't know. Nobody at work knows. If this gets out, I'll lose my job. I could lose my daughter. That's why I didn't say anything. But now I have no choice. I didn't kill my wife!'

"Go on."

"I never do drugs at home. It's just for work. A way to cope. That's why Bryden had no idea. But sometimes, during the day, if I need to calm down, if I need a confidence boost, I'll call my dealer. I'll go out for a while and get what I need."

"And is that what you were doing when Bryden died?"

His face contorts. "Yes." The pain and grief and shame he feels are clear enough.

"And can you prove that?" Jayne asks.

He answers shakily. "I hope so. After I picked up something to eat at the food truck, I didn't go to the park. I went to my dealer's. He has a place, a small apartment. There was one other guy there that I know. We're both regulars. But I'm not sure they'll talk."

"Oh, they'll talk," Jayne says. "Give us the name and address of this dealer. Now."

. . .

THE FOLLOWING AFTERNOON, Jayne and Kilgour sit across from Paige and her attorney once again.

"I have some news for you, Paige," Jayne says. The other woman leans forward expectantly; she seems to think that they have agreed to a deal for her in return for her testifying against Sam. Jayne says, "Sam has a solid alibi for the time of Bryden's murder."

She watches Paige's face freeze and then change from hope to disbelief.

"What? No, he doesn't. You know he doesn't."

"He's changed his story and now his alibi is one hundred percent solid." She pauses. "You alone will be charged for the murder of Bryden Frost."

Paige's face becomes twisted with rage. She roars in fury, stands up and tries with all her strength to knock the table over onto the detectives, but it is bolted to the floor, frustrating her. Kilgour leaps up to restrain her. "*Who? Who was he with?*" she screams.

"His drug dealer," Jayne says calmly.

She watches with satisfaction as the astonishment seizes Paige's face.

PAIGE IS SPEECHLESS with fury. How can this be happening? Sam lied to her. He told her he had no alibi. And now she has fucked herself completely. She feels herself panicking as Kilgour roughly pushes her back in her seat.

She knew Bryden would be home alone that day. She knew that she could overpower her, smother her with a plastic bag. She knew that if she wore long sleeves, and gloves, and if she vacuumed carefully afterward, there would be no evidence left against her. Anything found in the vacuum cleaner bag could be explained by her having been in the apartment regularly. She knew the suitcase was in the closet, and that Bryden would fit. The only risky part was taking her down to the basement. But she couldn't bear to leave the body there, for Sam and Clara to find. She knew there were no cameras, that if anything, there might be an eyewitness, but she'd worn a nondescript black jacket with a hood. And she didn't think they'd suspect a woman.

She thought Sam would be at work. She didn't know he'd go to the park for two hours and be unable to account for his whereabouts. That had been concerning, when the police were looking at him. Especially considering that they were sleeping together—she didn't want that getting out. But she knew he hadn't done it, so there would be no physical evidence against him. She hoped they could build a life together, after everything settled down.

But the fucking police. That fucking phone call.

And Sam *lied* to her. Why hadn't he told her the truth? She believed him when he said he had no alibi. So when it became clear that they knew it was her in the elevator with Bryden's body, she decided to cut her losses and pin it on him. She'd come to realize he didn't really care for her. She'd stupidly admitted hiding the body, the clothes.

This can't be happening.

THAT NIGHT, Michael takes Jayne out for dinner. There'd already been a celebration of sorts at the station. He orders wine and offers a toast. "To you, for solving the case."

"It was a team effort," she says. They clink glasses and begin to talk.

Jayne looks back at him. She loves him, and she knows he loves her. She asks herself: Can she do it? Can she commit to a long-term relationship, the kind of relationship that he's told her he wants? Is that what she wants too? Marriage and children? Can she do that and still do her job? The job she loves but that makes her anxious and exhausted and sometimes depressed? Is it time to choose?

It occurs to her that she still hasn't talked to Ginny, the forensic pathologist, about having that drink.

"Did I tell you?" Michael begins. "There was this woman in my lecture on abnormal psychology yesterday. She came up and spoke to me after—asked some very good questions . . ."

"Like what?" Jayne asks, sipping her wine.

"Like 'How does a psychopath experience love compared to a normal person?'" He pauses thoughtfully. "She wants to meet for coffee."

Jayne raises her eyebrows and smiles back at him. "Is she attractive?"

"Well, yes, I suppose," he replies. He smiles, reaches out across the table, and takes her hand. "But you have nothing to worry about."